# THE WEEK YOU
# WEREN'T HERE

# THE WEEK YOU WEREN'T HERE

## CHARLES BLACKSTONE

Low Fidelity Press
Brooklyn

Copyright © 2004 by Charles Blackstone
First Low Fidelity Press edition, 2005
All rights reserved

Low Fidelity Press
P.O. Box 21930
Brooklyn, NY 11202-1930

info@lofipress.com
http://www.lofipress.com

       Library of Congress Cataloging-in-Publication Data

Blackstone, Charles, 1977-
  The week you weren't here / Charles Blackstone.– 1st Low Fidelity Press ed.
    p. cm.
  ISBN 0-9723363-4-6 (pbk. : alk. paper)
  1. Man-woman relationships–Fiction. 2. Intellectuals–Fiction. 3. Authors–Fiction. I. Title.
  PS3602.L3256W44 2004
  813'.6–dc22
                          2004005146

Published simultaneously in the United Kingdom by Flame Books

Cover and Book Design by Todd Michael Bushman

Produced and printed in the United States of America

For Luis Alberto Urrea

*"It amuses me," said K., "only because it gives me some insight into the ridiculous tangle that may under certain circumstances determine a person's life."*

—Franz Kafka, *The Castle*

*This is perhaps naïve; distortion occurs in the moment as in memory; the mind is quick the feelings quicker; but I want the moment live in its dishonesty, minimal affectation: correction in reflection.*

—Ronald Sukenick, "Momentum"

# THE WEEK YOU
# WEREN'T HERE

# 1

Hunter thought all his dating life so far all he's been trying to do is replace one or two people. He dreamt of Jessica Emerson again last night. In the dream she was an actress and was starring in an upcoming film. She looked beautiful maybe wearing that black leotard he saw her in at the Halloween party—she was Catwoman—the first time they saw each other or spoke in two years. He introduced her to people. He felt smugly haughty that his friend Jessica was a famous actress but when he introduced her to his friends whom he was sure had just viewed the same trailer they didn't seem to be able to grasp the significance. That dorky solid slab of boyfriend he met at the Halloween party but had heard about previously could never love her the way he had the way he probably always would.

 He wished he could say this to her in his dream: You know that girl you know the one who made me be mean to you made me try to forget you you know that girl you know the one reason I dated her the reason I divorced my life for her is because I made myself believe she was you. It makes so much sense now but fuck it didn't work and I lost you probably forever and if only I had realized how much of a mistake I was about to make I would never have done it. I'm so sorry it just felt like I could never touch you and so I thought it would seem similar enough being with her but it didn't couldn't.

 What he did in fact tell her in the dream was that he had

something really important to say and that he hadn't told anyone yet and that wasn't a lie.

What she asked gently probing in her sort of insistent charming sort of way.

I don't want to say it's embarrassing he said.

You can tell me she said so fucking persuasive practically detasseling his stupid pride right there and wait he thought maybe she'll want to sleep with me ditch the slab if I tell. She'll be so fucking moved by how totally depressing sad ruined dejected trampled upon I am that she'll want to—no she'll definitely think what a loser couldn't even didn't have what it took to—.

She still wanted to know and so he told her. I didn't get in to B—.

She looked stunned. He tried to sound mournful and sullen but it felt more like being heartbroken it was really not so hard to feign he even tried to push tears into his eyes straining to cry but nothing. It seemed to work though. She leaned toward him to hug they kissed and he thought this the most perfect kiss ever it was worth this complete and total failure worth this pain so sharp and real and profound that it doesn't even mean anything yet and all for this the summation of everything. This.

# 2

So did he go downtown and try to see Lila today or did he just forget about it. He could deal with his car in the meantime and drove to the dealership. Soon this week would be over. He would have to return to real life and there probably would be a decision to make. Dewey would be coming back as well from her trip to Madison. Would he run into her. He didn't think he had seen her thinking back on it prior to a week ago since maybe the beginning of the semester. So would things be different now now that they had sort of merged paths slightly now that there was a distinct possibility of a thing happening forming developing taking shape gathering permanence and structure out of fragile molecules and sugar compounds. How long would he be stuck at the dealership. This was a last minute decision to right the muffler situation but he hoped a worthwhile one. There would be no other time when it would be convenient to go and even now this was sort of inconvenient. He would rather have been reading or running on the treadmill or something other than just sitting and waiting. His coat felt cumbersome though he didn't take it off. He could drink coffee maybe flip through a magazine. Chores like these he knew too well were a way to avoid writing. He'd been sending his old work around instead of generating anything new. Would Soft Skull like his book and publish it. That would be the most ideal of circumstances. It would be hard not to get into a good graduate program with a book sold. He knew the manuscript needed some substantial editing. He wished not to have to be the one appointed with that duty but actually that might not be so bad a concept considering to get the appointment of editorial responsibility stage one could not pass by the extremely hopeful interested in your work stage or the we accept-we'll do it-we love it-we love you-stage. That hadn't happened yet but he still held out hope.

# 3

He felt suddenly exhausted. His back hurt his fingers stiff his imagination restless. He thought about Lila about sleeping with her about what she looked like in only her underwear about kissing her about how their bodies would fit together. She looked amazing even with clothes on was quite pretty an amazing body really and now this tan he expected she'd have would be very inviting and hard to resist. He guessed it all depended on what would happen that night. Would they go drinking. He knew she was only twenty so perhaps going to a bar especially on St Patrick's Day would be difficult but probably not impossible to pull off. His catalog of bars that were basically self-serve amounted to only a few and none close to where they would be when she finished work at Borders. He didn't really know about a lot of downtown bars had done most of his drinking in Lakeview the west side down Southport but how would they get there unless he drove and perhaps drinking and driving on a first date wasn't such a good idea. Hell you weren't even supposed to drink at all on a first date but couldn't he make an exception. He wanted to be able to relax to be a little less anxious and perhaps that would lead to him feeling a bit more adventurous than he usually did which might lead to something happening. He didn't often take risks when it came to dating. He wished the guy weren't expected to make the first move or if somehow the signals that guys were supposed to pick up on could be just slightly less subtle.

Maybe they were completely obvious—the signs—and he just never noticed it was too thick or deluded by his own thought tempest to be able to see.

He wanted to find the *Dating for Dummies* but had no idea where it was. He bought the book pre-Hilary and remembered some of the things it talked about. Was licking of lips a sign. If the girl let the guy walk her to her door that was good. Not wanting to end things—that was promising—and a leaning toward was considered a plus. Too many others to even think about—when flirting use your entire body look her in the eye smile pay attention to what she says don't be too serious but don't be silly either focus on her don't think you can't do it if she wants a kiss she'll lean forward posture relaxed palms up casual touching nodding but not indifferently mirroring you you're fucked if her arms are crossed if she yawns if she reaches for her keys make sure to eat and tip well chew with your mouth closed talk softly use your napkin don't go to movies or concerts or sporting events don't say you'll call if you don't plan to and don't kiss her if you had a bad time and definitely don't have sex.

Probably he didn't need a book. He could figure it out. It hadn't been that long. With Hilary he did have to make the first move and that worked—they ended up together after that. It was rather exciting how they stood in her tiny suburban kitchen. When they kissed he wrapped his arms around her and realized it was the first time they'd even hugged. Maybe that's what happened more often than not that guys made moves before two people had even stood close enough to hug and then the couple spent all this time together without having sex and ended up hating each other and themselves.

Maybe being somewhat impetuous was important. It was dangerous to start as friends. He'd learned that from experience. Simona. For one it was hard to effect passion after you'd spent too much time together platonically after one started seeing the other as just a really good friend. With Simona he was all over her not literally but thought about her was very solicitous bought her food drove her around and gave her little presents even a silver one-hitter which he utterly disapproved of but wanted so desperately to make her react. She ended up losing it or loaning it out never got it back. She said she felt—sort of felt—bad. Maybe that was a lie. She'd lied to him before and during their relationship. She probably really meant to mention him on her senior page but when the yearbook came out and she'd professed her love for everyone but him it must have been because they just misentered the information. He knew that was utter bullshit when she said it. He was on yearbook duty he helped enter some of the handwritten data and it was after they had been together for at least a month or two that the sheets were due. He was surprised when he saw her handwritten notes. Actually his friend Ammo pointed it out to him Look she didn't leave you anything and Hunter sort of laughed it off didn't know what to think. He never said anything about it one of several secrets he'd never reveal to her about her. When the yearbook came out she lied he just nodded accepted it didn't confront her couldn't tell the truth like he had occasionally pictured doing. He just wanted to believe she loved him and maybe it really was an oversight.

How would he know if Lila wanted him. She was flirty but hard to read. He would be on the lookout for cues words. Maybe he would make some advances depending on where they ended up. He felt like a bar would for some reason be appropriate in this situation. That was weird. He never had imagined a bar being a suitable location for a date but things were definitely different with this girl the fact of which perhaps warranted a change. He got along with her but things were still very superficial. They hadn't really plumbed any sort of depth yet. Maybe that was good. He usually used up everything in the pursuit and there was nothing left to do after. This was better more responsible more adult like more normal more like what everybody else did. Not being so needy more reticent that was definitely good. He liked how with Lila it seemed easy to be non-freakish to behave decently to be enthusiastic but still reserved to not give everything away right away. Why was that. Maybe he was being cautious because he was scared. It was definitely something he hadn't experienced for quite some time. He wondered how she was defective. He seemed to only end up with defective rejects. Why was that. He hated that. Simona Hilary Eileen the first Dewey go as far back as you want. All the empirical evidence seemed to suggest that he was a defect magnet. The together girls always somehow knew better knew to avoid him. So many had avoided him this year so so many definitely some defective ones too but Lila seemed not to fit this profile at least not so far and he was excited about that.

Basically nothing could go wrong nothing he could conceive of anyway because he hadn't invested all that much. He'd become perpetually preoccupied. So many things pulling him in so many directions grad school obviously a major part but this sort of sudden influx of dating possibilities made him less needy and less easily distracted. He was thinking about Lila but it wasn't a fury it was probably—wow—it was probably just how ordinary people prepared for a date: a moderate amount of wonder a bit of trepidation some regard for the kissing potential. Even if she were a bad kisser she was hot enough for it to not make a difference. He could distract himself with other parts of her body. He was aware of the possibility that she might not be what he imagined her to be that their romance might exist differently on the stage than in his head but he really hoped she would be incredible. It was because of that dream kiss with Jessica that he had such high expectations. It was because Simona was actually exceptional to make out with. Hilary was okay good fine for kissing but because she didn't want to fuck it was hard to categorize her. Miriam was a good fuck but an awful kisser and a lousy person. It was funny how every good thing really depended on the bad things and the badness of certain things negated most of the good of the good things. So it was really impossible to pinpoint a good thing and regard it as a good thing because of all the contingencies. He still had a thing for girls he didn't know. He'd have to break that habit if he were to have a relationship with anybody. What had happened to the girl from the treadmill and the elliptical machine at the gym. She just disappeared and he hadn't seen her since the driving behind her on Dorchester incident last week. This had been such a crazy week. What kind of underwear did Lila wear. Was it sexy. She worked next door to a Victoria's Secret. She had the body for good underwear why would she not wear it.

God the boyfriend previous present past future issue crept up on him again. Why would somebody so unquestionably desirable be unattached. Maybe there was an out-of-town person somewhere or perhaps a recent break up emotional residue lingering the sort of thing where she would think I'm ready no I'm not ready let me try him out see what it's like and then quickly decide it was a bad idea tell him something that would make his face fall like Maybe this wasn't such a good idea. But then again if he could deify the moment worship the night they would be together maybe that would be enough. Her underwear he hoped would be glamorous. Miriam always talked about wanting new underwear but wore really terrible ill-fitting pieces. Why did she tell him about that.

Maybe it was because they were on their first date which wasn't really a date more like some sort of perfunctory prelude to their fucking and he was still sort of with Hilary. At the time they'd split up for a weekend so he was reluctant to cheat—would it be—but he and Miriam ambled through Old Orchard holding hands walked into Express and she pointed out a bra and underwear that looked like an American flag he approved of. This before he knew about the rags the Flintstone garments she wore beneath her clothes. It was really a let down to see what she really had. Hilary's underwear weren't stunning either. He barely remembered Simona's—that was so long ago now—but she at least had a body and knew it and dressed accordingly. It was funny with her because he actually didn't want her to wear things that were too suggestive or revealing or sensual because he was scared it was an invitation for others to look to want and he didn't trust her not really ever partly due to her beauty. It scared him. Maybe that's why he usually stayed clear of girls that were very attractive.

He always felt like the way Simona looked would perpetuate her unfaithfulness would somehow incite cheating—she had cheated once with a doorman who briefly got her into heroin—and always felt better when it was colder when she wore big sweaters hid underneath them. He always motioned for her to adjust her sleeve when a strap would slide into view and she'd roll her eyes and then fix it halfheartedly and he spent half his life with her worried about what she was doing thinking feeling when he wasn't around. At first he thought he was beyond all that with Hilary—it had been almost two years since he'd broken up with Simona—but found himself imagining her—even her— cheating. He realized all of this wondering obsessing wasn't purely arbitrary. He was aware of the fact that he had come into the lives of both these girls when they were attached to other guys and while he had applauded his skill in extricating them and convincing them that he was the ideal boyfriend that they were simply wasting their time with dolts that it was high time to make the switch to Folger's crystals it always came back to haunt him eventually. If they had done it to the losers he thought why not him. So he was always reading into things imagining bad things waiting to hear that they'd done it. How long would it take for them to come clean. In fact Hilary had cheated on him and he'd never told her how much he knew about what had happened. Maybe her transgression took place only in the mind and only over the course of a time leading up to and during a break up early in their relationship but it still counted. He took her back after the split—same thing he'd done with Simona after she'd cheated—said he loved her—it was what she wanted to hear—and this partially out of his disgusting competitiveness always needing to win. It was also partially because he was afraid of being alone.

He always wondered especially as things started to tarnish

and become hard to endure toward the end of things with Hilary if he would have just done both of them a favor by disappearing during the first break up and just letting it all go.

# 4

Observing others often made him feel worthwhile writerly as though he could use some of his attraction to random women to thicken his novel's plot somehow. He spotted a girl in the Commons. He wrote in his notebook: *Her hair looks like it has been wet recently and she tosses it casually. It's dark with highlights and long but not too. Touches her shoulders—more than that—reaches her chest when she leans forward. She wears a hooded sweatshirt which is pink. She has incredibly dark eyes. She eats cheese sticks in marinara sauce looks almost perplexed takes a pen out of her bag switches cheese stick from left to right hand licks fingers individually begins to write in planner. The scarf doesn't come off.*

He thought that if only this moment this uniquely serendipitous ideal vantage could last forever his life would be perfect. This was a girl who could never be quite real and though he could only glean certain cursory yet majorly significant details— the handedness the cheese sticks the predilection for sauce the Cheetos the regular Mountain Dew—he was instantly and completely infatuated. How often he wished the girls he ended up sleeping with shared his hand. It had never happened though why hadn't it. He always thought that being with a left handed girl would be the answer to everything that the girl would be smart and trenchant and maybe even a writer or at least a critical and informed reader that she would understand irony and be sophisticated have been to Europe want to live in New York or maybe already did have a Mac and ridicule those who were in thrall to PCs appreciate her own left handedness and admire him for being the same. Whenever things didn't work out with a girl the first thing he thought was it's because she's right handed she can't really understand me how I think she's left brained I'm right it was over with before it could even start. Of course then he started to think about other reasons and could no longer blame it simply on her DNA. More eye contact glancing now. Could she have known he watched. No but she might have noticed the particular hand with which he gripped the red pen.

He should probably eat something he thought something but he didn't want to appear vapid. What was she planning. He wondered was she free next Tuesday. He always marveled at and was jealous of those guys who could make things happen out of nothing. Walk up to a girl like that say hi ask her to dinner. He was not one of those guys. Christ he could barely make things happen out of distinct prearranged coexisting circumstances. The girl's clothes said disparate from under jeans legs that weren't long enough came these thrift store long brown boots they were okay but what did any of that matter. She read closely. What did she love. Did she get excited over Melville. What about Bartleby. Had she wondered about what his—Bartleby's—ambivalence really suggested. Would the sex be somehow more exquisite the conversation more sublime less manipulative with her than with all the insipid or gradually disappointing right-handed girls. She did look over then and intentionally so. He just knew it.

Was it the same girl he watched yesterday. No it wasn't. Same way of pulling her hair back same handedness similar disordered sartorial bent but it wasn't her. That girl was beautiful not just sufficiently beautiful but necessarily beautiful sort of like that one whom he just exchanged like five alternating glances with but then she got up left the room came back rearranged her notebooks and that was it. It seemed she looked okay he guessed sufficient Jessica hair and maybe shaped face but it was hard to tell from this distance. Sip of iced coffee to obtain another logical reason to hold head in upright 180 degrees due north his drink just sugar water now. Oh shit he just noticed her hand that she held her pen with. Left. Fuck. Why was she like every other girl these days: utterly describable yet completely unapproachable ultimately unknowable. It was as if he chose this on purpose but clearly it was random. God damn it more staring. Now he bet his hair looked ridiculous.

She flipped her Jessica hair all on one side now the right side held out of her eyes with her right hand while she wrote with her left. That flipping was so 80s reminded him of Lisa Spencer from Algebra in seventh grade. She was hot well cute. He guessed he was more taken by her binder and the unique fastidiousness with which she would punch holes in worksheets file pages according to subject reverse chronologically. There was this rumor that year that she and Pat DeFranco fucked in the eighth grade lounge. He believed it then could still picture it clearly could be obsessed with the image if he let himself and maybe at one point had been.

# 5

He looked at certain things and felt incredibly old sometimes. Maybe it was true that he was getting old. His grip on certain elements of the past was getting hard to count on. He looked at these kids around a cafe and felt incredibly old. They had messed up hair dyed green dyed magenta wearing thrift store clothes mechanics shirts with Nissan patches blue cords and jeans and other pants shredded at the cuffs old boots looking entirely 2001 grunge piercings intra gender hugging and touching all very suggestive of other things. They probably smoked pot did other drugs exchanged partners with an alacrity that made him feel like his time had come and gone. Why did he still spend time in this neighborhood. What was he proving by making himself an infrequent yet enduring fixture. Did he long for something which he was never again to possess. This one girl was particularly attractive he thought undoubtedly bi (did that fact scare him or turn him on he wasn't sure) and she sat on the bench side of a table with her legs spread her right arm hanging in front of the inside of her right leg her shoes off. This other girl next to her basically sexless only things like the shape of her mouth and the size of her tongue revealing her gender the rest amorphous nonspecific. He was completely enraptured by these kids whom he was sure went to Lab. God it was his sister next. She would be their age in ten years maybe even fewer. All this tension and a bag of shelled walnuts. This jerky awkward expressiveness of one who came in with a mother just then. Maybe she'd just recovered from some sort of accident.

All the girls seemed to sit up at once when the parent was present and when the spread legs girl sat up she retrieved herself from the green hat glasses girl's grasp. Now the girl with the green hair in a hooded zip sweater covered in patches and buttons odd non-specific emblems of some sort of generalized rebellion joined them. Would he have thought this group cool if he were not fixated on the lack of proximity between them. Was it that that heightened the allure. He wanted a napkin. He wanted to watch maybe the Nissan girl and the green hat under red hooded sweatshirt girl hook up. The red one put on her coat maybe to go outside and smoke. She had writing on her hand. He had noticed that when they stood next to each other in the queue. When he arrived he waited to order a latte for a conspicuously long time. This girl was so aloof and intricate her wallet chain hanging so low almost hovering around her knee. It looked like most of the girls'.

A guy a tall boy with shadow sideburns and baggy blue Dockers approached the table seemingly beckoning the girls to come outside. The writing was on her left hand which made her right unless of course somebody else was responsible for putting it there. Maybe that was a new mode of sexual expression writing on each other in ballpoint. Perhaps he wasn't privy to the details of that didn't know what that meant yet or maybe never would. He flirted often with the idea of—well not that much lately but always in some offhanded way thought about—being with a girl much much younger. But now something about these girls made them seem so much like on the other side of a line even he wasn't willing to cross. Yet.

This one girl the one who had the green hat and had been all over the cute dark eyebrowed magenta-haired girl now stood at the counter. Hands in her back pockets she said I'll have an Americano with milk on it.

The counter guy had to break the news: Um an Americano

doesn't have milk in it.

Did the guy sense the awkwardness of the gaffe did he understand. He tried to make it better in some ways. He hedged suggested that she could add skim milk to the Americano. She didn't seem to realize what this sort of mistake meant. Maybe she wasn't even embarrassed. How could she not be. How could the counter guy not be. Maybe he was used to serving kids. They undoubtedly filled the place provided the bulk of the coffee-consuming culture. Look at this Hunter thought looking to his left and then right. The kids cleared out. They left a certain mess behind. One of the luxuries of youth he guessed not having to bus your own table. He was completely self-conscious about junk on and about the tables he usually sat at probably would have under other circumstances gotten up and cleared their coffee cups napkins the can of Sprite the cute girl drank more balled up napkins the empty bag of nuts.

Some of them came back in. The girl retrieved her soda can. Different kids joined a girl with pink sort of Barbie hair taking their places. God how many of these people were there. Did they all go to Lab or was somebody bussing them in from somewhere. They all had similar hats knit gray and black with designs. The magenta girl's looked like flames. The new pink hair girl's looked like snowflakes cut out of a piece of paper.

Another girl the one with the green hair and now a biker jacket said Whatever it's no big deal I might just pass out on the couch and actually lay back on the bench black jeans stuffed into black boots. She sat up threw her left leg onto the bench talking to the girl who came with the mother with the unsteady muscle uneven gait. She needed to sit. Her voice sounded awkward and primitive too. Maybe she had muscular dystrophy or something but she didn't seem to have that sort of familiarity with her problems. It was still very hesitant like she wasn't quite sure what her ligaments did or didn't do didn't really have a grip on the limitations quite yet. The cafe was pretty much empty but did it have to be a cafe to make him feel empty. Now they were coming back.

There was an adult in the midst some sort of figure who seemed to know the rest. It was all this sort of ambiguous amalgam one even he failed to understand and he wondered why he sat there instead of being on his way somewhere else.

Shit so was he going to go or not. He was supposed to be reflecting on Colleen O'Rourke at the moment. That was the purpose for his intentional seclusion. Nothing but thoughts. But he kept thinking about Lila wondering if she were in fact working today and if in fact he should go see her. Why did he always second-guess his intentions and actions. He continually wondered if he were misusing time as though he weren't capable of budgeting and making good choices. So Colleen. He didn't know her until she died never heard of her before. Colleen died suddenly the article said. He had clicked on the article because it said breaking news. He was curious about the things that took place at B— wanted to absorb the culture was making the transition as best he could without the final say as to whether or not he would someday soon become part of that culture. He didn't know what would happen at this point and looked for clues in the articles things maybe about grad student admissions. This one time something scared him. It said B— turns down applicants because of not having enough money and what aid the school would provide wouldn't be enough for some so that's why they turned down people. This freaked him out. He filled out the federal application only declaring his own meager earnings from the last year. He was old enough not to have to include his parents' information. He thought that omission might be useful in gathering more aid. This grad school stuff was heady but ridiculously expensive.

He was relieved to find out it was just some kind of stupid editorial. Well he of course was still concerned about the money. He knew he'd have to take out a truckload of loans and didn't care about that but now he wondered if not disclosing had been the right thing to do. It was only an editorial. Some student trying to sound informed. Thank god it wasn't anything official he thought after seeing the byline. Did it actually make a difference. Would B— think that he wouldn't be able to come up with enough or wouldn't qualify for the right loans and would they turn him down on account of that. That was scary. He didn't want to think about that. So he stopped reading the headlines though they continued to arrive in his email every day. Well not his own email an alias a stupid fake Hotmail address he had and used when he didn't want anybody to know he was behind whatever.

Were those girls dykes he wondered how could they be so young. Could they have been older than fifteen. He strongly doubted it. There weren't lesbians when he was 15 or if there were they didn't offer it up for public consumption like these. Maybe he didn't remember but the grunge crowd he knew once seemed to be ten or twenty degrees tamer than what he looked at around him in the cafe.

She died in her sleep. They found her Friday morning. Colleen O'Rourke died in her sleep never to wake again. Well yeah that's what death was. That was sort of an obnoxious thing to think. The article said updates to come over the weekend. He kept checking his email and their website for any information but kept finding the same stuff written that Friday late afternoon. What journalistic diligence to at least have published something that very day. What integrity. His college probably would sit on the story for weeks months forget to publish it at all. That paper only came out on Tuesdays. How can you have breaking news stories at specific weekly intervals. It made no sense. Less sense that this girl had died. The Monday report revealed more details. The girl was an international relations quote concentrator. He guessed the term major was too confining conservative restrictive for an ultra liberal ultra progressive populace. She was twenty-two. She was from California. They had a photograph in the Monday issue. It was black and white a black background the only real lightness and contrast coming from her face. Her hair was dark and her clothes dark but her face illuminated. She smiled weakly. She was sort of pretty but then again this photo didn't get clipped from *Paris Elle*. No definitely not. She seemed like she was sort of a blur already whenever whoever snapped the shot. Maybe a tilt of the camera or was she standing slightly bent. A lean to her left he guessed quickly imagining himself in a picture while he looked at her face trying to make the necessary coordinate adjustments. Which way was left right north. She looked almost at him from the screen but away from him. He stared at her eyes barely able to ascertain the shapes the outlines and tried to find depth in a flat high res screen. He couldn't turn away.

It was then he realized that this had to mean something. Like he wanted everything to mean something. No. Like a specific meaning one he did not intentionally supplant. Something intrinsic. He couldn't say what exactly but this had to have a bearing in some way on what he'd been thinking feeling wondering about.

He lay in bed first eleven-thirty then twelve then one-ten. He hoped he had dozed off without realizing it. He hated lying awake when he knew he had a full day ahead of him. He had fairly broken himself of the napping habit and was proud of that. The exercise he did seemed to allow for more sustained periods of thought activity motion. Maybe. He could do more these days with less torpor in between and was proud of that too. He even weighed less. Maybe that helped him stay buoyant amidst so much heavy weighted bullshit that comprised his day to day. He lay awake wondering about Colleen O'Rourke. Even though he'd only seen her picture a couple of times it was embedded like code into his head. He could close his eyes and see the pallid skin the unsure eyes the unspecified background as if to suggest a life in transition no permanence nothing meaning quite what the subject thought it did or should. Was everything about college like that especially college away from home. Her off-campus apartment and roommates were merely filling temporary space the bar they drank at the night before she died in the off-campus apartment bedroom. She died in bed vomited on herself maybe overdosed on Benadryl. Was such a thing possible. They found a bottle knocked over beside her bed. He often mixed antihistamines and liquor. Note to self he thought stop drinking during allergy season. Was it possible he didn't know since it hadn't happened really to him but was it on the east coast was it in real colleges the case that you bonded with people friends and you loved them wanted to be no place other than with them near and that you never thought it was going to happen to you but when you graduated—this girl was a senior a senior in March of her senior year at college—these people would gradually mean less and less the experience further and further away. So many new experiences and choices shudder gasp work career one hoped interesting people to date and drink with from work and the gym and church. Did people still go to church. Definitely not anyone he knew or cared to know but still. These other experiences got in the way competed with before entirely eclipsing the old life. He could sort of understand how that worked even though he didn't have that strong a stranglehold on his college years. He started to feel a tiny flicker of nostalgia climbing up from his lower intestine and into his colon and duodenum every time he imagined it ending with the unique and certain finality of your last semester in your last year with no plan or intention on continuing in that one specific place.

    Colleen O'Rourke. It said on her ph record that her nickname was Coll though the articles didn't seem to corroborate this. She had this life in P— and was about to graduate. Where was she going it didn't say. Grad school. Did people who went to good colleges feel the same particular need to continue education as those did who went to mediocre schools. The one roommate quoted predominately in the article well obituary said things like Colleen O'Rourke was a quote brilliant writer. Of course that statement resonated as did other things about how she was socially active in campus politics. He wondered if she had been as upset as he about what happened in Florida. Was that idiot really— well thinking about that was almost certain to render rest elusive. He could not get over the thought that if he did get in now it would be certain. If they did accept him and he went there it would be an even transaction: one loss one gain no change and how was he supposed to live with that. Maybe it wouldn't bode well for his happiness should he end up there. He thought maybe it would cause nothing but unhappiness and insecurity. Things would be good but not great or what if they sucked. That was always a possibility. He was so fickle so incredibly hard to please that coupled with his giant expectations could create quite a volatile circumstance.

It was getting late. He thought he wouldn't get a chance to see Lila today at least at this rate. Was she even there. If he did find her and see her what would she think. Would she say to herself Of course he seemed sort of interesting but I'm glad to have had space from things it clears the head. You return to things with a better more balanced perspective and view of your surroundings.

Well that's what happened to him when he went away for Thanksgiving. He liked Helaine for the weeks leading up to the trip to Florida. He dreamt about her while he was there in Fort Lauderdale. He looked at things in little shops on Las Olas considered buying her little luck stones and things which made him feel like maybe he could present the small piece of shiny glass or polished stone and say Here I got you this while I was away. I thought of nothing but you during the four or five days wished I were with you or you were with me or that we just weren't apart but so I got you this stone or brick or beach shell or pebble. I found it. Dug it up. Would you believe this thing was lying in front of the jetway just as I was about to arrive about to leave and I picked it up figured it was lucky and so here. Here it is for you. And she'd be so excited or touched that she would want him. But in actuality what happened was he returned from Florida didn't see her didn't write her. Then it was Christmas break and they might have exchanged an email or two but nothing significant more like perfunctory on her part. She may have felt guilty about leading him on or rebuffing. Did she even have a clue about how he felt. She must have. It was so obvious the way he doted on her how quick he was to respond to even the slightest flicker of attention she paid him. But he didn't buy her a stone he didn't see her before finals and managed to get way over her by the time the spring semester started. *Vissi d'arte* and that was that.

    Okay now he felt like going. He probably had just enough time. He'd have to rush and pay to park but maybe she'd be there. What would he do if she weren't. Fuck. He hated to pay for parking but he hadn't planned well and this was Friday and it was almost the end of the week and he knew if he didn't do something now time would run out and he would forever blame himself for not trying. There were too many missed opportunities moments when he didn't do something when he should so why not say fuck it and go now. Why not.

# 6

He would find Lila where he expected her to be at the time he thought she would be there. He got there early even though the traffic was completely inhospitable. What was usually a fifteen minute ride took forty-five but he'd tried not to panic. He figured it would take her at least five minutes to leave if her break started at five but when he finally got off the Drive he turned too quickly made a left at Pearson instead of Walton no big deal just another right and he drove down the ramp and into the underground parking garage took a ticket wound around several floors before finding a space and began the upward climb inside Marshall Field's.

He took an escalator from the mezzanine to three and then the next was stopped so he walked it and then found the elevator got into the first car realized it was headed down. He sighed.

A girl with packages said Well it's not the worst thing and he liked this the interchange said Yeah well they should have different kinds of beeps or something so you can tell if you're going up or down and she just sort of nodded and then they were back on the ground floor and she got out a girl followed a girl who hadn't spoken but who carried the same kind of bag from the same sort of clothing store and then the car was empty so he began the ascent once more.

He started feeling panicky a little nervous about seeing Lila and tried to think of things he'd say. What did you say to someone who'd been away. He thought of a joke he might use maybe that would work. He entered the café didn't see her. What if she didn't like surprise visits. Coming to the bookstore was one thing but here he could potentially catch her in an awkward situation maybe she decided to lunch with a co-worker when she realized he wasn't coming. He wondered if she even expected him to come. How recently had she thought of him. Obviously he wouldn't try to seriously pretend like he had come for other reasons than to see her but being there felt a bit silly. Driving there he had contemplated turning around especially when the traffic gridlock became a dead standstill but remained resolute once he'd turned off the Drive even when he was still far enough from the garage to not have to enter far enough to still have choices to make. He went in anyway and was now seated having just purchased a really expensive soda a dollar ten what a fucking rip he'd spent so much money that day alone very unlike him the breakfast in the restaurant seven dollars maybe a bit more with tip he hardly ever dined out and then parking looking at the rate chart he figured he'd be lucky to get out and only pay ten dollars. Could he sneak a validation somehow. They didn't validate tickets in Marshall Field's the cashier who sold him the soda said Only in the mall. She suggested trying Foodlife. Yeah like that would work. He'd have to eat there. He had eaten before he left thought not very much but he was too tightly wound now to be hungry. He pulled an article out of his bag de Certeau Walking in the City. He looked up when he sensed movement. The first time it was a group of older women maybe employees and the second time it was Lila. She looked directly at him sort of smiled—the smile lacked conviction. It was like she almost did recognize him but then didn't and as he slowly rose she probably quickly figured out what was going on. He walked up to her.

 Hi he said.

 She was still smiling. Her skin was dark on her hands and what he could see of her arms her face sort of darkish a little reddish her eyelids had a streak of white that was a weird eyeliner color wasn't it but it seemed to work. She looked exciting. He wanted to touch her.

He administered the joke So you look sort of like this girl I know but there's something different... Like you've been away...

She smiled I was out of town I went to—

Yeah I know I was just joking he said in a low voice and looked away. Was she returning the joke. Her tone didn't suggest she was kidding it was more like how you would explain a trip to someone who didn't know you'd left perhaps how you would tell a total fucking stranger.

She wanted to eat and ordered salad. They were out of the soup she liked. She examined salads through the case. It seemed to take eons for the cashier to understand through their hand gesture and mutter exchange how much tuna salad Niçoise to put in the container but finally Lila had it and a cup of water and a small dish of peanut butter frozen yogurt on a tray paid for everything and headed for the table where Hunter had already spread out his bag and coat and de Certeau article.

Oh you're not doing homework already she said.

He said No it's not homework.

Yeah right said she playfully.

He decided not to insist but to continue. Okay you got me he said and began to push the papers into his bag.

They had a good conversation talked about school things mostly not serious things just general Did you know about... and Isn't it funny how... and I never knew that... Then she said she had something for him. A present. She gave him a peso. It was a ten piece a two-toned copper and silver sort of coin reminded him of some denomination of franc he liked and he was rather touched. It was sort of the first thing he had of hers the first gift and he remembered how when she mentioned offhandedly that she was going to Mexico the week before he said Bring me back a small thing a matchbook a stone something and even though she'd said okay she likely would have forgotten. He forgot too. He began to wonder what it meant. Here she was just giving him

a coin from the change pocket of her wallet saying how she liked to carry around foreign currency because it made her feel more—
Worldly he suggested.
Yeah worldly she said.
Helaine a girl he liked earlier in the year in the fall had given him a golden dollar once. He still had it but it wasn't an actual gift. When he'd had dinner with her and her friend Penny at Bennigan's after a trip to the Art Institute in November he paid for the meal on his credit card and they'd given him cash. She gave part of her share in golden dollars and he set one aside to remind him of that night and how he felt about her. Now it was dingy-looking. He'd actually lost it for a while and then found it in the trunk of his car. He hated the concept of change that was worth more than change was used to being worth. It stopped him made him aware of the fact that his transaction couldn't have the insignificant automation that transactions usually had the exchange of goods for money and so he tried not to use them and usually didn't but now he had a peso or ten pesos to add to the collection.
She kept saying It's nothing it's only like ten cents when he thanked her. It meant something didn't it that she was giving him something. She started to grow concerned about the time and getting back to work so she disposed of her containers and returned her tray to a stack by a receptacle and they started walking.
He said Could you hold this and she took the soda can he was extending. He zipped his coat. He decided not to ask for it back and liked the idea for two reasons. First the casual way he said Could you hold this and the easy way she said Yes and did it was like how people who were close behaved. Second she was holding something that was his. It looked good within her grasp on the escalator. Then she realized what she had said Oh I've still got this and passed it back. He stood a step above hers and it took them a second to pass the can from one to the other. He wished

she had held it a little while longer before returning it.

She had to go upstairs. He had to return to the garage and claim his car. It was time to part and then there was a pause a bit of stumbling as they were about to leave each other. He knew it was time to ask her out on a real date. They would have to do something other than pretend to run into each other and inhale a salad on her lunch break and he needed to take a chance sooner or later. Otherwise everything he'd been building up the kneading the maneuvering would become irrelevant beside the point. So he said in a voice which felt external to his body and his throat like something pre-recorded artificial yet trying to seem real So what are you doing later.

She said Well actually I'm going to see a movie tonight.

Oh well what about later.

Later.

Later as in you know tomorrow after work or—

I'm not doing anything after work tomorrow actually.

So maybe we could do something have a beverage or something.

Coffee.

Yeah coffee or some you know soup or— She laughed now shifted feet. He continued Or tea or liquid nitrogen something—

That sounds nice. So I'll see you at nine tomorrow.

Yeah okay definitely. She looked unsure for a second so he added But you know only if you want to.

She looked at him. I do want to.

Okay so then tomorrow.

Yeah but I really have to get back now.

Okay I'll see you tomorrow and he turned then to go headed through the doors a red light at the intersection and he stood waiting to cross.

I have a date tomorrow he thought. What am I going to do.

# 7

He had spent so much time thinking feeling acting so hung up on what would happen with grad school that he really had no idea how not to. His applications had been finished and mailed off for almost two months now and B— had said mid-February according to one email thank you for applying note. Now it was March practically the middle of the month. Well not really it was only several days into the month but he was still thinking and wondering every day. He'd always harbored this silly notion about pairs of occurrences: that life happened in a series of doubled events. A positive occasion always came coupled with a negative one whether he was aware of it or not. When things good and more likely bad happened he kept trying to apply the concept to his life. Something favorable had to be followed up with something thoroughly unpleasant. He did that now—waiting trying to figure out if he could somehow predict what would happen with his applications and what other things would happen. If he got a girl to like him he could lose out on a grad school or worse.

This was limbo. He was convinced of it. He called it that. That was his name for this feeling. People asked all the time—Where are you going What are you doing—but he could only explain that he did not yet know. He wanted so much to be able to go away flee his circumstances do new and different things. He saw grad school as the perfect opportunity. How else could he get away. Why else would he have a reason to be someone else. He'd been barely anywhere. He didn't travel didn't really want to so why not this. But it wasn't as though he was hedging. He would clearly do it though how could he really say at this point. It was mere speculation hypothesizing wondering waiting so he couldn't say with any kind of absolute certainty.

He didn't talk much about the schools specifically that he had applied to. The place he really wanted to end up at in his grand scheme he'd kept a secret from most people. It was kind of funny. You know he really had never planned anything always used to mock people who planned said things to himself like They're just deluding themselves they don't really have a clue live for the moment seize the day *in vino veritas* but who was he fooling. That was all bullshit. Especially now. He also felt like this was god's way of fucking him for having always doubted and being insincere and an iconoclast—not in a religious sense—he could have given two shits about that—but in the way that he mocked people who wanted things that were specific. Obviously it was fear. Why wouldn't he just admit he wanted things. Because to say you wanted something made the desire tangible and to give tangibility meant that you could lose something. This wasn't something he thought of. Lots of people talked about this. It was how the whole thing the world life was basically constructed. It was all about making choices and having to then concede losses as they would present themselves but he didn't like being so pessimistic. It was a problem. He sometimes felt like Kurt Cobain. When he was seventeen he actually worshipped the man. Well not like obsessively didn't go camp out in Seattle but his short and powerful trajectory was always a really important model. The things he'd done how much he'd changed the world how he never settled for being any less than he ever wanted to be and in such a short period of time. Being on this precipice not knowing if he'd get into grad school or not was so difficult in a remote way. Sometimes he let himself not think about it. He didn't walk around perpetually hung up on it but he just wanted to hear something good or bad. Yeah right that's a lie. Obviously only good would be good and bad wouldn't be. That's just the nature of opposites. Desired things always had some sort of opposite which would be undesirable. That's really the only way one even knows something is desirable by thinking about what isn't.

When people asked insisted he tell them he usually only mentioned the other two schools he'd applied to. Why. Because it was partially the fear of actualizing. It could live and be protected inside his head but to make other people a part of it well that was scary. But at the same time he thought he may have been fucking with fate or something by not saying anything about it so occasionally he did tell someone and tried to make it like it wasn't that big of a deal he'd applied to B— but it so was. He could hardly even say its name out loud.

He thought about it most every day especially on days when mail was delivered. He had some dreams about receiving the verdict. They were crazy dreams that kept layering on top of each other. This one Saturday when he was supposed to be screening a movie for his Film and Authorship class—*Wild Strawberries* or maybe it was *It Happened One Night*—he rented both of those tapes at Blockbuster and sat in the TV room at his house in front of them—but couldn't concentrate kept drifting and he kept thinking about getting the mail and checked for it a couple of times but nothing was there. It was really late in coming for some reason. First it was one and then two and even three and nothing. But so the dreams were basically the same event: going outside looking in the box shoeless his feet touching the concrete which was blistering it was so cold but he was numb to it.

The mailbox in the first dream. It was so heavily packed jammed up with stuff little packages and magazines curled tightly folded things and letters he was convinced that something important would be inside but he couldn't get to it. It was so fucked up. Then he woke up but maybe he didn't really because the dreams overlapped. He hated when that happened—when it was hard to discern what was really happening and what he was imagining—more than anything. It freaked him out worse than the contents of the dreams themselves.

Then in the next dream he opened the front door and walked out onto the porch but instead of finding the mailbox as it was as he'd always known it to be the same as it had always been all the years he'd lived there growing up going to high school both of them going to college for so long it was some kind of contraption like a sculpture of mailboxes and birdhouses and all sorts of weird compartmentalized things. He opened some of them—some of them may or may not have contained mail—but he couldn't reach what he was seeking—such a metaphor—and woke up into another series of dreams. Not all his dreams were about mailboxes. Some of them had him waking up and thinking about how oh that was just a dream thank god it didn't really happen sort of like other dreams he'd have where he'd get the rejection letter. He couldn't recall any of those now but he knew he must have had some of them. He likened those to the weird disfigurement dream where it's like okay so now I have to live like this without an ear or with broken teeth but then upon waking realizing that it wasn't like that at all.

He hadn't given a shit where he went to college. Nothing meant anything then. He knew he needed to go didn't really see it as an either-or but he really didn't care where he ended up. That's sort of a lie. He had always dreamed of Bennington but not dreamed—dreamed sounds so cliché—anyway he didn't apply. At the time having a relationship seemed to decide things for him. Simona wasn't going to college—not a serious one anyway—and that had an effect on him. Did he really think that they'd end up together forever and married and all that shit. She always talked about it and he sort of playfully nodded along. How could he have believed it would last. It was ridiculous then and now to think that something like that could or would make a difference. Maybe he just used her as an excuse: Oh I couldn't possibly let go of this so I'll not apply anywhere far away just to avoid all the fear and the eventual disappointment. His other friends from Lab had already gone away gone to real schools Yale and Penn and Harvard. Yes even Harvard. Well nobody from his class he didn't think but a year ahead of them and it amused him that Chicago was the big deal school at Roycemore. Roycemore was a school for fuckups—he fucked up sophomore year at Lab spent the year drunk and stoned went to class when he felt like it of course they'd have thrown him out—there was no way around that—and so he ended up at UIC. That was the only college he really consciously considered and that was just because it was close. DePaul and Loyola he applied to those schools too but half-heartedly and so when he got in it really didn't mean anything if anything just intrigued him like how could they think that he would really belong there. Later on those places seemed more desirable as he got slowly more and more commuterized. They have dorms and everything he thought. Well UIC did too but basically only international students lived in them. It would have been more like college at the other schools. He remembered the Bennington application he never filled out never sent in. The junk still sat in his closet with some newspapers some of the ones from when Ethan Kane got killed and an old yellow legal pad the one he used to write down phone numbers and prices and stuff when he was trying to find an apartment all this to go along with his decidedly Chicago life the one he was sort of planning out but not really in the last few weeks of high school. There was this summer ahead of him then something like a transition and how would he use it and what was Simona going to do. She was going to Europe. Well that was the original plan. He was supposed to go too though didn't want to but she insisted. Luckily she crashed a car and got grounded for the summer—no trip to Europe—and had to look for a job to pay her parents back. They checked out a few apartments together one-bedrooms in Rogers Park and he always imagined her in there really wanted to live with her but she said her parents weren't into it. But if he had an apartment they could surely play house and fuck all the time even with the bedroom door open. And he would have to have a one-bedroom. A studio would be too small. They could fuck whenever they felt like it and she could cook things. She really didn't cook much though she did manage to teach him how to make macaroni and cheese but they could do these things together and that would be okay.

Hilary didn't respond well to the idea of his applying to grad school at first. This was of course when they were still together. She didn't want him to leave but all he wanted to do was leave—even then—both her and the city—and it irritated him the way she mocked him. She was in fucking graduate school for god's sake. Her degree was to be for journalism and that was quote sensible and quote a worthwhile profession. But he loved literature and reading and fuck what she thought. He was kind of in love with the notion of life as a grad student. It sounded so luxurious all this reading and thinking and nothing like the deadlines and bitching and crying and driving around and interviewing idiots and trying to come up with copy and copy editing and professors who were so dizzy on their own non-accomplishments they probably asked for a pair of those cheap plastic wings on airplanes but reading and being far far away. Hilary had designs on a semester in DC after her program ended. She talked about that frequently and he was always supportive. So why would she say the same bullshit that everyone said when they didn't take his writing seriously. Do it in your spare time—that was one of his father's favorites. She didn't take what he did seriously and he didn't either in the I'm such an artist bullshit sort of way but she would say things when his novel would get rejections from agents like Well you can always start another one and that so pissed him off. Not that it wasn't true he obviously would write another one but that the book probably sucked because she had been around when he wrote it such a detriment such an onerous part of the process that he couldn't help having written the thing poorly. He remembered how she made him cut out this sex scene which was totally within character because she couldn't separate him from the writing thought he was fucking the girl and in some way cheating on the page. She wanted to read him into every scene. When he'd show her a chapter and she'd comment on it she'd say—and this always irritated him so badly—Well this thing that you do here and he'd of course have to remind her that it wasn't him. Maybe it was just one of the problems that go along with a first-person narrator. He would have to explore that later. He was kind of getting annoyed with the first person anyway and figured to pull off another novel he'd probably have to switch to third at some point. People were so narrow minded like that bitchy girl in his first workshop whom he wanted to fuck regardless who claimed things like no merit in the first person but it wasn't like her writing meant shit anyway in any point of view.

# 8

Dewey wrote him back. He wasn't expecting that. He was at a café in the middle of critiquing an article on his computer for the Writing Center trying to think of ways to express things without sounding like a complete and total bastard. It was early in the morning. The article was good. It was an interview but fuck he was having problems. The email flashed in. He quickly did control-O to postpone composition and read it. It was cute funny. She proposed coffee mentioned her spring break trip again. He remembered the trip didn't forget even though he was really attracted to her when she first told him about it. At the time he figured she'd just dissolve and become only a random image associated with nothing like the rest but he emailed and she wrote him back. He felt like he could discern so much from those two or three paragraphs.

People shouted around him. Inconsequential static blared out of a homeless woman's headphones. Maybe some music was underneath all of it but from where Hunter sat it was just dissonance—obnoxious grating competing relentlessly with the overhead stereo. In the email he noticed Dewey was funny a good speller wrote in all lower case but used block letters to draw attention. He liked that. Sometimes he felt his email seemed too neat too orderly upper and lower case sensible paragraphing. He couldn't help it he just typed that way naturally. Actually it took more effort and concentration to use all lower case. The times he tried it he felt self-conscious. He couldn't concentrate on what he was trying to think about because of all this movement in front of him. God was this woman deaf bopping her head from side to side completely zonked making odd grimaces shrugs and sneers perverse grittings of teeth frowns staring across the room. Didn't that obnoxious noise bother her or was she numb.

 She suddenly rose squeaked screamed slapped the man she shared the table with a high five and shuffled across the room. He missed the quiet of his reading room at the U of C and couldn't wait for the campus to reopen. Was every public place only one or two degrees away from qualifying as a homeless shelter. The way some people most people dressed these days who could really tell what they were. He couldn't believe Dewey suggested getting together for coffee in the email. He was floored fucking stunned. He'd need to buy a new sweater for the occasion.

 His face itched. He'd shaved today debated doing it but gave in and now wasn't that happy with the job. A new razor he had to remind himself to be delicate with. A woman he saw just then made him think of someone. He remembered the name Elona Valeri. An interviewer from a few summers ago. Random.

 Dewey hadn't written him immediately but she'd written. He first emailed last Friday after determining she logged on fairly frequently. He had to know about that first. What could be worse than writing and being all like Call me sometime only to hear months later Oh I don't check that address I hate computers. Oh you wrote me. I had no idea or better yet never discussing it simply ignoring the gesture completely leaving him to wonder what vacuum his completely superfluous idiotic random blathering ended up in perpetually neither here nor there not checked overlooked forgotten about before it could even be remembered. He would have felt like a loser if that happened—especially with Dewey—so he checked certain key publicly-accessible documents tried to assess her habits could discern that she used IMAP a recent date on that file she'd logged in earlier that day both good signs but then the dot imap file advanced in time yet no reply. He figured she was shocked weirded uninterested. Well what better way to lose him than to not reply. A less savvy stalker might have waited and ignoring other empirical evidence decided to send again: Hey I sent you an email maybe you didn't get it. Yeah right how often did an email get lost in the mail. The times it did the file would bounce back fairly quickly to explain why.

Was she interested. Could she have actually thought about him. He wasn't sure if she even knew his name when they talked and flirted at the Writing Center party and he had to look her up on a tutoring schedule after she left to find out hers. But since he wrote now they had each other's names. Where did he read that you couldn't properly obsess about someone without learning her name. Oh god did his thinking so much about Dewey mean that he was only really able to stop all the reckless haphazard fallings in love when he was consumed by fear anticipation wondering thinking waiting more wondering hoping wishing planning grad school. Now that that was basically over with he'd need a new focus a new center to deconstruct. He hated being that way all the tearing apart and studying every single word and capital letter and casual touch. Had there been any that afternoon he flirted with her. Not really but they stood in close proximity for the duration of the conversation. Who were those twelve people who got in to B—. Did they all know already they'd gotten in. Why didn't he know whether he was going somewhere or not. What did those people think about the whole thing. He laughed wondered why they didn't publish the winners of this terrible lottery this contest this purely arbitrary method of deciding someone's fate in *P&W*. Obviously the people destined for a noteworthy writing program were truly unique sublime perfect humans with no discernible flaws presently or at any point in the future any place in measurable conceivable time. Why was he not one of them. Was he defective to have been rejected this way.

Enough about that. Back to Dewey. He liked the name Dewey. A great Faulkner name. He dated a Dewey once. That was a nightmare but he'd wondered what had become of her—his Dewey from high school—ran her name through a Google search now and again which produced nothing. Did she ever wonder what had become of him. He didn't get a chance to see Dewey the new one clap or hold a fork or anything that day so he didn't know if she were left-handed. Probably didn't matter so much anyway. He could deal with her as a right-handed person.

He didn't really feel like he would resort to the old and inglorious destructive methods the former invidious routines. Thinking about starting a relationship with Dewey seemed to bolster his confidence. He hadn't given up not completely on his hope of going away. He had to do something and needed to go somewhere. He knew that. That hadn't changed. He was indomitable like Scarlet O'Hara. He admired her strength for some reason these days and refused to believe it was over his getting in somewhere. It wasn't. He still had one or two more schools to hear from and refused to let the upset over B— take over and make him behave badly again.

He made a few decisions then. He'd see Miriam never again. That was over. He'd stop overanalyzing things. He would have a date with Dewey and it would be meaningful and important. He'd find himself a school. He'd stop writing this sentimental unctuous drivel and move forward. There was also Kate to think about now.

# 9

He hadn't been on a date for quite some time now. He really didn't even remember the last time to be perfectly honest. The first date with Hilary almost now three years ago that he remembered. He supposed he was excited at the time but in retrospect it seemed just quite weird and unnatural. It took him longer than he'd anticipated to get to her house the obscure south suburb he'd only heard of vaguely thought of never been to before. He thought it was several exits earlier on the highway and it was a Friday night. They were going to see a production of *The Idiot* that David Schwimmer was going to be in downtown. Hunter was nervous. It was May. He had the air-conditioning on full blast trying to dry his palms. He was wearing a dress shirt and a tie encircled his neck uncomfortably. He checked his hair in the rearview. He wished he had alcohol before leaving the house. What did all this mean he definitely wondered. He had chased this girl in and out of Non-Fiction Writing and about the campus. He wore her down and she started letting him catch her just a little. They'd gone for ice cream at Ben and Jerry's the day before. Where was this going. What did he want. And at that point it had been probably almost exactly a year and a half that he'd been single again so he was eager to fall in love eager to be consumed. That's how the preceding months had been what basically since January when he'd met her and now it was May and things were starting to take on a distinct unmistakable shape a shape he was beginning to see forming like a scab taking the place of a cut on his finger. Their connection was still nascent but starting to take shape. He didn't know what he felt. They had pancakes at IHOP after the play. He had his keys and a box of S'mints out on the table. She rubbed his foot with hers under the table. Later that night back at her place they kissed in the kitchen and from that point until the end it was what it was and he could do nothing to change that.

    So of course he now wondered if what had happened with Hilary the quickness the sheer unthinkingness of the whole thing were to take place again. He had a date tomorrow night with Kate the graphic designer. She seemed to be definitely interested in him. In fact she was the one who clearly started things. She wrote him first responded to his personal ad—not the other way around—so he expected things at first to embody a different sort of dynamic than what he'd been used to what he'd been used to when it was always his job to take the first step. He read a book about sex and relationships really only the dating section. It wasn't that useful just quotes comments from different random insignificant people. It spoke of whether or not to kiss after the first date—different opinions there—whether or not to screw—basically concurred that was out of the question. His father said that starting out with dinner was asking for too much right away but this text seemed to think you couldn't go wrong with food. Even if the date were lousy you still got to eat and have a good conversation. They he and Kate spoke rather easily. She was funny had some sense of comedic timing laughed at most of his jokes though maybe just out of politeness. They discussed what laughing meant. So nothing particularly serious as of yet. Maybe abortion and political parties and the death penalty would be good in-person conversations to have. He valued conversation so incredibly much. In fact it was more important to him than any sort of physicality. Sure he wanted romance in the physical attraction sense wanted to be hot for someone but he knew a relationship any two or more person arrangement was doomed if there was nothing worthwhile to talk about. That was the thing that freaked him out the most with anybody. For so long through so many conversations he felt like he was the moderator the one scripting things that he had to act casual while covertly planning and plotting. He found silences not character building just uncomfortable. It was probably that he had had so many good conversations in his life some drug induced many alcohol fortified that made him expect and be so intimidated by the prospect of not knowing if the conversation would be good or bad.

Only recently only with Miriam did he feel like he absolutely didn't care what they spoke about. The rest of the time with her he found the juvenile things she said amusing maybe slightly charming. The last time they were together that awful night when she tricked him into returning after they'd been walked in upon by her roommate and his intellectually challenged cohort and Hunter had to leave. They went for food. He ate pizza with her but planned to take off afterward. She bitched and bitched wanted him to stay. Earlier that night they drank Côtes du Rhône and she was totally unappreciative. He might as well have gotten a bottle of Boone's Farm it made no difference to her unsophisticated palate. They drank. They barely spoke. He half watched the movie was mostly concerned with getting drunk wanted to fuck her and didn't mind not speaking. In fact that helped things. Tonight he was completely turned off by the things she said. She was so fucking obnoxious a complete and utter moron and the less she said the easier it was to keep his erection.

So what of this Kate. Why was she so eager. He couldn't wait to find out what was wrong with her. The picture she emailed was only a headshot semi-profile. Maybe it was old. She mentioned a guy she dated from another posting who looked nothing like his picture when they met but what did that mean. Hunter got a haircut the day before in order to try to look more like the picture on his posting not to mention the fact that it made his silly hair look a tad more respectable. He hated his hair though appreciated its existence maybe shouldn't be insulting it. It could definitely get up and walk away at any time. No on second thought he loved his hair but wished it didn't get so frizzy when it was beyond a week or two after the haircut. He hated getting haircuts. The wasted time the insipid conversation with the stylist the money. He never quite understood outside of social convention what the point of tipping was and how people hardly ever probably never actually used it to reflect their opinion of service rendered but just gave the obligatory 15 or 20 percent regardless of satisfaction or happiness factor. Yet you didn't need to in fact probably never dropped a dollar in the plastic Starbucks box. And of course tipping vagrants for occupying space and being annoying was completely optional and could if properly navigated be totally avoided.

    Did thinking about things too much make it almost certain that something couldn't be truly enjoyed. Why was it that he had to think so much about something. Just let loose relax right. What idiocy. Obviously it was impossible not to think and plan and wonder if he cared. But wasn't the point of this date and the other possible dates potential dates to make it so that he didn't have to be completely wrapped up that it wouldn't matter if things weren't ideal or went poorly because there were others and that fact would make him more rational and balanced. He would not need to become so consumed with one girl since there were others potentially more interesting exciting with more potential in general. But potential for what. He didn't feel like he wanted to get seriously involved right now. He had become quite comfortable being single. He had time to do what he wanted to do needed to do reading for classes writing. His writing clearly was better more pointed well crafted thoughtful and thought provoking innovative more daring definitely than when he was with Hilary and felt like literally and figuratively she watched with a suspicious eye behind his back over his shoulder eyeing what he typed speculating what it meant about their relationship. God she definitely did not have the slightest literary inclination. Though she'd read it it was wasted on her. If she didn't know that every story he wrote had a narrator and it was a fallacy to think that the words he wrote were his own or indicative of his own feelings—even when they were more or less—it just betrayed her jealousy her immaturity her ignorance her basic inability to understand him. Well what did he expect she was a journalist after all.

He didn't have a plan yet for his date with Kate. He had an idea thought Uncle Julio's would make for a good time. Fajitas he guessed would work. The *Dating for Dummies* don't eat food on a date you can't eat with a fork advice he'd have to ignore for now. He was interested in getting drunk but not conspicuously so on margaritas. He was definitely going to forget he ever read the book's entreaty about not drinking on a date. At this point in his life he could conceive of no way of suffering anybody he liked or didn't like without the succor of a couple of drinks. What was wrong with taking the edge off. He knew his personality could be intimidating and off-putting even under ideal conditions. He talked a lot and discursively. It was because of all his thoughts. He liked thinking. He didn't feel the connection with reticence if he thought. He wanted to say he had a good working relationship between ideas thoughts and his discourse. What was worth thinking if not expressed in words. He just hated silences so this worked out for him but he still occasionally thought too much when sober and wanted to not think so much and just perhaps have a good time. He was just so fucking concerned about being a bad date a fucking loser another one for her to add to her list of bad dates. She said she was writing a book. He hoped that wasn't just hyperbole that she was really doing it. That was definitely common ground. Wouldn't it be funny if she sold a book first. Wouldn't it be just so fucking typical. Non-fiction did sell better than fiction but these days non-fiction was completely artless. Maybe that's what made it sell so. But then again popular fiction was also artless cloyingly so these days. Who was left to make art. He thought of Tosca *Vissi d'arte* and wondered if Kate liked opera. He hadn't been since he was a child wanted to go again just saw an ad that morning in the paper for *Rent* which was coming back in May. He'd definitely get tickets for that date or no date. He didn't want to miss it again.

The most sublime experience was that night he and Jessica saw it together. The seats were outstanding the dinner before at Trattoria No. 10 on Dearborn so quiet and nearly romantic. He remembered the conversation. They talked of salaries a time when he was actually proud of his. This was when he worked in the phone room full time and she still attended Syracuse home for the spring break following that summer that was theirs. It was after she'd returned from London. They quickly dashed to the Schubert. It was very cold and windy. It was weird that Hilary called him that night. He was more excited about that dropped Jessica off at her apartment quickly It was so good thanks for coming I had a wonderful time and then pulled out his cell phone to return Hilary's call. Why why why why didn't he just skip calling her back and instead go upstairs with Jessica. He couldn't remember whether she invited him or not. He guessed she had. There was also that night in May and this was maybe a week after he'd started dating Hilary but was still under the impression that he'd be able to date Hilary and also retain some semblance of his former life. HA. Was that not the biggest joke. He went to Jessica's. She'd returned home from New York for the summer. They had dinner at her apartment and watched the last *Seinfeld* episode. He was heady from being around her but of course they were just friends of course and he was getting stuffed up from the cats. He lay on his stomach on her bed while she returned a call and then Hilary paged him. He called her wanted to have both Hilary and Jessica in his life but felt immediately that there was awkwardness which could never be surmounted. Hilary seemed suspicious uncomfortable already owned him and it hadn't even been two weeks yet. He got off the phone. Felt like he couldn't stay at Jessica's any longer and tried tentative excuses to leave but she didn't want him to go and he really didn't either but felt like Hilary was going to get angry and probably didn't want that either. Jessica rubbed his shoulders while he lay on his stomach and his back. It was surreal. He got hard. How did she do it. Did she straddle him. It was absolutely sublime from out of nowhere and for this tiny moment he felt like they could kiss. Maybe she was jealous enough of this person this Hilary to realize she Jessica wanted him. Now could have been their moment but he was such a fucking loser a pussy even then. He didn't try anything and then never saw her again. It was over. The relationship ended the way it was the way it ever was the way it ever could have been peremptorily and absolutely ended. He didn't know then that it was never to return never would.

The two years they'd lose touch followed by the brief Halloween party reuniting meant nothing. She was already millions of miles away from him never to return again over and done with. How could he have been so stupid and careless that night. Maybe she was trying to say Yes when she rubbed his back god fucking damn it it was fucking just like sex. It was so exquisite that massage. It made him almost hard thinking about it even now. Why didn't he stay that night. What if they had kissed. Maybe they could have been together. Maybe they'd still be together. Of course that was irrational quixotic but who cared. There were too many missed opportunities which he could clearly envision that had taken place over his romantic trajectory too many that he could think of without even having to ponder it. That one though. He didn't even know for sure would have no way of ever knowing to what extent it had been true and real but that one he knew would be the most disquieting of them all. So maybe if he'd learned one thing since then it would be to not not take advantage of anything for any reason because he was too likely going to regret the outcome forever and he couldn't stand regretting things. It was just too hard.

# 10

So this was damage control. He was figuring out what to do how to get beyond what had happened. He kept lying. He still had yet to tell anyone outside of Jessica in the dream and it wasn't even real then. He just couldn't bring himself to do it. Even with people whom he wouldn't have to see physically react to the news—Angela whom he only conversed with via email Ammo whom he had the chance to tell yesterday on the phone—he was silent. He didn't want to think of the probable disappointment the almost certain sadness that telling would bring. A perfect complement of course to his heartbreak he was still numb trying to salvage a future pursuing small less glamorous leads. He mailed an application to UMass non-degree seeking only two pages no essays transcripts apparently no recs. Why was everything every concept convention routine so unshakably rooted moored to its semantics. He hadn't heard from C— yet. That was a little strange. He wondered about other people's suspicion. Was there still plausibility in the notion that he had not yet heard from the other schools too—did that still exist—or did people just nod politely knowing the truth about what had happened and just felt sorry didn't really want to push him didn't want to have to not believe.

At dinner the night before with Julianne he wanted to tell her when she inquired. It hurt him to lie lie so blatantly. It was a lie only to protect himself no matter how much he tried to say it was to avoid hurting others—others who had experienced this vicariously supporting him through this whole thing. Julianne had other things on her mind. She looked good. Hunter Flanagan told her so but then quickly added Aside from the fact that you just worked out not because it was true but since she would have probably said No I don't I just spent two hours with my personal trainer and my hair is wet.

She had problems and shared them. Recent apartment burglary. These are the only earrings I have. These rings are the only ones left. She pushed forward her hand showed him her ring finger and index finger. Simple silver rings small stones on one of them. She sighed reaching her fingers. He felt terrible for her.

Also intraepithelial neoplasia. Pre-cancerous cells on my cervix. They detected them two years ago but never told me.

That was scary. Why the hell was she still smoking. A speeding ticket that afternoon on Lake Shore Drive as if anything could be worse. Julianne and Hunter Flanagan ate spicy tuna rolls maguro and ebi drank water.

He wanted a real drink. I just got drunk last night she said plus I just worked out.

So did I he said but didn't insist. Also he forewent the tuna tartare felt like that was a good ascetic gesture didn't want to appear indulgent in a rather sorrowful time. He didn't want to ask more questions about the pre-cancerous cells because he hated the idea of having to bring it up again during a lull. Maybe she'd taken her mind off it focusing instead on something less unpleasant and here he was contemplating redirecting her leading her back to the formidable topic because of his own selfishness. He wouldn't. But he did anyway.

They lost my test results.

It might be nothing right.

Well maybe maybe not.

She asked him about schools later and he lied said he hadn't heard anything though spoke generally of how difficult it was to get in with this feigned prescience that disgusted him. What a lie what a sham disgusting. She didn't mention his birthday was the next day and neither did he. It probably slipped her mind or had she just gotten used to not thinking about it.

 They hadn't celebrated birthdays together in two years so maybe this was a conscious conceit. They had a different relationship now since having resumed friendship after the split. It wasn't as daily clingy inseparable as it had once been between them. Well it made sense. She had a life worked found apartments for people had friends from bars clubs office gym neighborhood people who knew other people who knew people she knew or once knew friends from college but not really many of those it seemed friends from Lab she actually graduated with her mother Hunter Flanagan.

 He still hadn't mentioned the birthday thing and she drove him to his car after dinner was over and they'd split the check fairly evenly. She wished him luck on his upcoming semi blind date. She kissed him on the cheek. She didn't say anything. Hunter Flanagan wasn't the sort to bring something like that up. He never had been. He was of course gracious when others remembered his birthday and said something to him—depending on who it was—like Ammo on the phone. He was somewhat surprised as though it made perfect sense for him to remember everyone's but why should they think of his. He remembered random ones people from childhood people whom he hadn't wished a happy birthday in a decade or longer or never but was still a bit amazed and never expected such random solicitous outpourings of affection to ever point in his direction.

 He forgot his watch. It was the second time in god knows how long he'd forgotten to put his watch on before leaving the house. He remembered his Film and Authorship readings his app for UMass and to take a multivitamin but forgot his goddamn Swatch. Now he felt naked. Worse chronologically disoriented. Worse annoyed that he didn't have it. He was sure he'd end up late at some point today as a result of this reckless Wave Of Mutilation. It was odd how much he noticed its absence how many times in a day did he look at the time without realizing it like being deprived Internet access in a blackout suddenly you're conscious of the lack suddenly all you want to do is check email do searches that you might not have needed to in normal circumstances.

# 11

He'd never been faced with so much possibility at once. This was an extended period of many things happening things that always made him feel oddly detached surreal out of character. He'd simply never been situated beside and around so much attention. Two publishers for better or worse possessed copies of his manuscript another still was probably about to read a poorly phrased ill-conceived partially plagiarized blurb sort of thing and hey who would even guess he had a date tomorrow with Kate and he had begun planning negotiations for coffee with Dewey. He supposed she concerned him more probably due to the fact that at the moment she Dewey was the only one out of the two that possessed shape a human form. He could picture her clearly. He'd seen her more than once and they shared space that Friday afternoon. But Kate though he'd spoken to her on the phone now twice and seen a picture she emailed one he thought that was nice he hadn't been able to parse the image he saw on the screen with the one he imagined. Her voice and face were now two disparate components elements he couldn't link together. So maybe that was what made him think more of Dewey even though he probably knew more about Kate. This wasn't a race or a contest. Hunter Flanagan felt everything was a challenge a test no certain outcomes precarious circumstances and so he didn't know what to think. Today he was twenty-four. That had to have some relevance.

To Dewey he suggested they go off campus but she didn't want to. She qualified this For now—this was in an email—it was better to stay on campus. He didn't mind really though of course wondered what it meant. Obviously she was busy. Yeah right. That was just a silly trope. Didn't people rearrange schedules—wait—that was his problem: he was too comfortable with the idea of rearranging too quick to upend change miss cancel just to—he wanted to stop that. He had to make sure not to do that to only ignore existing commitments and significant details in moderation. Otherwise he'd be fucked would sabotage both these possible relationships. He didn't even know couldn't even entirely say for sure if he were even ready but certainly this was one way to find out.

Maybe it was this I'm-surrounded-by-so-many-lame-things attitude. He wanted so desperately to be distracted by something engulfing be made not to notice the imperfections. The things he wanted to have as permanent signifiers though arbitrary—the fixation on handedness having a significant physical attraction—perhaps ended up making everything lame in his world. People—specifically on his college campus—were so empty but not even in an ironic way. They had no sense of irony. They merely existed told dumb jokes said bang bang bang over and over had no inner comedic sensor to help them detect what was funny. They held sustained odd facial contortions laughed loudly completely unconcerned with quality of thought worthiness of articulation. They were just fucking stupid or young. He became painfully aware of this as he watched them eat in the dining hall. He knew he had nothing in common with them but what function did Hunter Flanagan serve in the world. What was his purpose outside of maintaining ironic distance closing himself off from things while always remaining—and to his detriment he was sure—porous. He had no filter. He couldn't shut things out that were unpleasant but always felt like his grasp of the things he did wish to recall—Dewey for example—either for bolstering his confidence or for his writing—those seemed to dissipate as soon as they happened. And why spontaneous disruption of flux perpetual motion. In a way he wanted relationships to remain at all points insufferably contentious and dismantling romantic. But did he still. Was he still capable of romantic spontaneity. Everything seemed so blasé responses scenes from stock footage catalogued dusted off. Even his words for his notebook at the moment seemed poorly selected regrettably dull unintelligent. Ah to be young and unsophisticated again a shiny moron. Yeah right like Hunter Flanagan was ever less than fully relevant. God it was getting annoying. He almost had no longer the stomach nor the patience for his sandwich. Only Pepsi One in the vending machine. That sucked. Where was the diet Mountain Dew. A group of sophomores a few tables over played Battleship. Games in college. How bored and pointless are we he silently wondered.

# 12

There was something weird during the dinner with Julianne. It reminded him of their separation. He regretted a comment he half consciously made about Burbank. Though neither of them explicitly said Hilary did Julianne regard Hilary as the cause of their riff the source of the continental divide. Well she was he guessed to a certain extent just as everything was to a certain extent. He appreciated their new relationship. The distance wasn't uncomfortable rather it seemed like a healthy evolution. But they had yet to discuss the split explicitly. Maybe they never would. He certainly wasn't going to mention it. But when would he stop thinking and wondering what not discussing it meant and what Julianne hid underneath that gaze.

He had a date that night a semi blind date. The graphic designer Kate. They'd spoken on the phone the last three nights. That was weird. Not the conversations but the habitualization before even standing in a room together. They talked about commercials. First ones that they found obnoxious. The McDonald's one with the shouting was his. Hers was Save big money at Menard's because she didn't like getting the jingle stuck in her head. They both liked the one for Webvan. I want to go to the PTA meeting but I need beef. He liked that she paid attention was observant retained details with almost the same obsessive voracity that he did.

He bought wine a Beaujolais couldn't find Côte du Rhône at

the Dominick's. Philistines to be sure. His eyelid twitched. Why did that keep happening. Had he pinched a nerve. Was he anxious. He didn't feel particularly so. She told him she was right handed on the phone last night which he'd of course been wondering about so it wasn't because of that. He hadn't asked or said anything at first enjoyed wondering not knowing. Hoped of course. She seemed to have the left personality spirit enthusiasm. She laughed a lot was actually kind of funny seemed to understand irony. He liked that after Hilary and how obnoxiously sentimental mawkish Miriam had become. He welcomed frivolity. He didn't shave didn't really need to. Did he stop for flowers. That seemed so anachronistic a gesture. Daisies. Maybe she didn't even have a vase. Dating elicited or the prospect of dating stirred this punctilious concern within him he didn't much care for. Maybe he could just do whatever act naturally. He had fifty-two dollars in cash. His account balance made him laugh out loud at the ATM. He'd be okay.

He still hadn't heard from C—. What was taking so long. He imagined some sort of final round semi finalist app folders spread the length of a conference table faculty with coffee mugs with suggestions of vodka and lime milling about touching the file folder labels nodding umhmming. It was so tightly wrought a time. Like he felt if things really went well that night what would that mean about other things. Getting laid and then no grad school. Of course he wondered about that.

# 13

She hadn't responded to his subtle gestures during the earlier part of the date. He had moved close to touching her reached for her hand a couple of times when they sat at the bar before dinner. They had to wait quite some time for a table. That's what Uncle Julio's was like but then again what wasn't like that on a Friday night. She hadn't grasped back or lingered. She seemed uncomfortable. Her hand might have been a tad bit clammy. He linked his feet through her bar stool moved his body in trying to hear but mostly he was just trying to find a place to put his feet and she pushed her feet back into the same bar stool recesses held them back there and seemed to be running her shoe across around what seemed to be his shoe. But he didn't know if this had been intentional or not. Perhaps she didn't notice that his feet were even underneath her stool. Maybe she wasn't thinking assumed it was just part of the metal stool frame. He recoiled didn't feel like beginning that stuff yet. They hadn't even eaten yet. He drew his feet away and when hers began to reach his again he returned his feet to underneath his own stool.

It was the kiss that ruined everything. It definitely had to do with that. It rather surprised him. It was everything going terribly right and terribly wrong at the same time. First there was awkwardness. He'd sort of invited himself upstairs—the end of the date—parked illegally in front of her building. She suggested he turn on his hazards but he said no because he was afraid of his battery terminals and then they went upstairs. He would have to have said he wouldn't have expected what happened to have happened. Though he supposed they had connected over dinner that preceded the Lilliputian quantities of drinks they consumed he had only half-heartedly gauged her reactions her potential how good of a job he had been doing. It seemed she didn't like him that much. Maybe it was that he didn't like himself that much at the time the lack of alcohol the hours amassing time encroaching closer and closer on the delirious hour. He had to face it he just couldn't stay up all night anymore. It was difficult. He would have supposed he'd have been completely infatuated by that point delirious because of romantic intoxication instead of due to lack of enthusiasm. He would have been coasting off a second or third wind sort of the way he felt on the drive there after he'd set out after he cleaned out his car the haphazard bagging of the variegated materials he found beneath the seats bottles keys a Kappa plastic cup. For a second when he unearthed that he wondered if it had been there since the summer. Could that have possibly been the last time he'd cleaned out his car.

After it happened he felt absolutely terrible. It had gone so unimaginably horribly terrible as far as kisses go and you know wouldn't it just work out that way he thought all this thinking about kissing not just about whether or not it would happen but so much emphasis he'd been placing on quality artfulness structure plotting not necessarily actual kisses past deconstructing or blocking future ones just conceptually the notion that a kiss could change things could make things different. Well for one thing he thought this part was funny considering it actually made him less anxious relieved the tension made them less awkward around each other the fact that it had happened.

Kate reminded him of a girl he saw briefly in high school. There were so many parallels. He thought this girl had pretty much pursued him to the extent of that one. They had met at this party after a St Ignatius dance that some of his St Ignatius friends threw in a room at the Oxford Hotel and he met this girl another girl named Jessica. She had red hair. She drove a minivan. She listened to Cat Stevens and Rod Stewart on audio tapes in this minivan. Well he didn't find out about any of that that night. No that night it was surreal. She was dancing on a table probably drunk. Was he drunk too. Maybe. Probably. He was drunk so much of that year. It was the night before his birthday. He would be sixteen the next day or maybe even it was his birthday by that point. He slept on the floor in the living room of this suite. People kept ordering movies on Spectravision and not paying attention to them milling around people only falling onto the sofa or the shag carpeted floor long enough to blink their eyes or smoke a joint in the darkness. *The Bodyguard* played four or five times and Hunter lay on the floor of the living room at several points and laughed with his eyes closed laughed at the fact that the end of *The Bodyguard* was what he kept seeing over. Not different parts but the same end scene. He still basically remembered it: the plane and the walk and whatever else happened. But before that Jessica was still there with her date in the other room. Her date was this bizarre and frightening guy named Bob Rye. He was fucking spooky wandering around spouting non-sequiturs—I've got a gas grill and a jukebox and leather shoes and ballpoint pens. Why anybody ever liked him or let him hang around them was a mystery. He seemed perpetually out of place incongruous at any of these things. How he was there baffled Hunter. Maybe people felt sorry for him because of his weirdness. The things he said made no sense but it was more the way he spoke slowly like he was mentally challenged like it was difficult for him to form thoughts to have ideas to articulate those poorly formed thoughts and ideas that seemed most disturbing. Anyway Jessica was dancing on a table and Weird Bob was somewhere else in the suite. She was dancing on a table in front of several guys. She might have lifted her dress or flashed them just her bra something very seductive and coy at the same time. Then the other guys were gone and it was just Hunter and Jessica the two of them kissing. She was a good kisser. He was really excited. It was always his goal his ideal outcome at these parties to score. That was the term he and his friends Jeffrey mostly used to describe the pursuit the dance the anticipated outcome of kissing in the dark somewhere dry humping maybe obviating some garments. It really didn't matter especially when he was particularly frenetic who the girl was whom he'd end up with no the important thing was that it happened. But after kissing Jessica that night something felt different. He asked her to stay but she said almost regretfully that she had to return to Bob he had to take her home and they begrudgingly left it at that. She disappeared into the night and beyond the hotel Oxford and he just thought about her all night and in the days that followed. He asked Jeffrey's on-again off-again girlfriend Julie who went to St Ignatius about Jessica. Jessica had said something to Julie about him and she reported it then. That was exciting. He eventually called her or saw her again at another party. She fell in love quite seriously. This scared him. He didn't know what to do. Before she fell in love they had this night together. They stayed up all night making out watching *Kids in the Hall* eating and kissing in the kitchen of her house her parents were away out of town it was just the two of them in this Lincoln Park row house. He had taken a taxi there. How funny was that a time when he didn't have a driver's license. Now that was a long time ago. Clearly. He brought a pack of condoms. He didn't know if she would want him to have sex with her. He was a bit reluctant he had never done it before at that moment. He was sort of relieved when she didn't want to though at one point both of them weren't wearing underwear or anything else. He didn't know. The gestures the tacit directions coming from the movements and the motions seemed to point in one direction yet it was all still a big gray area. He hadn't ever been this close and probably been this intimate with anyone definitely no one whom he didn't know and knew as well as her. He appreciated that she liked him so much. She seemed to be what he had been looking for while he was obsessing over that other girl the young one Eileen yes that was her name. Yeah right like he could ever forget her unless brainwashed unless lobotomy unless dead but maybe it was because of her hold on his psyche her claim to his emotional stores that he couldn't let himself fall for Jessica and eventually he had to start ignoring her which made him feel like shit but he rationalized the act with Well I am just a shit so it's appropriate and still mooned over Eileen and whatever delusion went along with that and it was all just very sad. Eventually Jessica moved on—she wasn't an idiot—and they might have gotten together for coffee a year later or something like that but it was over. Most of that life was over. He'd already moved on from Lab to Roycemore was in the process of what catharsis life rebuilding and so he basically admitted that he'd been thinking about someone else back then and that's why he had been such a jerk and this conversation happened in two installments both at a café called Equinox and in her minivan. She took it well maybe elaborated on how destructive he'd been how bad she felt making him feel even guiltier and they might have ended up back at his place making out after she dropped him off. He would have liked a girlfriend who had a car although by then there was no chance of that.

In her apartment Hunter and Kate hugged again. She hugged him when he first got there to pick her up before he even had a chance to really see her face. Maybe it was a hug test. He must have passed. So at the end of the evening he went back upstairs with her. She hadn't invited him. He didn't really think about it. It just seemed natural to follow her. Maybe it would be just to the door he thought. That would be good chivalrous gentlemanly regardless of what happened. He wanted nothing to challenge his reputation his status as the best date anyone could ever have. Because even if he were lousy as a boyfriend even if he fell apart when it came to follow through and being there he could have that especially nowadays ever since moving out of the world and into his own head a place he looked at the world from but rarely ventured beyond. These days other than to occasionally eat breakfast or a sandwich or something and read the Sunday

*New York Times* aside from those things he was all show all flash and nothing else. He felt like less and less like his value his substance was dissolving and what he presented on the date with Kate was mere approximating mimicry of his previous charming self. Was that why he felt it was so much more necessary if not completely so to drink on dates drink whenever possible. Was that not the biggest cliché. He wasn't like that. He didn't need anything except as Peanut said a muse but muses who wanted to be girlfriends too were dangerous. They could distract and make him want to stop working and start fantasizing. He was actually pleased with the fact that the kiss sucked so badly because it allowed him a chance to read Lacan it was a long reading without becoming all enraptured and dizzy and romantic. He had work to do that was the most important thing. He sort of credited failing out of Lab when he was a sophomore due to the fact that he fell in love with a different Kate a Kathryn actually. She made him want to walk around in alleys in the rain made him avoid his Accelerated Advanced Algebra Trig. That was not a good thing. Of course he was only fifteen then. The *Singles* soundtrack was the only thing he listened to. He smoked cigarettes and didn't shower regularly fancied himself an existentialist a philosopher a dreamer a writer. Well that much hadn't changed significantly in nine years that was for sure but he seemed to think at the time that all that romantic yearning was valuable. And sure maybe it helped his prose nominally but how much and was any of what was going on now helping. He definitely felt like to write about what happened with the kiss he wasn't ready to do yet. It was all too weird. Still he didn't know how he felt. Well it was clear he wasn't in love. He'd learned to recognize the symptoms of that by now. It hadn't been that long. Of course he was in love with Iris and with Helaine already this year and more recently sort of with Lila but that all seemed to have faded.

    Hunter realized several kisses into things that he was going to have to take control of the situation. For starters he was horribly allergic to Kate's apartment. The cat bothered him more than he expected more than when he'd first arrived but perhaps the endorphins still coursed through his brain channels at that point and prevented him from getting stuffy. They definitely didn't any longer once the kiss started to take its queasy shape. No they definitely didn't then. While they kissed he thought about how odd it was how long it had been since he'd kissed a mouth other than Miriam's. At this point Miriam had taken to sending Why haven't you been writing emails which he didn't really feel it necessary to respond to but he couldn't have conceived of a kiss worse than the one she administered whenever he felt sad enough about his life to take comfort in her lack of comforting qualities which of course only made him feel nothing but worse about everything. But regardless he could have never imagined garnering less pleasure from a moment than what happened with Kate. Poor Kate. It wasn't her fault. She was nice enough. She seemed to enjoy his jokes she read books of a marginal quality certainly not Jackie Collins she could mock Creighton with the best of them she might have even loathed Harry Potter though doubtfully entirely cognizant of the ramifications of either of their existences on society their lives their children's lives literature in general. She said she hadn't read Faulkner. That wasn't good. But again she seemed basically literate knew how to use commas in a series didn't mangle the subjunctive verb tenses not that much anyway. So what was the problem. Her skin was a tad on the ruddy unclear side. That was a problem. Her face her body her posture well those things were unique. He didn't entirely dislike her hair. Why did he have to deconstruct girls such as he did. He seemed to be more optimistic definitely early on in the date and even still when he was tired and bored but persevering. Of course he hadn't examined her from up close as much as when her tongue was or actually wasn't in his mouth.

# 14

*Man and woman. He reads the paper a section of the* Reader *the feature story balanced between them spilling over the side of the table. She arms crossed at the wrists stares at him.*

*So whaddya having is the first thing she says after a long time.*

Hunter struggled to pay attention the details of last night still replaying unfolding in his mind. Before Kate mentioned strep throat on the phone he hadn't even felt sick well some sinus pressure that he felt strange but he hadn't really thought much of it. Maybe allergies still going through dialysis to get the cat out of his head. That was weird the other night how quickly he'd gotten allergic began to itch on his face in the back of his throat. A lot of ailments that night the stuffiness the itchy eyes. He'd accidentally touched his right lid with an unbeknownst to him contaminated finger. Well that and drowsiness. Not much sleep coupled with staying up and having to be a participant continuously on and so late at night. He'd gotten used to not having to do that. When he wasn't dating he was usually in bed by 12. He admired his diligence on this date his reluctance to submit to narrative lulls or yawns. He supposed he also lost the pre-date pre-meeting endorphin flow probably soon after meeting. He sighed inwardly. She was cute he supposed sort of nice apartment. That fucking cat though. Her most pressing flaw was that she didn't drink enough. He'd brought her a nice bottle of wine. She offered some to him when he first arrived but he didn't feel like sharing anything with her already beginning to lose interest even then. They drank water instead. She only had one margarita at the restaurant and he didn't want to appear well to be too much of a sybarite too early into things. Plus maybe she'd freak out about his driving and he wanted to avoid that. Something he'd rather not have to deal with. So alas one drink before a long but not entirely tedious dinner and one at the bar. After dinner he'd initially led them to a trendy dark dive the Star Bar deemed romantic on an Internet message board but they had a wait the entrance cordoned off by a fairly inhospitable rope so they ended up at Philosophur's where she only had one Bud Light and didn't even finish it.

Now he felt worse. He started to get silly. He called her on his cell phone both to complain about her infecting him and also to ask if she knew Jessica Valley. In the shower that morning he made the connection both of them went to Wash U. She said no. She didn't know her. He drank chamomile tea had sandwiches but wasn't hungry and hoped it wasn't strep. He'd never even had that before. What was worse was that they spent 25 minutes on the phone. His cell timed it. Fuck. He wasn't trying to mislead her intentionally. She was becoming like a friend but you're not supposed to give your friends bacterial infections. Motherfuck. What was worse was that he had a date with Dewey. She said yes to Thursday coffee and now what. Well he'd have to have recovered by then. He had a couple of days. Today is Monday he remembered. Fuck fuck fuck. His head was inorganic his nose snotty the roof of his mouth abraded. He needed a tissue. He wanted more tea but wished not to pay for it. He wanted to call Deanna—she was another Internet date who'd contacted him and that he'd sort of ignored last week when he was spending all that time on the phone with Kate. He should been more rational even then. Christ nothing had really happened yet and he already had regrets. What did that say. And maybe he could have avoided all of this had he been less available responsible cognizant. Was he doomed.

# 15

When he was almost 16 he got sick terribly sick. A terrible flu. His mother and Jeffrey took him to the emergency room. As he waited lay on the cot waiting to be looked at must have been late like 2 or 3 in the morning he worried about missing school didn't want to miss seeing Eileen even though by that point Eileen had already pretty much decided it wasn't going to happen the two of them being together. But he was 15 almost 16 and so didn't take her pulling away to mean what it meant. No he took it to mean well you're just going to have to work harder a tactic dubiously effective would work in other contexts later on quite successfully in fact both girlfriends that followed he acquired that way—was acquired the right word—more like beat into emotional submission. Basically he could never really trust those girlfriends wondered how genuine how real any of their supposed reciprocal emotions could be because of them just happening. Of course the girls who seemed to take the emotional initiative and pursued him and put more forth in terms of feeling and romantic inclination than he those who made themselves more available vulnerable those he couldn't let himself fall for because they were too simple. There must have been something wrong with them. It was unnatural to respond to him in such a generous way. Too needy scared him especially now. Especially now that he reached a different plateau. Maybe at this post fever still nasally congested moment he had discovered a way to not become so helpless. He knew from so much experience that he quickly relinquished control desire want need just as a part of the pursuit the chase but then these girlfriends made him remain faithful to the contract would not allow him to break the lease wouldn't even consider letting him sublet so he wanted to avoid that now. It was comforting to know maybe he didn't have to lose himself compromise have to part with living inside his head but of course that was scary too. That meant perhaps he didn't care about anything anymore. Perhaps it meant he was in fact shallow. He didn't want to think about that. His tea was too hot to drink yet. He was still sick.

That night he had lain on his back and on his side and on his stomach in the empty room. His mother and Jeffrey and Ron there too. Ron was their renter. He lived in the basement periodically. He tended to appear in moments of great crisis. Hunter lay there and thought about dying. He didn't want to die die from this fatal bout of flu. Jeffrey thought it was meningitis. Probably it was just pneumonia. But he imagined life without Eileen life without life and he didn't like that didn't want to be stuck in the hospital or at home. Home didn't contain Eileen and that depressed him. His daily happinesses were contingent on seeing her even though it was the anticipation anticipating seeing her that meant more to him than when they actually saw each other. Being together in real life was always so conflicted. So that's how he felt—sort of—now. But the feeling pointed to Dewey the new Dewey. They had a date for Thursday were supposed to see each other have coffee and he hoped he'd be okay didn't want to be diminished in any way in her presence.

He imagined he would already be there when she arrived. He'd have taken a table a small one by the window and would be nervously scribbling in his green notebook. She'd come in and he'd pretend to be startled pretend to have been engrossed but really he would have been attuned to every sound tremor motion within a 3 block radius might have even spotted her walking quickly peripherally might have forgotten about the balled up napkins he'd have been snotting in and hoped his nostrils and upper lip weren't crimson wanted nothing at all to distract her from his charm only wanted words details to further any semblance of attraction. Did she like him. Is that why she would have come. He felt like he had shell shock from these things had been deafened from the blasts of too many ill-conceived quasi dates. Maybe it was something about Writing Center girls. Maybe they were somehow harder to read more fickle with agendas of some sort. Well didn't everybody have an agenda if you really stopped to think about it.

What are you writing she might ask pulling out the chair setting aside a book bag stowing it beneath the table.

Oh this. Just a story I've been working on.

Oh yeah. I feel like I never have time to write creatively. Is it for a class.

No well it's sort of fictionalized personal narrative so yeah I think I'm going to turn in some of it for my non-fiction class.

At that point he'd start feeling self-conscious. He rarely read to girls even ones he was trying to hook up with. Maybe he'd start doing that again. The trouble with doing it was his work tended to be very tentative he wasn't sure whether he liked it or hated it plus this new thing seemed definitely to be more of a personal narrative. These days he didn't want to unintentionally reveal too much. He liked being in control of the details about his life he shared with other people and his fiction maybe revealed more than he wanted to. Plus what with the way Hilary reacted she liked his stuff even the inchoate badly executed blather from those days but she insisted on invoking the Intentional Fallacy but worse insisted on reading the narrator as him didn't see the implicit boundaries maybe didn't want to. Probably thought she could understand his motivations better if she read him into and out of everything. But he felt insulted didn't appreciate her comments. Hilary revealed her artlessness her lack of culture the longer he knew her and her inability to read a text closely partially had something to do with that. How would Dewey read him.

# 16

He put on a T-shirt this morning and it smelled like Jane and that summer when they were together. God he missed her. The old her. The Jane he saw when she came to Chicago last summer was not the one he once knew. This latter her went to Yale and sang second soprano in New Blue and didn't shave her legs. This Jane had a bruise on her lip that looked like a cold sore but she explained she got punched in the face demonstrating kickboxing. This Jane was sort of the same but now totally lesbian and not just experimenting like she did that summer. Hunter felt old when he looked in the mirror after they got off the phone before they saw each other. She sounded the same on the phone though it had been years since they last spoke. It was the fourth of July. He picked her up at her mother's building. Why did he run from her when she liked him all those summers ago. He made up myriad excuses. Part of it had to do with Angela like it seemed to always end up having to do with Angela. She gave him shit over the fact that Jane was so young. Jane was fifteen that summer. Hunter was twenty. Angela felt that his seeing her was wrong and the more he thought about it the less sure he was. He started to feel somewhat uncomfortable with the whole thing and pushed her away avoided her calls didn't see her. Of course that wasn't the first time he'd thought about appropriateness. No it was somewhat on his mind each time they went out. Her mother was a manic depressive had these terrible mood swings made Jane feel like shit and made her cry a lot of the time. Her mother had freaked out when she found out they'd spent time together when the two of them were in high school he a senior she a freshman. Her mother called the principal. The principal the asshole that he was told Simona. First what was the point of that. He wanted her to know he the principal probably wanted to sleep with her probably jacked off after their advisory sessions. She Simona was hot. It was understandable but she freaked out even though again nothing happened per se. It was just that Hunter picked Jane up once after a piano lesson. She took lessons in Hyde Park in a building across the street from the apartment he grew up in. He picked her up after and took her to his house. They watched TV sat sort of close to each other but he was absolutely too freaked to make a move. Okay so anyway Simona was out of town for the weekend had gone to North Carolina. Her family had a house there. Why she'd gone he didn't remember. She came back they watched TV sat on the floor of her parents' bedroom watched part of *Quiz Show* on cable. He felt like he'd cheated but really hadn't. Jane was just this tiny girl whom he couldn't stop thinking about whom he couldn't get out of his mind. For some ineffable reason he wanted her. Wanted her badly. He didn't even understand what it was about her that made him want to cheat made him want to sabotage the relationship with Simona though technically it was already corrupted. She cheated on him the previous summer so that was already out there but since he decided not to leave her it was as though that drama had obviated itself and so it didn't provide him with any leverage. Though he just liked being around this Jane who radiated all this sexuality even before he ever spoke to her even before she ever knew a thing about him. He wanted her. Fantasized about her. Jacked off with a yearbook in one hand turned to her blurry seventh grade picture. This was horrible he knew but regardless he broke up with Simona sent birthday cards to Jane in New Hampshire. She'd already moved away. She finished high school at Exeter but returned for the summers worked at a pizza place slept with some girls. That business had started at Exeter started with a rather lecherous unattractive roommate but apparently the concept resonated. She began sleeping with girls regularly. It made him feel sort of uncomfortable. He didn't know how to respond. Of course initially it turned him on severely but later on he felt competed with a bit challenged. It was sort of a cliché but it was how he felt. Their first kiss was so fucking insane. They finished a dinner at the IHOP. He had worked that night. He was a new supervisor and into it worked nights worked late so it must have been after midnight maybe even after one. He picked her up at her building. She well really her mother now lived in Rogers Park in a definitely scary sort of building called the Sovereign. He picked Jane up. He looked about him nervously. He didn't know how he felt about idling in front of this building. They went to Broadway ate at IHOP returned to the car. He leaned toward her. They kissed. It was a perfect kiss. She knew what she was doing. She leaned closer to his side. It was sort of hard to navigate their bodies around the hard plastic fixtures. They kissed. He tilted his seat back. She climbed on top of him. They eventually got chased out of the parking lot. That was semi embarrassing kind of scared him he didn't want to get the police involved. Could they arrest him for statutory. Did that sort of thing happen. Overactive imagination perhaps. He didn't want to take any chances constantly thought about what would happen to his job if he did get busted. Would they find out. What if he had to miss work. Nothing could have been less desirable of an outcome. He didn't want to lose his job. It was important to him. He'd been there three years and now recently promoted. Took it well rather seriously and this Jane thing perhaps came into conflict with those things. Also the way he dressed. He wore blue oxfords and khaki pants to work. He didn't have to he just felt like he should like it made a good impression on his employees the interviewers his boss. But his clothes juxtaposed to Jane's seemed ridiculous. Her T-shirts revealed tan arms and a insuperable neck and sometimes when she bent or leaned betrayed her midsection a belly button that had no ring in it. Her jeans were tightly girlish and dark recently washed or were they who knew for sure. He felt like a pedant old like a dork but she didn't seem to mind embraced his tongue eagerly. The subsequent nights they parked next to the marina and walked around beside the boats near the water stopping to kiss every couple of feet. But then Angela intervened. Made him stop calling her stop talking to her. She gave him this haughty attitude said it was wrong it was sick it was gross but he thought it wasn't like he had anything else going on so why not. But he must have whether he liked it or not taken what Angela had to say to heart internalized the vitriol somehow because he stopped returning Jane's calls. And then it was one day after the summer had ended his fall semester already had begun he was still working late though and he decided to call her back. It was probably because of the message she left—I'm going back tomorrow. I wanted to see you before I go—and so he reluctantly but not so reluctantly called her. And maybe she asked what had happened and he probably lied said Busy or The semester started and I have reading already or I lost your number or maybe—he really didn't remember exactly— it was something like I was afraid to call you because I didn't know what was happening. Okay probably that he didn't say. But they probably saw each other and yes they did they kissed in his car they went inside a Jewel and looked at flowers. It was late at night hardly anyone in the store at all they walked around browsing stopping standing kissing. He held her from behind reached around her waist and set his hands between her stomach and the top button of her jeans reached a little further down felt her hair down there and wanted more wanted her wanted to sleep with her. That's the thing he had been afraid of. Did he take her home. He rented a room that year but hardly ever slept in it. Like an idiot he never mentioned it to Jane that summer was afraid that she'd want to have a copy of the key start spending time there when she hated her mother so he never brought it up as an option when they tried to figure out where they could go. In fact several times when they drove around looking for a place to park to make out they passed the street with the building and it would have been so simple and easy for them to go there but maybe he didn't bring it up because he was afraid of having sex with her. Maybe that was a sign he still had some integrity left. But he was intoxicated by her smell the apple cinnamon shampoo the laundry detergent aura on her T-shirt the thin ribbons of perspiration which bordered both of them. He loved the summer. Maybe at one point not as much as then but she was so—he hated to use such a stupid metaphor but—she was so ripe and bursting with flavor. She had sex with an old boyfriend semi-regularly that summer a boy who went to military school named Greg and maybe at points she would hint things about not being happy or just in it for the sex with Greg from military school and this freaked him out because he wondered if her talking about Greg meant she was trying to say she was in love with him or something. He didn't want that enjoyed making out the breakfasts the making out but didn't want anything serious. Besides he figured how would it work. Jane was still in high school. She didn't even live in Chicago. But it was great being with her. They didn't have conflicting moments those moments of level headedness where-is-this-relationship-going sort of cant and he appreciated that. Basically they just had a good time and nothing meant much of anything of course except that he didn't know then exactly how he was always going to be kind of in awe of that moment. How it actually came to be he would always wonder about and sort of regard himself at that moment with a bit of jealousy like why has nothing similar happened since and why did it have to end. Seeing Jane three years later was anticlimactic. It was simply a different Jane. No matter how hard he tried he couldn't make the same Jane come back at all. She no longer looked or smelled clean. He wondered despite the hairy legs the I'm-a-total-lesbian-now odd swollen bruised lip New Haven persona if something might happen between them that night. But it didn't. Though she sat rather suggestively close to him at the bookstore café where he read a collection of *New Yorker* short stories and she *I Know Why The Caged Bird Sings* it obviously meant nothing though maybe she was expecting him to try something. Well he'd never know and apparently there wouldn't be any repeat performances because after that she stopped emailing him pretty much entirely. He wrote her at different points. In several messages he asked pretty much outright why she wasn't writing him and she responded briefly once to say she was very busy but after that nothing. He always attributed this sudden severing of communication to that night in Chicago but what had really happened to set her in such a motion. They didn't fight. He didn't try anything. It was just almost as it had always been. No specific place to go they ate at the IHOP. She was hungry and ate everything she ordered as always. He was a bit nervous and chewed slowly but left satiated. He paid the check. So what then. They tried to find a movie to go see but nothing looked intriguing enough to bother so they spent the night reading and he liked that liked being with her in a bookstore some of the old comfortableness perhaps coming back to him in flashes. Moments he would turn toward her and despite the too short uneven militant haircut despite the bruises despite the subterranean rage it felt like they had something. He could remember her back when they really did have something the abounding sexuality the surplus of youthfulness. She said something during the meal about that summer and how she was as old now as he was when they first started talking and it was true. She was almost eighteen. He had been eighteen when he picked her up after her piano lessons and it was sort of amusing sort of an odd thing to point out. He thought about it and didn't say what he thought about it but what he thought about it was Yeah what happened after we met and alternatively Why did I think everything meant so much that summer—that apartment my stupid job Angela's electronic disdain—meant so much that I would let her go. Though it wasn't even in like the most whimsical of moments he might have hallucinated a future for the both of them but it was that he had let go of something that was his and for specious motives and he had to live with that be reminded of that know that he had chosen something and gotten what he had chosen and this was that thing this aberration that resulting situation. This was that.

# 17

For some reason there hadn't been enough coffee. Hunter Flanagan had ordered a grande same as always. He drank it quickly. Maybe it hadn't come to him scalding. That was possible. It was good fragrant reminded him of boldness strength temerity he didn't possess. He appreciated that. In his car engine running humming prominently he really needed to get that muffler looked at again how embarrassing was all this shimmying and trembling Sinéad O'Connor sang *Tell me baby where did I go wrong* a girl with a blue Mustang an old one small angular like *Back To The Future* a fucking Metallica sticker affixed to the passenger side back seat window panel parked beside him. She put a yellow Club on locked it into place across the steering wheel. Was that really necessary in a campus parking structure.

He ran into Lila at the library and she'd been abrupt with him. Hunter hadn't seen her after her class—she had intro to lit right before his critical theory class that's how they'd met he supposed. Random flirtatious superfluous between class chat. So here he was. In the library she seemed curt right away went to the bathroom left him standing there but peremptorily returned.

He wanted to show her something. Something really upsetting he said and pointed at a computer.

She looked at him strangely.

Try to close that window he said. He watched her tentatively grasp the mouse and attempt to slide it across the laminated paper. The cursor didn't move just remained trembling in place.

He told her maybe to end the suspense It's the mouse. Somebody stole the ball. Can you believe it.

Maybe it's just broken.

No he said and reached for the round plastic piece which lay behind it. Somebody did this on purpose. I just can't believe it. He really didn't care that much though he was sort of amused by just how juvenile people who went to this school could be it really didn't surprise him. This school sucked. Why wouldn't it be inhabited by children.

She said she had to write an article and then lifted her hands to show him her fingers. I had my prints taken she said. There was faint black ink on the sides.

He didn't ask why only returned Oh well so you have no identity now.

Guess not.

You should try to find out who stole them.

Yeah you're right. There that was kind of a smile. He wanted to ask her out have a drink dinner something get to know her because they really didn't know anything about each other find out what all this meant.

She said I have to go type this and started walking toward the lab.

Oh he said a bit confused. Her motion movement was happening quickly almost too quickly to make sense.

She turned around looked at him but was still essentially in motion.

I'll talk to you later he said but it sounded more like a question.

She said Yeah but that was all the specificity she included.

So he left the library confused unsure wondering what her advances retreats meant why. Why he was even thinking about it thinking about her to her point of rationalizing She gets like this when she has to write a paper though what was up with all the writing at the last minute. He would never suggest she might try starting earlier. Perhaps that would seem condescending untoward but he really didn't understand it.

Did he really want to begin to experience more than one side of her. They had yet to talk about much of a serious tenor. He didn't know yet what her parents did if she had any siblings. He guessed either none or she was the oldest. Definitely she came across as the oldest child emotional wherewithal though only to a certain degree. He knew that the person whom he desired the most would be someone completely different—well not completely not categorically different but not possessing the attributes qualities of his own life he didn't admire. Maybe someone like Lila couldn't be the one because she went to the same school as he and that was a mark of discredit ignominy but did this person necessarily have to be the one judged by such rigorous and unnecessary criteria. Wasn't the plan to not to start behaving like that again judging again. Wasn't it.

# 18

I have a date with Dewey tomorrow I have a date with Dewey tomorrow I have a date with Dewey tomorrow he chanted to himself after working out at the gym. A fairly unimpressive feat of endurance Hunter Flanagan didn't get through his twenty minutes of running his strength seemed to flag after only 15. Spent the next 5 alternating between a flailing sprint and power walking while gripping the sides of the treadmill tightly until his wrists began to burn and ache. He was okay on the bike made it through the exercise. So tomorrow he thought. Hunter Flanagan has a date tomorrow night. Something bad happened as he was driving home. His cell phone vibrated. He flipped it open one hand on the wheel his attention on the tiny display. It was an 847 number. He knew right away whom it was. It was Kate. God damn it. Why she was relentless. Called last night he ignored her called now again. And who called from 312 this morning and didn't leave a message. Well he didn't care. This was getting out of hand ridiculous.

He had a good conversation with this girl he worked with Nicole today from the computer center. She was cute. He liked her had a little crush on her at the beginning of the semester when they first started working together but his interest quickly waned when he began to think about Iris all the time. Now she—Iris—well he didn't even want to start to figure out what any of her signs her suggestions meant because he was wrong if he thought they did have meaning because they didn't. She rejected him but it wasn't terrible. It turned out she was married had a fucking husband probably something Middle Eastern and pre-arranged. He didn't know. She didn't change her last name didn't wear a wedding ring. What the fuck. She had exchanged email had been coy with him for several weeks and then finally flung that sort of explosive device upon his small and unsuspecting village. Well it didn't matter now—that was months and months ago. But it did matter because he didn't know how to read for signs didn't know how or what subtle suggestions meant or didn't mean. Why was that always happening to him. When he thought he knew what something meant though never with certainty it always turned out not to mean what he thought it meant. Iris that's what happened there same thing with Helaine or with Lila or with whomever. It was just he was constantly doing that and he guessed the times when he didn't have even the slightest inclination that a girl liked him she turned out to. Kate obviously whom he thought of presently or if he really wanted to get depressed about it he could add Miriam to that list. Anyway why did he have such faulty sensory equipment.

He really didn't want to fuck things up with Dewey in any way. It hadn't even been a week yet since the disaster date with Kate but he felt like he was recovering having not seen her since then definitely helped but he was still confused about it. How did he get away from her. Hunter Flanagan and Nicole had a good conversation about it today after their shift. She was waiting for a friend whom she was to have lunch with and he needed to talk to someone. They were talking about jobs. She was freaking out about what to do after college. She'd been agonizing for weeks. He thought about Market Facts and suggested she apply there. She looked up their website at a consultant's computer. She liked it. He said he could email somebody. He still had friends there. She attached a copy of her resume and uploaded it to an email and sent it to him. He from a different Mac forwarded it to Essma said hi. They had emailed each other a day or two before about his potentially coming back to work there for the summer but he wasn't that keen on going back. This favor made Nicole happy. He was glad about that. He liked to be able to help people be able to give somebody something that she wanted or needed and not really wanting anything in return. Perpetuating serendipity. Why not. Nicole was still cute. He still found her somewhat attractive but knew his motivation to pursue her had come and gone. He liked being sort of friends with her. He liked that distance between them. He felt oddly comfortable around her had even alluded to wanting to sleep with her jokingly of course on several occasions. She didn't like Macs. That would be a problem a reason not to get together. No seriously he felt like he could definitely relate to her better now that he wasn't interested actively in her.

She mentioned something about seeing someone.
A boyfriend he asked.
Sorta she said looking away.
How long.
Eight months.
So since you've known me.
Yeah I guess so.
So he liked her and she went out and got a boyfriend. Well fancy that. It didn't matter much to him. He told her the story of the blind date the bad kissing. She laughed said she had a few bad kissing guys before.

She said You can always work with them. You can teach them things.

He said I think it's beyond hope in this case.

She laughed some more. Then he told her the story about his real not blind but unclear purpose date with Dewey. It was the next day. He left out certain details even though he didn't figure there was much of a chance Nicole could have known Dewey but he didn't say exactly where it was they he and Dewey had met. He didn't say where they were having coffee but did say she suggested the coffee first.

Nicole said Yeah she likes you I can tell and that's the same thing Angela told him.

Really you think so was his response. He wanted her to like him. He realized then that he wasn't just doing whatever like he thought. He wanted to fall in love. Fuck everything else. Fuck the novel which was in a scary way not for some reason giving him as much grief as other projects. But really wasn't it just the before—the starting part—that was the most difficult most gut wrenching wasn't that just the story of his life afraid of beginning too scared of trying. It sounded like a cliché something he would have said when he was sixteen but wouldn't have recognized the irony in at the time not in the same way he did now. He needed to do certain things now not just regarding Dewey or his novel but certain things in general. Okay he was thinking specifically about setting Kate straight being honest. It had to do with honesty. If he'd learned anything it was that a relationship could not exist on a foundation of lies. Maybe he had to not be so concerned about being funny or interesting and to just let things happen. That sounded like relinquishing his power though. Letting things just happen could result in disappointment. But what really was he to gain from pretending. He knew from last Friday that he had no reason to lie to himself to pretend he liked a girl more than he did just to fill a void. He didn't care to fill the void at this point in his life. He had—what did he have—he had his work and the energy which arose from god knows where this mysterious wherewithal. He had his classes. He was doing fairly well current with the reading. He had some papers coming up which he'd have to start worrying about and that could be rough. He would have to maybe stop writing for a while or at least try to get other things done before writing. He had to read this book about *Heaven's Gate* destroying United Artists and other things. Maybe the timing was all wrong for anything.

Maybe he was in fact too consumed for a consuming romance. But what the fuck. He'd figure it all out. Everything somehow made sense when you really needed it to. He always chastised himself and others for trying to read too far into the future so why give in to it now. That didn't make much sense. So what was going to happen tomorrow. He hoped he wouldn't have insomnia over it tonight. He should have bought sleeping pills at Walgreen's on his way home. He hoped he wouldn't start chewing the inside of his lower lip. He did that compulsively nervously as a nervous habit. Sometimes gum chewing wasn't even enough. He started gnawing. He had to not do that. What if he needed the inside of his mouth tomorrow. God he wished. He knew Dewey would be an amazing kisser the perfect kiss. He desperately hoped she would be or hell that he would even get the chance to find out whether she was or wasn't. She would be he just knew it. What if she did like him. Wouldn't that be weird. What if she'd been thinking about him these last weeks since they met. Hunter Flanagan hoped that could would even in the slightest most insignificant way be true. All he could do was hope. He would certainly soon find out or at least have a better indication as to whether or not it would be true whether or not he would have reason to think more about her if they would have possibilities maybe even get to spend more time together. Hunter Flanagan felt like he was on the precipice of something something about to happen like he was becoming tangible again like he was about to become something part of something potential again. He liked that. It was scary but he liked it.

Maybe he didn't understand women. He really didn't apply that term to any of the females who traveled from one end of his life to the other. He called them girls. Part of that distinction had to do with him what it meant to be Hunter Flanagan and part of it had to do with the fact that they were all just girls. Now he felt restless wanted to go to sleep didn't feel like checking his email wanted to think about something other than Chandler's mother on *Friends* is Morgan Fairchild. Maybe instead of TV he'd try books. He scanned his shelves. There was an Ann Beattie book he bought once but never read it. Most of the books he bought he did actually read but never that Ann Beattie. Maybe it was during his only Salinger phase or his only Shakespeare phase in high school. He read *Othello* all the time over and over again. Sometimes he felt like Cassio other times Iago. Mostly Iago. He felt comfortable in his shape inhabiting his body reading the lines saying them out loud sometimes when nobody else was around. What would happen tomorrow night. Ross and Rachel were never meant to be together always so close but coming apart tearing apart like a page in a notebook. God was he comparing his life to *Friends*. Had things really gotten that bad. Apparently they had. What was he thinking right now. Well for one thing Kate was expecting a phone call a phone call he did not really feel like delivering. He was still a bit stuffed up his nose still drippy. He was confident that the last of it would clear up before the date. The date. Was it a date. Why didn't he know for sure. At least with Kate it was more explicit their reasons for being together. Maybe Dewey thought that Hunter Flanagan just wanted to have coffee with her. Was coffee ever just coffee. Probably not. It was an easy thing to throw around.

He thought about the last email to Lila. They barely spoke to each other in person. Their conversations after her class before his class had turned into brief greetings hi how are you.

That morning he'd commented on the brightness of the new lights in the building.

She laughed said Maybe you need sunglasses.

But not at night he said.

Especially at night she said and then she turned he turned and they walked away.

That was all they said. It felt different. He had arrived shortly after her class finished and she was on her way out. It was better this way. He always felt strange talking to her in the emptying classroom preferred the hallway. They could fade into the throng. Maybe the people coming in coming out made it less weird or potentially weird. He chewed a piece of Cold-Eeze hated the grittiness of it but wanted to be able to breathe tomorrow. He had told this guy Jimmy P. from Film and Authorship class that he wanted to go to this Prince concert that Prince might actually play at but that wasn't confirmed. He wasn't really thinking when he said he wanted to go and was now stuck with a ticket. Fifty dollars. That was a lot but supposedly there'd be an open bar at the Park West. He hadn't been there in over a year. He knew the date he'd been there last exactly. March 17. That was the day of the Matthew Sweet concert. He was supposed to go with Hilary but they broke up two days before. He went alone. He still had the unused other ticket. He couldn't sell it didn't see anybody outside the club looking for a ticket but then again he didn't really try to find anybody since was mildly afraid of getting arrested. Prince supposedly according to Jimmy P. was to take the stage at four thirty in the morning. Yeah right there was no way he was going to wait around all night. Maybe this was a good excuse to try to make a date with Dewey a second date if what they were to do tomorrow was actually a date. If he had a date Saturday night with Dewey he would definitely not stay around if it got too late. He liked this Jimmy P. person but didn't know him well hadn't expected him to come up with the tickets. He said he was only 90 percent sure he could. But the bastard did. Just Hunter Flanagan's luck. He'd rather just stay home with or without a date preferably without. He could stay home read the Bach book work on his novel drink a glass of wine and pass out. He didn't want to drive to Lincoln Park struggle to find a parking place but then again he was sort of stuck. He needed to blow his nose. He was clogging up could barely breathe. It was going to be some sort of crowd of people Jimmy P.'s friends at this Prince concert which was actually just a launch party for Prince's website. Hunter Flanagan guessed Prince wouldn't even show but who could refuse an open bar. A few vodka tonics in actual glass—they didn't use plastic at the Park West—would make everything okay. Maybe these people wouldn't suck. He knew one of them at least this strange Canadian guy from class a swimmer named Gerard. He was an idiot but Jimmy P. liked him for some bizarre reason. Oh whatever he'd go for two hours and leave. Fuck the fifty bucks. Karen another girl from class wanted to go. Gerard had no sense of tact and blurted it out to her that they planned to go after class that afternoon. She now was interested. Hunter Flanagan guessed Jimmy P. couldn't come up with another ticket but it didn't matter anyway Karen had a boyfriend or at least she did last summer when he was sort of attracted to her when they tutored at the Writing Center. Jimmy P. was sort of into her. Hunter Flanagan was sure that a few drinks might make her interesting so he didn't mind so much her coming but of course what if Dewey liked him revealed things wasn't coy was forthcoming. What if they touched flirted what if he proposed they catch that night's Sherman Alexie reading and they went to the Metro and kissed at some point and he would want to see her the next night. It could still work out. He could maybe see a movie have dinner with her and then go to the Park West at ten or something and still leave early. God what was he thinking. How was he going to get any work done. Too much stimulation. He didn't completely mind. He put on a Dire Straits CD and listened to Walk of Life. How appropriate. it was a little loud though and he wanted something quieter. He should probably go to sleep he figured but it was a night too warm too springlike for sleeping. He sat on the couch with only his thoughts. Well not just his thoughts. He had the computer too. He felt strangely healthy having not checked his email since before leaving campus. Today was Wednesday. He was at the gym tonight. He didn't usually exercise on Wednesdays but he skipped yesterday ditched on account of his sickness didn't know if he'd have the energy to make it through. Well wasn't that the point of going. He didn't want to walk out into the cold air still sweaty didn't want pneumonia for christ's sakes so he went tonight. Nobody interesting to look at a rather boring scene in fact. He was glad he went regularly more or less it was a good thing to do.

    There was a reason he avoided his email. Why was he afraid of Dewey writing to say she couldn't make it fucked up with the times somehow they'd have to reschedule. Why did he think he'd encounter that. Should he dial in. Why would that happen. Because of the last time he got excited about a date or a sort of date and that time was with Lila and this wasn't all that long ago in fact it was only a couple of weeks ago and they had decided to hang out do something get a drink whatever and he was happy but then she called that afternoon. He was supposed to pick her up at nine. She said she couldn't do it after all that night could they have lunch instead. He said okay. So they had lunch instead salads at the Marshall Field's café back to square one. She seemed to think it a suitable alternative but it wasn't the same now was it. They didn't seem to find a time to reschedule. The spontaneity he flirted with—whatever.

Now he was getting tired. Hunter Flanagan wanted to sleep. His contacts were getting dry. Christ. Good thing he remembered he wanted to take them out let them soak not meet Dewey with dry or dirty lenses in his eyes. He didn't want to have red eye either. Maybe he'd get some new drops or something. She was really very pretty. She probably wouldn't be dressed up or anything. She was coming from class after all. So was she just seeing him to get it out of the way to say well I did it now leave me alone in a manner of speaking or did she want to find out what they might have in common find out if it were true what they wrote about Aries and Virgo being incompatible. Nicole was a Virgo too look what didn't happen with that.

He couldn't use this as a reason to neglect his work. He liked writing not that he really had a choice whether or not to do it like a passing interest in a girl. Maybe he should try to be less reticent when it came to plotting. He rarely discussed what he was working on with people didn't want to appear narcissistic only responded and albeit vaguely to questions others would pose about his fiction.

Now it was Romeo and Juliet. He'd definitely stay to listen to that one and then it was off to bed. Was Kate pissed. She probably didn't know how to get mad at anybody. She would have had several opportunities to get at least a bit peeved with some of the stuff Hunter Flanagan had done already and they hadn't even been in each other's physical presence more than once. This zinc gum was so disgusting. He wanted to spit it out but didn't know if it had been 20 minutes yet. It made him wince made him want to gag. The gum had suddenly turned very acerbic tasting. *The dice was loaded from the start.* What would he do if things went well. That would be probably more confusing because he was resolved to allow himself to like her. *And I forget I forget the movie songs when you gonna realize it was just that the time was wrong Juliet.* He definitely felt that he was being too over analytical here. He didn't need to think about things so very much. There were certainly other things to which he could direct his attention. So why did she make him so this way. What was going on. Where was she at this moment. Sleeping perhaps. Where did she live. Would he ask for her number if she said no to the Sherman Alexie thing which honestly he probably didn't have time for either so he couldn't entirely blame her for not wanting to go. Did she even know who Sherman Alexie was. Lila knew basically of no authors though worked in a fucking bookstore. Kate was similarly deficient. Well at least she'd heard of Faulkner and some of the others. Miriam that was a laugh she was really fucking stupid. He realized one thing: he would no longer be able to see Miriam or think about Miriam or have sex with Miriam after May because he would have graduated college and she would still be doing whatever passed for attending college and he would have more reason more empirical evidence in his favor to affirm her marginality. It must be nice not to have to do any thinking he thought then it must be nice not to have to worry about anything significant to be able to amuse yourself by staring into a beer bottle or talking about butt fucking. Being intelligent wasn't so great after all. Maybe this was an argument against grad school. Miriam basically protected herself from life by being an idiot being too dumb to really have to deal with anything substantial to experience real emotions to understand monumental disappointment to feel things of a profound nature. It was just something that being incredibly simple she didn't have to worry about and sure he felt like an ass saying that but it was the truth. Her ignorance protected her from the world and what sorts of barriers did other people have to filter out the elements to protect them. Not many to be sure. At least tonight on the eve of his date with Dewey he felt like Hunter Flanagan again.

# 19

He slept rather well considering. Hunter Flanagan figured he must have been tired. It wasn't as though much time passed without his thinking about the date. It wasn't as though any decisions up to the present point—parked outside the Dominick's to get cash and a tea from Starbucks—had he made without thinking about Dewey. He still hadn't checked his email. At first last night it was because he was just tired of all the monotonous junk group computer consultant mail notifications of nothing he particularly cared to know about and Angela wanting to know why he'd been silent for a couple of days. Hunter Flanagan started out selecting a light blue almost purple t-shirt matched it to a simple flannel blue and tan but quickly dismissed the combination opted instead for a green sweater and white t-shirt. The sweater was ribbed like the brown turtleneck he wore that day the last time he and Dewey spoke in person.

    He didn't call Kate back hoped she had been on the phone. She didn't have call-waiting and would think she'd just missed him. That would absolve him. He still sort of wondered about Deanna the other girl he exchanged email with from the Internet dating service. He felt like he waited entirely too long to call her but he just had so much going on. It was hard—it really was—that wasn't just an excuse—to do really anything. He wanted to reinvent himself start anew without all the what duties responsibilities commitments made in haste and regrets start over as someone else but now he needed more money for his date. He also needed a manilla envelope. It was time to send out a chapter again.

# 20

At lunch he wanted to think of funny things for the date anecdotes to share jokes. He figured the conversation would go well. They hadn't exhausted the resources like he and Kate had prior to meeting. He hoped she Dewey would have a good time that this meeting was out of desire to see know get to see get to know him and not just a he-asked-I'll-be-polite-and-get-it-over-with sort of gesture.

    He didn't feel like eating. Food didn't seem appealing. He switched tables away from the girl whose shirt revealed a good forty percent of her lower back a girl who from the front looked sort of like Jennifer Love Hewitt. He couldn't spend long sketching her as she was surrounded by others. These girls studying probably for some sort of math test. Everyone was always studying together with others for a math test of some sort. Literature was a more solitary endeavor.

    He felt considerably better but still cloudy. His exchanges with others were challenging. He had to over enunciate. People misunderstood his words. He struggled to mean anything. He had sandwiches from yesterday still uneaten. He knew he was hungry but nothing empirical seemed to suggest that was actually the case. He sat and tried to block it all out so he could finish this description of the math test girl. Did his writing mean anything. He hadn't had a surge like this in quite some time such a proliferation of output. It reminded him of when he was working on his last novel. Every time he sat down he wrote. Really it came together rather quickly. But that book was really concerned with plot. What he worked on now was definitely a different sort of narrative introverted self-reflexive self-conscious but really did any of it mean anything. His life seemed marginal right now. He was definitely in a funk didn't feel sad exactly just sort of uninvolved meaningless. He needed to see other people read other things. There was that non-fic book for Film and Authorship due in a couple of weeks. There was the Bellow bio already overdue from the library. He could read the Lacan again. Maybe his writing needed time away from writing. He feared fucking with it and losing the momentum he'd been given. He'd come across it somehow and didn't want to lose it but he didn't want to fuck himself in the process either.

# 21

Several things happened fairly quickly. He was sort of reeling from several things at one time. It wasn't easy to sort out. He felt conspicuous waiting for her. He ordered iced tea. He felt like suddenly he was on display wanted to write about it but didn't want to take out his notebook. His writing was so disorganized. The longer this new thing got the harder it was to manage. This was much like what he imagined happening how he'd want to do something to diffuse the panic but writing didn't seem enough now that he was really waiting. But oddly enough he wasn't having a lip biting panic. It was this curious euphoria. He was sure he'd sound like an idiot when she arrived though he still had time to pull himself together prepare or something. There was oddness abounding. He kept thinking about Lacan and the mirror stage. Outside the elements of Taylor Street provided no comfort. He wanted the stores the cars the people to make sense but they never were synchronous never had been. That's why he mostly avoided the surrounding blocks the street at least this close to the campus. Jeffrey had managed a Mexican restaurant West of there for a couple of months prior to taking off and he still hadn't written Hunter Flanagan why not what was he doing. Maybe he'd been barred from Internet access. Resolved to begin again. Okay it was good to occupy himself with other thoughts different textures of thought.

The tea came. Colleen brought it. The glass was very large.

Seemed incongruous but other things probably contextualized it maybe things he wasn't aware of. This was like a café with the personality of a diner wasn't that intimate at least by design more functional had this newness this sterility which hadn't yet effaced itself no dim lighting no history like the Medici or somewhere else though it still seemed comforting especially now that he was getting used to it. Colleen from his class was the waitress. It was comforting he supposed that she was there too. Christ did he have no agency. Did he always need a chaperone. It was silly to think but it worked. He scribbled on a placemat. He liked this found space. It had possibilities. It wasn't restricted by keyboard or little notebook rules. It was epic in a way the strangeness side by side with familiar objects. The dead goats he saw outside—were they—or were they calves. He couldn't tell. He watched men carry them off a truck into a meat packing store front on his walk over from campus. This iced tea glass was so fucking large it towered over the rest of the table constituents. He moved it from one side of his critical theory binder to the other. He was pretending to read Lacan. The drink now close to his right hand was sweating was heavy was made of leaden glass anodized steel cinder block something that could easily sink a ship but he appreciated that. Maybe it kept him from floating off somewhere like those dreams he always used to have where he lost gravity.

## 22

They sat very close to each other. For a while it was Hunter Flanagan and Dewey existing in this perfect circumstance the best he could have imagined. She had walked in several minutes after he last looked at the time surprising him. He was surprised now how comfortable things seemed. They talked about infomercials. They talked about languages. They talked about modern culture. He wanted to pull her close to him. Maybe she really cared for him.

People sometimes are so self-interested she said it's all about what can you do to improve your condition. She paused then corrected herself Well I didn't mean you Hunter Flanagan but you know.

He laughed pulled toward her. Of course I knew you didn't mean me.

He liked the way she said his name it was as though she'd said his name many times before.

Later he asked if she still had his phone number.

She said Yes I saved that email.

You save email.

Well not all of them but the important ones.

She thought his email important. What was he going to do about all of this. He wanted to see her again be with her again. They walked from the café back to her office. She worked on campus. They walked in a straight path essentially one long straight line of streets and crosswalks and up to the building. It was the first thing that had stopped them from moving.

Hunter Flanagan said I'll call you…but I don't have your number.

She said You could write me.

Yeah he said I guess I could do that.

Pause. He didn't know if that meant—

It's just that I don't get messages you know and I don't want to have to explain—

No it's not a problem I feel the same way. I only really use my cell phone.

She stood close to him. Fuck. *Dating for Dummies* said that meant kiss. She didn't fumble for her keys. She stood still her arms at her sides her eyes pointed up at him. They stood outside a building a campus building not that he cared but he didn't want to act hastily. He knew that much maybe still shell shocked from Kate. Well that could only be a good thing not rushing. Did she want—even if it were ridiculous—could she have wanted to kiss him for him to kiss her. He didn't. They parted. The strangest thing was how much it seemed to be the case that she liked him. He wasn't used to that usually didn't experience that so of course it made him wonder how why. He could acknowledge the fact that things went well. He could say that much. He was scared. It was certainly a strange and unfamiliar feeling.

# 23

Immediately after leaving each other's presence Hunter Flanagan missed Dewey. Walking back to his car he knew that he wanted to see her again and fast and that something had definitely happened. He wrote her an email asked her to have dinner with him. First he thought of inviting her out on Friday but that was the next day. That was too soon. Well not for him but he felt like proposing the next day ran a higher chance of turn down so Saturday. Yes Saturday. He imagined the two of them at a small table in the back of Hi Ricky between rounds of satay slightly buzzed from the spicy bloody marys leaning close toward each other like before more touching more laughing. He was really falling this time. He knew it already. It wasn't just more of the same. Dewey was real not just an image not just a theory. She had form and a shape and they had started something. Coffee wasn't just coffee. He dreamt of her fifty times during the night. One segment stood out. It was strange. He couldn't really put much of it together. They Hunter Flanagan and Dewey were at some sort of store a Halloween costume shop or the Alley black clothes odd phosphorescent light black lights and his parents were there too and so he guessed trying to recreate the dream while awake that he was going to introduce Dewey to his parents. The idea waking or as far as he seemed to be able to gather dreaming didn't entirely frighten him. He could picture it happening.

# 24

What's she like Angela asked. Hunter Flanagan thought the first thing she reminds me of is you. Of course he had long since realized there could be no Angela in his life aside from the electronic one so he'd basically stopped trying to invent one but still there were just certain things about her Angela that he really admired. Of course he didn't simply admire Dewey as an apt substitute. She had a magic a uniqueness. Maybe that's why he liked her so much. She wasn't like the others the others who really didn't understand him weren't capable of understanding. It wasn't that he was such an enigmatic presence. He made some sense but on different levels of course. It had to do with degrees of what he wanted to reveal. He felt like he could tell her things even though it was just looking. He could imagine her Dewey in his life but perhaps in a different way than he had in the past. So they might have dinner together he thought.

# 25

A message on the answering machine. He stood in the kitchen and listened to it. He didn't of course believe what it was saying. It didn't feel surreal exactly just sort of anticlimactic. The director of the writing program at C—.
    She said Welcome.
    She said Barker Award.
    She said teaching position.
    All of this overwhelmed him. He thought immediately of several things. He thought first so this is it this is what I'm going to do.
    He thought next about how he saw Helaine the day before. He'd been late for Film and Authorship. It was almost three o'clock. He had been reading *Final Cut* in the Pier Room and didn't really know what time it was until it was almost three. He took the escalator downstairs and she was at the bottom and walked toward him. It was crowded in the lobby people pushing their way around each other. Hunter Flanagan and Helaine stopped moving said hi. He hadn't seen her for a couple of weeks. He remembered the last time remembered the date exactly it was his birthday. While they talked then he felt like he was smiling but tried not to smile. They talked about nothing really then. They were in the Morgan Street Station.
    He had bought potato chips and a soda she said she was looking for a small pack of M&M's. He asked her why.

She held up a bag of peanuts. I'm trying to make trail mix she said.

That was cute. He didn't ask why but she explained They didn't have any trail mix so I thought I would make my own. She reached for a packet of raisins.

Well I guess you have it he said.

She paid for the items. They spoke more about nothing. When he saw her these days he always thought about how he was once attracted to her not just attracted but utterly consumed by her. She made him absolutely weak once he felt so strongly about her. He couldn't even for the life of him figure out why from just looking at her. Blonde hair excellent eyes glowing smile yeah but why such exigency. These days he didn't see her often. From time to time they'd pass each other but they had no classes together she was younger and a pre-pharmacy major. He tried to avoid the places where he used to run into her. Though when he was obsessed with her he never saw her in those places for some reason those weeks what was it a month when he was actually looking for her. No not then but now he tried to stay away from the couches the computer lab in the SRC dorm. She always went there or sat outside of there. Penny too. Hunter Flanagan was glad he didn't get assigned to work in that lab anymore. It all happened there his attraction infatuation with Helaine. When it first happened he was working a computer consultant shift. She came and said hello—without Penny he couldn't help noticing. She gave him her email address then wrote it on a small blue card gave it to him and then disappeared leaving him to languish in what really hadn't happened at all.

This time right now she asked him about what he was doing in a few weeks. She said You're graduating. She still had a few semesters to go maybe two years he wasn't sure. He said he didn't know. How could he not know he wondered later he was supposed to know by that point. He never expected it to stretch on and on like this. Maybe he'd start looking for jobs. That sounded so depressing.

He wasn't sure if she asked and he said it first or if she remembered and brought it up but somehow they ended up on the subject of C—.
She said Maybe I'll go there for pharmacy school.
They've got mountains he said.
Do you ski she asked.
No he admitted but there has to be other stuff to do there.
Definitely. She smiled. Maybe he sort of knew could sort of remember why he was so attracted to her but it was hard. How much of all of this of any of this was just Hunter Flanagan making himself think something convincing himself something were true when perhaps it wasn't at all. He didn't like questioning his perceptions. He liked to think he did feel something genuine once and it was just something he'd packed away the emotional response and he'd pushed the memory so far into the background that it was as though it had never been there. But he knew it had. Yeah he guessed he did after the phone call.
    He listened to the message again and thought about Helaine mentioning C—. Maybe she was a talisman. Why would he have seen her he never saw her and she said C—. Other people just asked him vaguely. Some people pressed for specifics but he was always elusive. Talking about C— with Helaine made it more real and then it was real. It really happened. They wanted him and to such a great degree of fanfare. God it was crazy. Phone calls. All this time he was just waiting for a letter an envelope to arrive with something more promising than a cheaply printed form letter in it and now awards TA positions and what courses would he teach. Would it be creative writing or composition. He couldn't sleep that night wondering about his syllabi whether there would be a course packet or if he'd just bring Xeroxes of things. What would they read. Would his students like him. Would he be a good teacher. He didn't like being preoccupied before bed and it was hard to sleep anyway because of the warmth. This was April. Now it was spring. It was getting warmer. It rained but it was becoming warm. Winter definitely over. He'd be moving. He'd never moved

anywhere. He'd be moving to C—. Was this what he wanted. He slowly began to get excited the next morning after hearing the message after checking to make sure he hadn't just dreamed it all waited for his mother to leave the room that took an excruciatingly long time so he could hear the message privately. He didn't want to involve her too much. It was weird enough as it was that she'd gotten the news in a manner of speaking before he did. Of course that freed him from the burden of having to tell her himself. The director said one of the top five applicants. Could that have been true. He wished he could find the statistics somewhere how many applied. Probably at least fifty or sixty. Could it have been more. He wondered what it was. Maybe his samples. He didn't even remember what stories he'd sent. His application process had become sort of disorganized and haphazard by that point. The C— app was due a week or two after the others a week into the semester and Hunter Flanagan procrastinated and avoided and then it was getting late so he just threw everything together sent it in and now this.

Just that morning he had non-fiction with his professor Bates the one who suggested he apply to grad schools and specifically mentioned C—. He had gone there. He loved it. After class they walked together. Hunter Flanagan had a copy of the U of C newspaper that published his flash fiction. He gave it to Professor Bates. He said thanks. Bates then asked if he'd heard from any schools as he did from time to time. Hunter quickly told the truth sort of glossed over the N— specifics but said openly honestly about B— how that wasn't going to happen. Bates didn't seem that surprised about it or even disappointed like he'd expected it but not in an unkind way more like no big deal.

Hunter Flanagan told Professor Bates he'd still not heard from C—.

Bates said Yeah they never tell you anything. How do you think I ended up teaching here. I interviewed there and got hired for this job and I'm still waiting for C— to call me.

Hunter Flanagan laughed. It was then that Bates went into

University Hall and Hunter left campus went to exercise did his running and got home and there was this message. He couldn't believe it.

    He made phone calls. Julianne. She screamed. She was excited. He jokingly said Well you'll have to move with me now and she said Hunter you know I can't do that but she had to meet with a client her cell phone battery was low so they didn't really get a chance to discuss. He left a message for Trey but he wasn't home. He called Helaine. He hadn't dialed her cell phone in months probably not since November though he still had her number saved on his phone. She wasn't there either. He said what happened on the voice mail. What was the use of being coy about it. She was his lucky charm now. Oh prescient Helaine. It didn't mean he liked her again. There were other people he wanted to call.

    He called Professor Bates. Even he was really excited and said You should check into housing early unless you like pot. They laughed. Hunter Flanagan felt strangeness in the conversation but he figured it was because he still hadn't started believing any of this was true. For all he knew he was dreaming. No obviously he was awake but whose life was he acting from upon within without. He suddenly felt like telling people many people but couldn't think of anyone to call. Who would want to know. He thought of two people then two specific people whom for different reasons he wanted to call. Dewey. He wanted to share the news with her. Why didn't he have her phone number. This was not the sort of thing you would want to tell someone especially someone like her in an email. He'd have to wait until they saw each other next week and what would she think. Would it scare her. Would she not want to get involved now that this factor had factored itself into things. He also thought about Kate. He could call her. In fact she'd left several messages kept mauling his cell phone. He didn't even want to hear her messages didn't check them only knew she'd called from the number he was starting to remember definitely recognized as hers on the caller ID. He could call her and tell her but he had a strong inclination not to say anything to her. He didn't want to involve her in this. Only people that were close to him. He barely knew her. Only people he wanted in his world. That criterion didn't exactly include Helaine. She was some sort of peripheral character half in the past now strangely implicated in his present had inadvertently gotten herself wound up in this turn of events unless of course she was a talisman and then she would have known intended on becoming involved.

He didn't want Kate to know and decided not to say anything. He hoped that what he was thinking—that eventually his leaving would come up—wouldn't be an issue which meant that he hoped he'd have found some convenient and gentle way of not knowing her any more by the time he'd need to start packing but how did Helaine get involved in this. He'd stopped thinking about her pretty much three months ago maybe longer. He just couldn't stop thinking about the strangeness of the not such a coincidence coincidence of these unlikely and completely baffling events. He returned to thinking they felt like they were the goings on of someone else a completely different set of people Hunter Flanagan had nothing whatsoever to do with. That was the best he could come up with to explain the phenomenon.

# 26

So why wasn't Dewey writing him Hunter Flanagan wondered. It was now what the third yes third day. Soon it would be a week. A week could certainly turn into a month. A month well if you reached a month of no communication you might as well just forget about the whole thing. He did feel hurt. This wasn't about winning about conquests about getting her. He really liked her. He probably needed someone to want and to like and sure others would come along and fill up the space distract him sufficiently to make him not think about other things other things namely the things that bothered him the grad school stuff. The acceptance had helped him come to terms with the rejections. He could even say that word call them rejections now. That didn't seem so strange.

He felt bad about poor Christine the girl he barely noticed when he was depressed about B—. He had pizza with her on a blind date set up by his stepmother's friend a Lab parent called Laura Phillips. Laura Phillips set him up with Christine her babysitter. They had pizza together on a Saturday. Christine was babysitting. Hunter Flanagan was to come over for dinner. Fine. He talked to her on the phone she seemed okay. Fine whatever he was actually kind of excited about meeting her. This was long before he'd become blasé about blind dates and impassively unexpecting. Well that day he found out about B— like two hours before and he was so shocked so totally stunned and hurt and upset. He finished the last of an old bottle of Absolut Citron he'd stashed in the old woman wine bottle holder. The wicked witch of Providence to be sure. And so by the time he went to meet her—he picked up the pizza margherita tomato and basil she was a vegetarian god that would never work out would it—he was a little drunk. Anyway so he practically bounced over to the house and met Christine. No big surprise kind of too thin and teacherly this long button down sweater too tight but not to be sexy jeans just too tight as in probably old or she was too modest to want to draw even a glimmer of attention to any part of her body. He was jovial completely hiding probably well the disappointment the utter feeling of failure and loss like somebody had died. It was like that. It was a sharp and mysterious numbness the kind of numbness that only comes out when you are grieving mourning some sort of loss the kind you never really anticipate because if you could there wouldn't be grieving.

# 27

So Dewey. Maybe he scared her off in some way. What way could it have been they barely spoke exchanged a few tiny emails really their only encounter of length and intimacy to date was the coffee afternoon which he thought went rather well. Did he scare her away. Was it too presumptuous or forward to ask her out later that same day. Of course she—he didn't think—would have read the email until the next day or maybe even the day after that but obviously it was the intent. He used certain words. He wrote I want to see you again. Those were romantic words. See you. That couldn't be misconstrued as casual or suggestively flirting. No that was This is a date we went on whether you think so or not. Hunter Flanagan said so and he wanted to have another one. He backed her into a corner over that one. He was so immediate she would have had no other choice than to say something. She said she had fun. Though wouldn't she have just omitted that part if she were trying to be truly only polite or did that mean she wanted perhaps to experience what he was in all the blissful imagining and so forth. He read too much into not very much present. He based his entire happiness his sense of self his feeling of security on it. That was stupid. Maybe he was supposed to react to this with a certain degree of emotional maturity—whether or not he in truth possessed any—to wait. So fine that was the only course of action he could take. He couldn't write back and ask why she wasn't writing. It would only encourage more hedging and indirectness and maybe lying. He wanted to avoid that. Certainly he could try having dinner with that Deanna person. Fuck the fact that he hadn't written her in quite some time ignored one of her phone calls. That was all during the Kate days. That was funny that entire courtship from start to finish in what three or four days. He was beginning to surprise himself with the speed with which he fell into and out of fixatedness.

He was still thinking about Dewey though. He'd see her name on flyers about the Writing Center wanted to rub his finger across her name. He'd reread all five of her emails a couple of times. He imagined logging in checking his email finding something from her and enacted different versions. There were the versions where she'd say Yeah let's have dinner and he'd be happy and start thinking only about where they'd go what they'd say how beautiful she'd look what he'd do that would make her laugh. Would they be loath in leaving each other's company. Would she look at him longingly like she did the other day but this time on a quiet street in front of a sleeping house in a tiny neighborhood and would he lean in and kiss her or would she say no give something else as reason. Why not. More commitments more tests papers too many other things basically saying her life was of a certain size and shape and thickness and width and there was simply no room no free corner every part of the shelves full of other things too much stuff other pieces elements components papers to think about things to care about other than him. That wasn't the version of course that made him very happy the one he looked forward to hearing from her or reading about. However he had this sinking feeling that at some point sooner or later that was the news he was going to receive in a thin envelope with nothing personal decorating it or the letter in any way completely artificial and mass produced even the address label printed by some machine somewhere unfeeling impersonal a letter which would say We regret to inform you she's not interested but thanks for applying. He'd get that email from her in one way or another. He'd have to then sit and think about it and wonder where he'd went wrong and wonder how to make sense of it all and wonder what he was to do with his life now and what he'd have to tell people. All of that.

# 28

Hey Hunter Jimmy P. said.
    Do you have the tickets.
    Of course. Do you you know have the cash.
    Yeah what did you think. You thought I wouldn't.
    No I knew you would come up with the cash.
    Look don't be mad if I want to leave early.
    You seriously can't think about leaving before he plays.
    What I can't think about is four thirty in the morning.
    Look we'll talk about this later.
    Okay fine whatever.

# 29

*I think it has to do with big things she says.*
*What kind of big things he asks.*
*Big things. It's like we want certain things and they're monumental. They are quite prodigiously large.*
*He laughs. Maybe that's why we fall in love.*
*She looks at him. Yeah maybe that is why—wait what do you mean.*
*Well he starts falling in love is basically about trying to find something that you don't have and make it exist in another form.*
*I've never really thought about it so—*
*So what.*
*So clinically I guess. That's quite an operational definition you have going.*
*No I'm serious though. People like us you and me we want certain things in life. We're not happy with things not being of a certain profoundness.*
*I guess I know what you mean she says I feel that way too. Certainly it's impossible for me to be satisfied to be contented with the notion that I would not have what I think it is that I seek.*
*He says I see these people all the time. I see these people and they look like they don't need anything that they're satisfied and this part he doesn't say out loud to her she looks way too beautiful right now way too serious looking at him way too much he doesn't say that he doesn't usually allow himself to fall in love because of things like this happening. People seem content a lot of the time. Do you ever notice that.*

*Of course she says. I often wonder how it is possible for such content people to exist in such a frame of mind like wouldn't it drive them insane not to want not to desire big and lofty. Like how could they just sit around with their plain m and m's and not think about what it is that they're not getting what it is that is making them want to be complacent and—*

*You're so right he says and doesn't say I can't believe this happened I can't believe I fell for you and now you don't really want me all it means to you is some kind of intellectual repartee. You fell in love with my discourse with my theoretical perspectives which is completely understandable I'm sure to a certain extent I am in love with your theories whatever makes the attraction work I guess. Who understands these things. Maybe only Freud. Maybe only the new French feminists but regardless what I am supposed to think when I look at you and I see so many things and know that you maybe don't see the same things or just different things.*

*Maybe it's the wanting that makes things real she says suddenly. Maybe it's the fact that if we get the things we want desperately we turn complacent and boring and fatuous and all those things.*

*You're probably right he says but doesn't say and just looks at her tries to take in everything about him and her because for all he knows it could be the only opportunity he'll ever have.*

# 30

So when he tried to consciously remove himself from writing it just seemed to start up again. He didn't care for the editing process surrounding his last book. He'd always disliked having to try to recapture the intensity recreate what he was thinking feeling at inception reinsert himself into the narrative. His second draft was still a mess. He'd thought about sitting back down with it making drastic changes but always felt like his time was better spent on new thoughts new crafting of scenes new characters. Too much time in the old could be internecine. The old stories always seemed to find a way to reintroduce themselves. Really it was less philosophical than this. It was laziness it was lack of experience and talent that made him reluctant to revise. He wanted someone to come along and take care of the inconsistencies the factual inaccuracies for him. Why should he be bothered. His task was to think and feel and work out in an intangible plane and if continuity became something of a problem well that's what editors machines non-creative contingents were for. Not him.

How could he expect a publisher a legitimate one any to seriously consider his work when he didn't believe in it. Maybe if this new thing held if he could make it into something he could just shelve the other one with the rest of his dusty sophomoric attempts over the last decade and start over. That could be good. But still he'd spent a long time with the other felt it was decent nothing a new and untired eye couldn't put together.

There was in the BSB dining hall the Jennifer Love Hewitt girl—she was back. Probably she was too tall for him. She smiled and looked somewhat like Jane the old Jane when she looked like herself. When laughing she lowered her head to the table enraptured happy. She faded in and out. Of course the real Jane looked much different now less of her old self than this random tall girl. What was all this conjuring up of the old Jane for. Why did he care. What did any of it mean. How much did he need to unearth in the quest for reaching some sort of sublimity. How much. He figured lots of girls looked like Jennifer Love Hewitt approximately speaking but none quite her only somewhat like her. And what if he actually found the real one at a restaurant in LA or New York. Would she be everything he ever wanted. Would he care.

He liked writing in his notebook though the computer seemed better suited for the barrage of words ideas scenes that flowed forth but he always worried about going too quickly like sex thinking faster than writing writing faster than thinking. His handwriting sucked. He needed to type if anyone was ever going to understand. His fingers moved quickly over the keys but he had to backspace over typos so much. He always felt like the hardest part of writing—not even strictly speaking novels but really anything especially if there were several drafts involved—was keeping track of the pages. Disks with different versions could drive you insane. He saved sometimes in RTF when he switched between the lab PCs at school and his Mac at home. That created formatting issues. If he were better organized this wouldn't be a problem right he'd keep records. It was the same story with the fiction he sent to magazines. He was a habitual simultaneous submitter but really never knew at any one time what agents publishers editors assistant editors interns had their hands on his prose. That was a problem undoubtedly. He'd bring his green notebook places he went try to write to observe to relax become the characters but it would inevitably hasten his being ill at ease. Everything was all over the place. Notes scenes lines of dialogue on receipts in the margins of his critical essays Derrida and Freud and Saussure. He had some of it typed out but a lot remained in scribble everything disparate impossible to cohere. He hoped it would all somehow connect somehow come together eventually make some sort of sense to him or at least to someone before it all just came apart and became nothing.

# 31

It wasn't as if he were intentionally keeping the news from Dewey. Hunter Flanagan completely intended to tell her about the call. So many other people knew now. Professor Bates announced the details in non-fiction and everybody seemed excited. Peanut wanted to make an announcement on the Writing Center listserv. Hunter Flanagan demurred. Why she wrote. Is there someone you don't want to tell. They discussed the events after the phone call in a serious of rapid-fire emails. He knew whom she alluded to. Dewey obviously. Well he wrote yes and no.

Later he explained I want to tell her but don't you think that will make her not want to get involved.

No Peanut said. Girls like to know they're time bound. It lets them act freely without consequence.

Well okay but what if Hunter Flanagan wanted something more. Couldn't long distance relationships work. He'd always said no they couldn't if someone asked but in actuality had never even tried it had never really felt moved to. Usually he just avoided the issue and let romances come apart before geography became complicit.

Really it had more to do with the fact that he wanted to tell her in person. He thought about how he would tell her. Maybe she would be really amused excited want to celebrate but he didn't want to say in an email. He'd already done that to some anticlimactic degree with Angela. They both sensed the letdown. He wrote one version of the email where he told her but immediately deleted it. It sounded completely wrong. He wrote another mentioned only the fewest possible details. She wrote back quickly adulations block letters and said that it was hard to express her felicitations this way.

He replied Yeah I know I should have called you and half meant it. So he wasn't looking for a repeat performance. Would Dewey feel like he had purposely excluded her if she overheard someone talking about it in the Writing Center. She worked there today Friday and he didn't. Tonight he was having dinner with Trey. Maybe he'd have a good idea about what to do but it was after all sort of her fault. She could have given him her phone number. Still though he really liked her emails. They reminded him of Angela's. Maybe Dewey was Angela. They seemed to have similar personalities at least electronically. He wanted to go check and see if she'd written back about next week yet. Where would they have dinner. Dinner. She was starting to break down beginning to yield. Maybe she liked him. Maybe she read his emails five times. He also invited her to go to a reading Professor Bates was giving in Glen Ellyn at the College of DuPage. He didn't pitch it as a date though. He was trying to arrange a group of people to go out there. A group thing would make her feel like it was casual which was exactly how he wanted it to seem. He really wanted Dewey to hear Professor Bates get to know him. If she went Hunter Flanagan would definitely have to tell her about C—. Someone there was bound to bring it up. Professor Bates was really excited proud mentioned it every time he saw Hunter now. If he didn't tell Dewey before that it would definitely create an awkward situation. Maybe he would stop by the Writing Center see if he could catch her in a free moment get it over with. It could only become more difficult the longer he waited and he really wanted her to know about Professor Bates's reading. This relationship with Bates was an important part of Hunter's writing life and he wanted Dewey to know about that.

# 32

He went to the Writing Center ostensibly for the papers Frida wanted him to look over really to see Dewey. She was there looking at a chart some poems on a heavily ornamented bulletin board.

Dewey said Hi Hunter almost louder than he'd expected.

He didn't know what to do with it. Her reaction surprised him for a moment like she was really excited to see him didn't expect him to show and now her day was brighter because he had.

What's going on. What are you doing now.

He said Nothing really why what are you doing.

She said I don't feel like going to Anthropology.

He said Do you want to go somewhere.

Where she asked.

How about CCC.

Okay she said and so they went outside.

They walked over to the union.

Do you want to go in he asked.

They stood next to concrete structures. Some people walked around them and others sat and talked. It was a beautiful day sunny. They were standing in a dark spot the light blocked by the height of the building.

She said Let's go sit somewhere and they walked to the middle of the quad to the benches and sat on one where there weren't people around. Hunter liked how she took the lead directed him moved him about. They sat.

I just didn't really feel like going she said.

I know the feeling. He was supposed to go work sit in a computer lab but didn't want to. He didn't want to do anything except sit beside her. She was wearing a gray turtleneck sweater. After saying she was hot and then Now to figure out how to get this off she began to extract herself starting with the sleeves. She had a lilac t-shirt underneath. She looked absolutely beautiful. It made Hunter nervous. He was wearing a blue flannel shirt a thin one and it felt small on him. He knew he must have looked dorky in it wanted to unbutton and roll back the sleeves but didn't. She sat close to him. They crossed their legs sat facing each other legs folded sort of lotus on the bench.

He started to tell her about dinner at his father's house but exchanged that conversation with one having to do with what he'd been agonizing about. He came out and said it all in a wave: I got into grad school.

She was enthused. She didn't hit him. That's great. Congratulations.

Yeah he said I'm still trying to find out whether it's really happening.

Wow I can't believe it. So C—.

Yeah.

That's in C— wait oops I mean where is that obviously it's in C— but what—

Boulder he said. It's in Boulder.

That is exciting she said I've heard good things about it I mean I don't know for English but as far as the school's concerned. People say that all the time don't they like Oh Madison is such a good school or Urbana is such a good school.

Yeah that's funny they never say that about this place.

Yeah strange why that is. You never hear they're great for— yeah it just doesn't happen that much.

Her lilac t-shirt made him want her. He wanted to kiss her. He knew he wasn't supposed to want that that wanting that should come later and this was too soon for that but fuck it it was how he felt. Then maybe he flirted sort of shamelessly but felt okay doing so. Maybe it was okay to flirt. She had to know he liked her. Maybe she thought he had to know she liked him. So what was going on. Why still the coyness. Maybe it had to do with the phone stuff.

He brought that up too said about his acceptance I really wanted to tell you but you know couldn't call you.

She told him about a guy an old friend she inserted parenthetically someone she'd known since childhood. Maybe like a Julianne he thought. He doesn't get email she said. He just gives me all this grief about not calling him and he lives at home so when I get home at eleven I'm thinking I don't want to call his house and wake up his parents.

That's what's nice about email Hunter Flanagan said you don't have to worry about waking anybody up.

Right she said then added unless they want to be awakened.

They laughed. He liked this. He liked sitting across from her. Were they starting something. Did something already exist. There was an intimate quality about things. It didn't at least when he wasn't thinking so much about it seem strange why would it or uncomfortable because they didn't know each other well but who did know anybody well. He wanted to know her more. That's what people did. He tried to make himself believe this. People meet each other and get to know each other we're not all born knowing everybody else intimately. He felt like he could tell her things. They were a lot alike in many ways. They cared about grammar. That he loved. He watched her write. She wanted to show him what a quotation mark looked like in Greek. It was sort of like open triangles two of them one in front of the other. She drew it with her right hand. Oh well. She still had so many other good qualities. Maybe that hand stuff was just arbitrary. It didn't signify what Hunter Flanagan wanted it to most of the time. Most of the time it was meaningless. He could think of plenty of left handed people he didn't like and he liked Dewey and she was right handed so what did it matter. The only person he knew who was left handed and it meant something to that person at least the way it meant something to him was Angela. She cared about it admired her own handedness and his and other left handed people all this time all these years that he'd only known her as a voice only known her as a handwriting only known her as letters in email and some cards. He hadn't gotten cards for a couple of years not since the two years they didn't speak.

God how many relationships friendships connections of his had Hilary's existence caused him to sever and mutilate and forever render just slightly off kilter never quite regaining the same tenor like they were nervous. The relationships now had phobias about Hunter Flanagan abandoning them. So they were while in many ways the exact same way as before if not better still a little circumspect still a little wary and were just sort of diffident now. Angela for example they had been friends again close friends emailing several times a week for over a year again now but had yet to talk on the phone. He should have broken the phone silence to tell her about C—.

He couldn't believe he'd told Dewey. He got that over with. She seemed okay with it. He even told her he'd been thinking about how to tell her. He wondered what she took that to mean. It was more flirtatious perhaps to be candid—very unlike him. He felt good saying it and repeated it several other times maybe to make sure he really did say it though he knew it was more for trying to find a way to gauge her growing reaction. Did she feel like it meant something to her that he told her truthfully even though it was difficult or did she feel like their time together potential time now was limited and did that fact matter most. Though how could it be the latter she knew she was leaving in the fall too so even if this hadn't happened separating would become an issue eventually but regardless he told her and that was good. Maybe he felt she was ready to know. Maybe now she'd be ready to know other things.

That night at dinner with Trey how much should he say about her. He always felt a bit self-conscious talking about girl stuff with Trey. He had no idea why. Trey was a good person to talk to about things of that nature but maybe it had to do with the fact that Trey's relationships had always seemed to be more exciting more dramatic and Hunter Flanagan's appeared sort of weak tepid in comparison and probably always would. The whole Hilary debacle. Trey couldn't believe that Hunter Flanagan and she weren't having sex almost two years what was Hunter doing but he of course could sympathize. Trey was having problems of his own extricating himself from an overly zealous girl still in college a theater major. Trey was in med school now in his second year. But Hunter still was going to tell him and probably everything because it would be on his mind and he hated silences and would say and do pretty much anything just to avoid them. He'd be more comfortable discussing Kate with Trey especially since she hadn't called or really written in a few days.

Maybe she was starting to get the hint that would certainly be nice although he regretted things escalating to the point that they had. Of course he hadn't really made out with her had sex or anything like that so leading her on strictly speaking he couldn't exactly hold himself responsible for because as he saw it he'd given her plenty of hints that he was just sort of looking for a friend which he didn't mind having but right now he just wanted to think about Dewey. Of course he didn't tell Kate any of that. He and Dewey didn't discuss the dinner for next week during their conversation today and he wondered if she had been thinking about it. Maybe wondered why he didn't bring it up. He didn't want to look too deeply into every little thing. It would drive him insane. The fact was and it was pretty obvious that things were working out serendipitously as she said about their chance meeting today and he liked that and wanted to focus on that and not all the other things which could diminish the magic the excitement his contained but sort of warm and smiley enthusiasm if he let them which he didn't of course want to.

# 33

She said she had to go back. Hunter Flanagan demurred as he had done the time before. She laughed threw her torso forward not violently just a laugh-induced lean and then returned straightened her back slightly.

She looked at her watch. You know for some reason I have no problem no moral dilemma when it comes to missing classes well mainly Anthro but as far as the Writing Center is concerned I just would feel awful about skipping a session.

Yeah I know what you mean he said though he didn't miss any classes.

I would feel like less of a tutor if I couldn't even show up for my sessions. She laughed.

They walked back to Douglas stood outside the Writing Center momentarily.

She said Well this was nice and then just looked at him like she was waiting for him to say something. This was just like the last time. He didn't know what to say. Why didn't he. Usually he'd say I'll call you but they didn't do that so he could have said I'll write you. She already owed him email though. He didn't want to be annoyingly overzealous.

He said You haven't checked your email.

No she said not since... She drew out the word since while she thought. Since yesterday at two-thirty in the afternoon.

Oh he said I've sent you a few. What he meant was the invite to Professor Bates's reading but she didn't know about it yet so he figured he'd just leave it for the moment. Was that weird.

He didn't know if he should say something or not say something but regardless he said Listen I'm glad I got to tell you what I wanted to.

She smiled. I'm glad you did.

Me too.

Then she said I have to go Hunter. I'll talk to you later.

Yeah he said. She turned and then he left started walking to the computer lab where he was now an hour late. He felt like he had no shape. He really did like her and like the other time wished she hadn't gone.

# 34

The restaurant was crowded when he went in. Trey hadn't arrived yet. Hunter Flanagan was a few minutes early which he was glad about for some reason. He felt like he didn't want to keep Trey waiting. Trey was studying for his boards and seemed sort of freaked out about the whole thing panicked about where he'd end up doing his residency. When he and Hunter had talked on the phone Trey mentioned wanting to go to New York when Hunter Flanagan said he might go to N— for grad. Hunter Flanagan liked the idea of moving to New York with Trey. Their friendship had suffered many hardships a longer separation than he and Julianne or he and Angela any of them. In high school when Hunter Flanagan met Jeffrey and began hanging out with his group of friends he and Trey basically grew apart. Hunter Flanagan felt bad about it then as well as now but he didn't know what to do. Anyway he figured these days it sort of worked out. He was friends with Trey again but of course was careful not to reference Jeffrey in any way reference anything connected with that life any of the people places things. He just sort of edited them out. He hoped that Trey didn't still hold a grudge. It didn't seem as though he did. Hunter Flanagan expected people to simply go along with whatever he felt like thinking or doing at any given time without regard for their feelings and while he could hold grudges hate people indefinitely he seemed to think that that it was simply unconscionable that anybody would ever feel that negatively about him.

Trey came in. He was wearing a red coat a medium winter coat probably a little thicker than the spring day would have suggested. His combed back hair stood up but not maniacally. He hadn't shaved in what looked like a day or two probably the same as Hunter Flanagan.

He said Hey Flanagan when he came through the glass doors and they shook hands. Since Trey was taller than he Hunter Flanagan had to look up to talk to him. That was okay. They still had to wait to sit. No tables were open.

Well congratulations again Trey said. That is really cool about C—.

Yeah Hunter Flanagan said.

So tell me what it's all about.

Well I get this award and I'm not really too sure what it's for exactly some sort of incoming student thing I guess.

Yeah sure.

And then there's the TA thing. I'll teach two classes each semester.

What kind.

I'm guessing comp or maybe creative writing.

You'd probably enjoy the writing.

Yeah I think I definitely would. But that's not it. I wouldn't have to pay tuition too.

It sounds awesome. Was it your first choice.

Well now it is. They laughed.

Where else did you apply again.

Hunter Flanagan told him. It's so hard to get into these programs he explained hundreds of people apply and they only let in twelve or something.

Is that how big this program is.

Probably. I don't know for sure though I'm guessing it couldn't be much larger—the writing part anyway—than twenty. You know they want people to be able to... He couldn't think of a good word bond no. Get along. Finally settled for Work together.

Well I'm really happy for you Trey said and extended his hand again. Hunter took it a moment when he wasn't feeling sweaty palms though Trey's felt a bit warm.

Hunter liked seeing Trey though these days the way he imagined things conceived of their relationship was a bit different before they met to what he felt it was when they were actually together in person. Maybe it was in his own head his own *mishegas*. They had now been new friends for almost three years. Hunter found that fact reassuring. In fact Hunter thought he'd had more recently been friends for longer with Trey than with Julianne whom technically he'd only been talking to again for only about six months. The three of them had been very close in high school before Hunter Flanagan left Lab but really earlier than that before Jeffrey came to Lab Hunter's last year there. The events of that September to June still barely made sense to Hunter the rearrangements of friends the abandonment of all school responsibilities the obsession with Eileen the drugs drinking throwing up parties the cigarettes the probations the mandatory tutoring sessions visits to the guidance counselor every Thursday the driver's ed and permit and license and then at the end of the year the knowledge that he was not going to be invited back for another year and then the subsequent transition to Roycemore and drive to Evanston every day. Things had certainly changed hadn't they. Now he didn't smoke did no drugs basically drank only socially. Too much free time might prompt him to buy a bottle of wine and last summer he finished 750 milliliters of vodka left to his own devices but he didn't think he had a problem in fact was far from it and now he was going to graduate college in two weeks after five circuitous years. He still wore Doc Martens not the same pair obviously but the same style not the combat boots the three holes and maybe his life had wrapped around itself somehow. If you looked at the elements you could almost in a remote way mistake this year for the early 90s. He wore Docs he liked a girl named Dewey he was friends with Julianne and Trey and could have dinner with both of them and have a good time. Maybe the absences not just from the two of them but from what his essential self the real Hunter Flanagan during those vague years and the last five in college were good. Maybe he'd completed some sort of winding path back to himself and the things that were important to him now. Trey was a med student Julianne sold real estate and lived in Bucktown Hunter Flanagan wrote books and was going to C—. Was he really. God it was still unreal to him. Maybe the absences had made all their hearts grow fonder. Sometimes Hunter supposed that his relationship with Trey for example from having been apart for so long—and it was a long time five years not exaggerating—was actually stronger more adult like more real than it would have been if they had all of that high school experience together. Trey had his old friends still. Hunter's old friends. Most of them had left for college but oddly enough returned to Hyde Park. Hearing about Thompson and Jeffrey Zurich still being around was something that went along with seeing Trey. Thompson was a grad at UIC and what was Jeffrey Zurich doing Hunter didn't really want to know but after hearing Trey mention them Hunter silently decided he definitely had to go to C— and maybe for longer than two years or at least move somewhere else upon finishing his degree or degrees. He did want a PhD he wanted a university job a university life at least for a while but he didn't want it to be in Chicago because everyone else was still in Chicago and hoped that maybe he could end up moving to New York and that Trey would want to do that too someday.

    His cell phone vibrated. He checked it discreetly didn't want to seem like he wanted to be somewhere else with Trey there which he didn't. He enjoyed Trey's company was grateful and appreciative of Trey wanting to see him and of his praise. Trey was tired. It seemed every time he and Hunter got together Trey was tired. The last few times he had been hung over from a night or a weekend or a week of partying. Trey liked ecstasy which was sort of ironic—a drug Hunter hadn't done and wouldn't do. He never considered returning to a life of recreational drug use. For one thing he didn't think his body could abide it. These days he exercised and watched what he ate to a certain extent and enjoyed tea. How could he weather the storm of a night of drinking and drugs. The latest he'd been up in a while was that tawdry superfluous night with Kate. The call on his cell phone was Renee his old co-worker. Damn. He hoped it was Dewey. He always wanted it to be Dewey. Every time the phone vibrated he hoped it would be she. He really wanted to have a phone relationship with her but he sort of liked this not-having-a-phone-relationship relationship. It was quite possibly good for them.

So did you ever straighten out that girl Trey asked.

No Hunter admitted. It didn't really work out that way. I told you how she calls me like eight times for every one time I answer. She writes me email all the time.

You have to be firm Flanagan.

Yeah I know but it's fucked up. I like talking to her he said.

He didn't say But not as much as Dewey. Oh god maybe he was compensating keeping Kate around as a phone friend since he didn't get to have one in Dewey. He had to stop thinking about that. No it was definitely good they didn't call each other. It was like seduction. It was like unraveling the secrets and the personalities slowly letting them steep. This would have to lead to better things. Hunter Flanagan always acted impetuously not just with women but with everything. He didn't like delayed gratification. That's why he was so gimme gimme gimme so damn impulsive all the time. He had no self-control. That's why he'd sent queries to dozens of agents before either he or his query letter or his manuscript were ready and look at what happened he ended up with a psychotic agent out on a farm somewhere who had produced all of zero promising leads in the last year and a half. He didn't even know if he would want to see the book published under his own name at this point so what was the point of rushing things. What did that achieve. Probably nothing and he knew that.

# 35

So he really liked Dewey now. Yesterday maybe solidified things. He wasn't expecting to see her or if he had expected to see her the extent of it would have been a moment a second to tell her or not tell her in a corner of the Writing Center where nobody stood only for a minute or two and by the time Hunter Flanagan would have decided to act it would have been too late. Others would have descended upon the space making their aloneness their togetherness not so alone anymore but now disappointingly populated. But things didn't work out that way. They sat together without any interruptions for an hour. It was glorious. They played with pens. She took these pens out of her bag to show him pens from pharmaceutical companies with product names like Axid and Zyprexa and Evista and Paxil.

She said that Paxil was used as an anti depressant as well as for stopping smoking. It's the same part of the brain she explained the same neurotransmitters which make somebody depressed are the same ones that make somebody want to smoke.

Well smoking goes along with depression I guess.

Yeah. She had four of the pens and gave him two of them. She held two too and they would click the clickers and touch the grips on the ones that had grips.

She said That one is my favorite when Hunter Flanagan held a blue one with Gemzar on the side in white letters. As they spoke each would reach into the other's hands take one of the pens and exchange it for another. They did this for a while as they talked.

She told him more about her family didn't mention a father but did speak of a brother and a sister. Her sister currently was in college also at UIC. Her brother was already graduated.

At one point there were three of us here she said and of course she still had the younger brother who was in fifth grade. She told Hunter Flanagan about him before. So Dewey wasn't the oldest child but wasn't the youngest either. He'd never been involved a girl who wasn't one or the other. Eileen had two older siblings but much older they were in their twenties back then maybe both even finished with college when she was only fourteen. The first Dewey was an only child. Simona the youngest just one older brother Hilary had a younger brother and was the oldest and that was it. Those were basically all of them. This Dewey was he guessed a sort of middle child but not really since there were four of them unless of course she had yet to mention more. He liked how her family was structured. She had a lot of assertiveness an independence about her. He liked that too.

# 36

He kept seeing the image of Dewey pulling her head through the gray turtleneck the way her face looked her hair hidden by the sweater neck her glasses off. She set them on the concrete ledge beforehand. She closed her eyes while the fabric passed. It was only her hair and then her face emerged her eyes still closed. It was only her face for a second. It surprised Hunter Flanagan. Dewey's face without her hair without her glasses she looked like Jane for a moment. It happened very quickly and then was over. She finished taking the turtleneck off. She was out of it. She reached for her glasses. She was back to Dewey lilac t-shirt and all. Hunter was relieved. It didn't scare him exactly he was just surprised to see Jane in Dewey's face. Did that explain the attraction. Dewey didn't seem very Jane. He hadn't likened the two up to that moment hadn't seen any Jane in her and it wasn't the new Jane it wasn't the Jane he saw last summer the Jane with short greasy hair and bruised lip and hairy legs. It was the Jane from the summer four years ago when she was young and attractive and not a lesbian yet that summer when Hunter Flanagan and Jane spent late nights together and kissed everywhere—in his car in the IHOP parking lot at the marina walking around looking at docked boats parked in front of her mother's building on scary Argyle. Maybe Jane had the same lilac t-shirt. Maybe all girls had that t-shirt. But Hunter Flanagan didn't care about Jane anymore. Now he could only think about Dewey. She was the only person his mind contemplated the only one he wanted right now. She still hadn't responded to his email. They were still going out this week right. She didn't say yes or no about the Professor Bates reading. He'd invited Jimmy P. didn't want to at first in the event that Dewey did want to go paranoia like she'd fall in love with him or worse. Then he started thinking maybe they knew each other from before. He should probably tell one or the other of them about the other but he figured he'd wait to see if she wanted to go and then say Jimmy P. wants to go too. He wrote about Frida. He hoped the configuration would work a tacit understanding to both Jimmy P. and Frida that Dewey was Hunter's sort of date and that they would consort with each other as they wished or not. Frida presumably had a boyfriend. Well not just theoretically she'd introduced him to Hunter before. She and the boyfriend attended a reading Hunter read in a couple of months ago at Jak's. She talked about him in class too how they'd been dating since high school blah blah. Her parents didn't know about him—that was sort of odd though not really intriguing—because he wasn't christian or something but now was. It wasn't entirely clear why or what prompted this living in stealth but regardless. Would Dewey think that maybe something was going on with Hunter and Frida. She hadn't of course read the email and Hunter hadn't of course mentioned the event or wanting her to go but he hoped his email explained what was missing. He said explicitly that he did not want this to supplant their already existing sort of plans and really he had hoped that the idea of a group thing a field trip would make her want to go more in case she was reticent didn't want to have things move too quickly as far as dating was concerned. Did she know they were already psychically going out that the physical stuff was merely supplementary to be delivered at a later point but as far as connections were concerned they had one. Hunter imagined sitting beside her in a darkened theater maybe trying to hold her hand seeing what she thought but when they drove—if they drove—would she sit in the front or would Frida thus mangling the ideal ratio of boy to girl who sits with whom arrangements. He hoped that wouldn't happen. Maybe it would be better if she didn't go. Maybe it would get too confusing and impinge on their dinner which he hoped would be the next day that Thursday or ideally Friday. He didn't like making any plans at all these days. He liked holding all his available free time open for her. Though it was kind of frustrating and a bit awkward not to know—not to even begin to know—what he'd be doing on any given evening. Now he was reluctant to agree to go to an open mic or book signing or Charlie Chaplin film. He passed up *City Lights* on account of Dewey being available and wanting to do something with him and his not being able to imagine saying no. That was a bad thing. That was as though he were saying I don't have a life I'll wait around for you no matter what. He didn't want to set that sort of precedence. It was a fine line a gray area how much you wanted to show that you liked a person that you wanted to see her so much without letting that person know that she controlled you. Maybe it was about maintaining control like regulating therapy keeping everything controlled. He could perhaps be more available at this point without relinquishing too much if he made sure to be less so later once he was sure that she liked him that she wanted a relationship with him. It was definitely confusing. He was sure he had no idea how or in what manner to conduct himself how to think or act.

# 37

When Hunter had to cancel his—what—date sympathy meeting with Kate so he could instead have dinner with Trey Friday night she got angry. In an email she said it wasn't fair and was similarly irascible on the phone. He said Sunday and this seemed to placate her for the moment. It was now Sunday. He needed to read Spivak in the library but got up several times to check email and on the third visit a message from Dewey appeared. She thanked him for the e-card—the Sordid Nights of an Illicit Truck Driver—he sent her but said she couldn't make the field trip on Wednesday. Well at least she finally wrote back.

Kate's complaint was I haven't seen you for two weeks.

Two weeks Hunter said—it felt like it hadn't nearly been that long—but I've talked to you.

Yeah barely.

Okay that was a bit unnecessarily caustic. Hey he was doing the best he could considering.

# 38

He drove to Evanston to see Kate. He didn't really want to see her. It was Sunday. Though he had finished the Spivak he had to read he felt like he could have much better spent the time elsewhere doing something else. Basically he just didn't feel like seeing her. She'd forced him to come over. He was seeing her under duress. He'd cancelled on her to see Trey at the last minute on Friday. He told her Wednesday and when he tried to suggest that this weekend wasn't the best she started to complain.

She said on the phone I haven't seen you in two weeks. He said But we've talked a lot. She muttered something he didn't quite hear that had to do with the fact that he never called her. He said he didn't want to get into it right then.

So he agreed to see her Sunday. But late. I have to work in the afternoon he said.

Since he'd babysat for his sister Maya—the six year old not the rebellious twenty year old—Saturday night—he picked her up at a birthday party in the afternoon and spent the rest of the day with her—he'd had no time to read or do anything. Today was essentially the same. Basically he was mad at himself for this Kate thing still going on. Why hadn't he been able to turn it off to stop it. Why did she still think he had attention to spare and wished to direct it at her. He felt like he'd misled her somehow but didn't know how.

He drove into Evanston took Touhy east from the highway

and made a left onto Clark which becomes Chicago Avenue in Evanston and took a right onto South Boulevard and another left onto Hinman. She lived on Hinman. He didn't like the fact that the longer this went on for the more trips he'd have to make into Evanston. That's why he'd quit his job to stop having to drive such long distances. Funny how life screws you over sometimes makes you drive regardless of how or what you do to try to get out of having to drive everywhere. Maybe he'd get rid of his car.

    He found a place to park on the street. Well that was one good thing. He dreaded going into her apartment didn't feel like dealing with the cat allergy but there was nothing to do about it now. He missed Dewey. He felt like he was cheating in a way and hoped that nothing physical would transpire. Was it cheating. He and Dewey hadn't even had a real date yet. He didn't want to be fettered by all of this Kate nonsense. It was nonsense wasn't it. He didn't want to date her barely even wanted to talk to her. So why did he still. He guessed he found her amusing. She made him laugh. He didn't feel particularly attracted to her but she had a good sense of humor. She ate up all his dumb jokes and mannerisms. Maybe that's what the attraction was: she was an audience he could count on. He spoke to her freely. He didn't feel inhibited the way he did when he spoke to someone he liked say Dewey. Then his words thoughts came with footnotes had to be properly couched and that led to silences delays in the live feed which if he didn't work to keep up with would become noticeable. With Kate he didn't care what she thought of him. If anything he hoped in some way that perhaps she'd become disillusioned start to dislike him if he said obstreperous things became contumacious sardonic. But nothing seemed to faze her which was a bit disconcerting.

    Maybe it had to do with Eileen. He thought about how back then he was sort of the Kate type willing to do anything make any concession just to see her. He cherished the times they spent together even if she were just sitting on the phone talking to someone else or packing up a suitcase even if she were watching television and he just sitting there dumbly on the phone listening to her laugh. It was because she didn't give him very much he felt like anything that had anything to do with her was important. And it didn't matter how she treated him or the fact that she didn't really like him because he needed her and that was how it worked. This of course was heady quixotic adolescence. He was twenty-four now. It was unlikely he'd end up in that sort of situation again. While he had been keeping his weekends relatively open in the hopes that Dewey would want to see him he knew obviously that that wouldn't go on forever and if she remained more or less distant long enough he'd eventually lose interest more or less and then it would fade away. Like Lila he sort of talked to her now but he didn't try to make plans with her anymore not in a serious way. He'd stopped taking the train downtown to see her at work.

There were maybe three weeks maybe even a month when Eileen seemed interested. After that it was just Hunter Flanagan being interested and Eileen being completely insouciant and Hunter Flanagan refusing to accede or realize what was going on and do something. It was then while he parked listening to the end of a live version of No Woman No Cry on the eighties station that he realized that Eileen had broken up with him gradually not all at once. She didn't do what he wished he could do to Kate just say Listen this is the way it is and I'm sorry but no. Eileen moved away from Hunter Flanagan a little at a time gradually. She created a series of distances between them and time passed and Hunter Flanagan remained steadfast and more time passed and she didn't yield and more time passed and then he left Lab and went to Roycemore and suddenly they weren't speaking anymore and he wasn't even sure how it happened. At first it was so subtle so barely detectable but she stopped returning his phone calls and he stopped thinking that he should make more phone calls. He just realized what she'd done and then began to deal with it stopped trying to talk to her and then began what he guessed was still going on the phase which comes after the afterness: the Now.

He hoped that he could create a series of distances until Kate would intuit what he wanted and leave him alone.

This was not the high road he was taking no this was what the spineless did. This was the role one would take if one had no balls. He should have said something before. How long had this been sort of going on for. Maybe a month now. It was spiraling out of his control but slowly. She was just too fucking accepting. He didn't want to be doted upon. He wanted tension and uncertainty. He didn't want another Miriam that he could treat like shit and she wouldn't care just tolerate anything. He didn't want some female acting the way he acted toward Eileen all those years ago. He wanted someone with agency. He wanted his own agency. He definitely didn't feel like he had any then sitting outside her building on a damp street on a Sunday early evening in Evanston. Maybe he'd tell her that night. Maybe he'd just get it over with say something like I'm not looking for a relationship right now. I'm not ready. I just don't feel as strongly as you appear to. Something. Anything.

At dinner at the Lucky Platter he had a burger. It was over cooked. He said medium rare but it was more like medium. Fuck. He could never get a hamburger the way he wanted it. She didn't get the tuna melt had a barbeque chicken sandwich instead and sweet potato fries which she put ketchup on. Gross. How could he possibly be with a girl who had a BFA in design claimed to know something about abstract impressionism but couldn't match potatoes with their appropriate complements if her life depended on it. Jesus. Was she really going to eat them like that. His side was macaroni and cheese. They had margaritas—March Margarita Madness extended by a month. She had lime. He had tamarind.

What is tamarind he'd asked the waiter.

It's sort of pruney the waiter said.

Fine Hunter Flanagan said. It was too sweet overwhelmingly so. He thought about adding salt to the glass to try to even out the unctuous sweetness but didn't know if that really would work so he just drank it the way it was.

They talked about sex. First through innuendo then more innuendo metaphor in a silly way. She said Quesadillas and he said You want me to do what to you. She laughed. He laughed. He started asking more questions later. They discussed old partners. He knew you weren't supposed to talk about those topics on a date but this wasn't really a date. He didn't feel like being particularly candid but took the opportunity to share with another person some of his disdain for Hilary and a few of her decisions.

She went to grad school to Medill but went home every fucking weekend. Can you believe that he said rather vociferously. Again he wasn't concerned if Kate became particularly troubled by all of this. He wasn't acting entirely spontaneously but he wouldn't have spoken about Hilary so freely if he had been trying to make a good impression. She said she had only one boyfriend during college a guy named James a guy who didn't even go to Wash U.

He was on a co-op she said. He was catholic. We didn't have much in common came from different backgrounds. He didn't know anything about art.

That's too bad Hunter said. He didn't know what to say next. He wondered if they had had sex but doubted it. God he hoped she wasn't a virgin. That would explain all the unearned affection—if she were—all the solicitousness. He wondered what Dewey was doing at the moment.

After they finished dinner he actually persuaded her to order another margarita with him. This time they both had lime. When they left he was a bit buzzed but not really and wished he had been walking down the street toward the lake with Dewey instead of Kate. Dewey liked the e-card Hunter sent her. She wrote him. He read her email before leaving the library. She said she couldn't come to the reading on Wednesday which was something of a relief since Hunter had invited Jimmy P. and he worried for a minute about potential confusion over whose date was whose even though he had billed the evening to all parties involved as being simply quote a field trip. Well this way he didn't have to deal with Jimmy P. potentially hitting on Dewey though Jimmy P. was mostly all talk. It seemed he fancied himself a lothario but was in fact more shy than outgoing. Possibly Hunter's perception had been off. Well anyway he hoped Dewey hadn't forgotten or decided against their dining plans. They were still to have dinner this week that's what she said last week maybe the 3rd Coast or that Dish place he'd been reading about but none of that mattered now because he was stuck here with Kate and didn't know what to do.

 She looked a bit more inviting but that was probably because he was a bit drunk and was having trouble thinking. They were on the couch in her apartment. It was a small couch overstuffed cushions gray smooth fabric. She put her head on his shoulder sitting close to him. At one point she kissed him. He took a breath. Get ready for bad kissing he thought. She didn't approach his mouth as aggressively as he'd remembered. It was gentler. Perhaps it was because they were sitting rather than lying down. Perhaps he'd already acclimated to her mouth her quirky scary style of kissing. Perhaps he was too drunk to say no but that was exaggerating it. Perhaps he didn't care. They were twisted up. She was sort of on top of him sort of still in a sitting position.

 She almost fell off the couch. She said Do you want to go in my room.

 Okay.

 They got up and went in her room to lie on the bed. She got on top of him. This was more comfortable more room anyway.

 They kissed. He braced himself expected the worst. The lights were on. She pulled herself off him and turned off a lamp flipped a switch on this hanging moon shaped light. It was made out of different colored blue plastic and hung against the wall. She lowered the blinds. Her window faced the parking lot. She lived very close to the ground floor. You could hear people's conversations as they moved from their cars to the building. Kate returned. He slid on top of her. They moved about kissing rubbing against each other her glasses off. She looked different than what Hunter had grown accustomed to. He never quite reconciled the two Kates. The Kate from the picture she sent him before they met that really didn't mean much to him and the Kate he imagined when they spoke on the phone who was rather a different person all together. Then he met her. That's the face he pictured nowadays the Kate in glasses the Kate who looked something like Ellen Greene but with darker hair. He rarely saw her eyes. Maybe he wasn't looking at them though when he spoke to her or to anyone he always made eye contact. He hated people in fact who didn't. They seemed odd. He liked eyes liked intimacy well that kind anyway. Now they were making out again. This was different than before the way he applied his tongue consciously tried to imply that that was the way they should be kissing. He was definitely attracted to her. The dim lighting helped the kissing. It wasn't as bad as he remembered from the first night. Maybe he had gotten used to it. It wasn't as strange. She seemed to have better aim. The arc wasn't as convoluted. She didn't miss and end up sucking his lower lip—that pissed him off from last time. She was still rougher with him than he would have liked. He felt his lip swelling or maybe just imagined it but then at one point he could have sworn he felt a tear a rip like she had fucking braces or something. He thought he could taste blood.

He pulled away. I think I hurt my lip he said pleased with the gosh I don't know how it could have happened it couldn't possibly have anything to do with the strange and actually quite bizarre way you kiss or anything tone the statement took like it was random or maybe a medical condition.

She said You didn't cut your lip.

No I think I did.

He touched it. He didn't feel blood. He didn't want bloated lips. What if Dewey wanted to see him. What would she think. His dick was hard. He liked the way it felt against her crotch. She was still clothed but Hunter's hands were under her shirt. Her shirt began to rise. He could see her stomach seemed okay a bit of excess but he wasn't exactly an Ironman in this situation. He felt her chest. Her bra was smooth. He circled her nipples. They hardened. He liked that. He wondered what her breasts looked like. He wanted to see her bra. She was lifting his shirts too. The flannel and the t-shirt got all bunched up a few inches above his midsection. He wanted to just take them off but that seemed untoward even given the circumstances. Actually he was thinking about the time didn't want to get stuck there too late and knew that undressing even partially would make it seem like he wanted to stay longer.

It was hard to extract himself from her bed. She kept wanting to kiss more said Don't look at the clock. He didn't make any effort to hide his glancing over at her bedside table alarm. Well he had to go sooner than later. He wasn't so much concerned about the time—though he did have to get up early the next morning—as much as he was concerned about getting more allergic to Grover the cat. Why did girls need cats anyway. That was something he never understood. He really couldn't stand any animals cats and dogs especially because of the somatic issues and he didn't get why others bothered all the cleaning listening to barking meowing. They were cute certainly but too much work for such little return sort of like relationships Hunter's anyway.

Hunter joked If I stay here too long I'll just fall asleep.

Kate said You could always sleep over. Okay that was a little weird. He definitely didn't want to do that. He didn't want to wake up with her. Why did she want to wake with him. Miriam was always begging him to sleep over and he refused each time. He was not a Sleep-Over Artist. He liked privacy at night. He looked like shit in the morning and neither wanted to inflict that on anyone else nor expose himself to the indelicacies of the brightest light that the next morning would certainly offer. No he wouldn't be doing that. Instead of having that conversation he just kissed her some more and touched her breasts. Her bra looked purple. He said something about it to her after she commented on his vegetable boxer shorts.

    He said I like your purple bra and she said It's not purple it's brown. That was confusing. Hunter looked at it some more. Now it started to look brown to him but why did he think it had been purple. Maybe he was going crazy. His usually keen defenses were clearly malfunctioning tonight. Why was he hard. Why did he suddenly seem to want Kate. This was only further complicating things. Tonight would have been a good chance to tell her the truth disabuse himself in order to offer himself unattached in any sort of indirect way to Dewey. What did she want. Would they have dinner she didn't say yet. What would they talk about. How much longer could this Kate thing hang over his head. He definitely wasn't improving the situation by engaging in this bout of pressing midsection against midsection. She had an okay body though. He guessed it was true that her fairly adventurous underwear definitely graded above Miriam's ragged Salvation Army reject intimate apparel and he appreciated that. Kate's bra was intact for god's sake and she pulled down the waist of her jeans slightly revealing some cotton leopard print panties. Christ Hilary had the same ones but probably in a larger size. Hunter thought about being in Hilary's bed. He barely remembered what it was like. They never had any room to move around except when they were in his room at home or when he still rented in Evanston. Lying in bed all day what an inspired notion. That he must have really cared for her at one point possibly lent explanation to some of the bizarre things he assented to do. He was actually kind of impressed that they could spend so much time in bed back then considering they weren't fucking. How much mutual sucking could they have done. He guessed they watched TV too. That was the problem with relationships: since there were only so many things you could do sexually before growing tired or bored you had to start finding other things to occupy the time. Most of those things cost money parking admission tickets. He vowed if he ever had a serious relationship again to ensure at least two things:

    (A) He wanted to have a relationship where it was okay to

spend time alone. He didn't think with Hilary in the almost two years together that they spent more than an hour apart during simultaneous free time. That was ridiculous. No wonder they suffocated each other or really no wonder she suffocated him. That's what happened when you spent so much time together. The oxygen ran out.

(B) He wanted a relationship where he didn't have to go into debt just from providing them three meals a day. His next girlfriend would have to cook for the both of them or feed herself or something because he probably threw five thousand dollars away on restaurants with Hilary over all those months and what seemed romantic early on—pancakes picking up checks drinking coffee for hours—really became a big fucking inconvenience. One he wished not to repeat.

He gathered his things. His face itched. He looked at his lip in the bathroom mirror. Fortunately it wasn't split. He applied another layer of Chapstick. His lips did feel tired frayed fucked up. They didn't kiss at the door. He just bolted for it.

She stood at the frame looking out I'll call you talk to you soon he kept saying turning his head back. He wasn't sure what he was running from. He'd already committed the indiscretion if you could call it that. He'd already advanced things physically. Next stop fucking. No he doubted seriously they'd fuck. She was for all he knew still a virgin and probably didn't even want to fuck. The fact that there were virgins in the world who were over twenty boggled his mind. At seventeen he thought he was late. Hilary was twenty-four now and to the extent of his knowledge had not yet done it. Not unless she went out and picked somebody up acting impetuously on the eve of their breakup but she probably regretted losing him even before he was gone probably was too shaken up for weeks or months afterward to look at other men but eventually he knew she would have if she hadn't already gotten over him and probably had other interests presently. It didn't bother him. Why would he begrudge her that. She deserved to be happy. He just wasn't the person to effect that situation. He wondered what she was doing now working at that Southtown newspaper being a reporter. Well you hoped she'd find whatever she was looking for or was willing to accept in place of what she really wanted.

Hunter on the other hand was not ready to accept what was simply in front of him. If he'd learned anything from the Hilary debacle of nearly two years it was that no matter how you tried to reframe the truth no matter what accommodations you made in order to try to better convince yourself of the situation's similarity to an ideal situation it was bound to fall apart and that it was better not to pretend. That even though it might be painful to be honest that it was really the only thing to do because there really wasn't any other choice to make.

# 39

On the drive back to Chicago from the reading Hunter Flanagan and Jimmy P. talked about sex. Hunter told him things he had almost started to forget about. He told him about Hilary how she didn't want to have sex with him.

How long were you guys going out Jimmy P. asked.

Almost two years.

Man he said shaking his head I could never have put up with that. Was she like totally religious.

It wasn't just that Hunter said. She was catholic and everything but she always said I could never imagine getting an abortion.

Yeah those girls are fucked up.

Maybe it was better that we didn't—that we weren't...

Yeah maybe.

Hunter had forgotten how crazy she was how she wouldn't let him put his dick anywhere near her cunt. She'd essentially freak out. There were these times and he told Jimmy P. about them as they sped down 53 and then 55 blazing past billboards bright lights neon restaurants everything sprawling and artificial and ridiculous just like the suburbs always were. Hunter couldn't tell the difference between out there in Glen Ellyn and Willowbrook or Clarendon Hills or Aurora or Indianapolis or Des Plaines. They all looked exactly the fuck the same. The same Chili's and Joe's Crab Shacks and Targets and Old Navys and vast open highways parking lots and Bakers Squares and McDonald's and everything was so meaningless and empty. Nothing had any character or any sort of history. It was like most of Fort Lauderdale. As though they leveled out everything at one point heaped concrete blackness down and started over. They listened to a tape. It had good songs on it. Siouxie and the Banchees. General Public.

He told Jimmy P. this story. This one time he said I got some of it on her leg and she fucking flipped out was all like give me a towel give me a towel. She was convinced it could fucking climb up her thigh up and into her.

God Jimmy P. said I don't know how you put up with that. It must have driven you out of your fucking head. What's worse.

Hunter didn't say what was worse was the time maybe what a week or two after they finally broke up and he was seeing Miriam—well not seeing as in dating but seeing as in fucking unabashedly without having to feel guilty about cheating or the possibility of cheating—and he felt so insignificant like the biggest loser like he had thrown away his relationship for such vapid utter worthlessness. One night Miriam was on top of him and she took off her panties and his boxers came away and she straddled him began to rub against him and it freaked him out. He was so used to having to keep at least two layers between the areas used to having that be a big deal and he didn't know what to make of that feeling of that awful response coming instinctively. Was it simply that he'd been conditioned to react that way or had Hilary's insanity rubbed off on him. Did he now think it was possible to get pregnant that way. Did he think that was really true. How did Hilary really believe that. Was she deluded. It was ironic that someone going to fucking journalism school for a master's degree could really think that she could get pregnant without a penis actually being inside. How they stayed together how Hunter put up with that was simply beyond him. He must have been the deluded one. It was insane the whole relationship and his life and he was still stuck on a Wednesday night fleeing the suburbs and all of its unctuous idiocy all of its trite blandness and Hilary was still haunting him.

    Was she in fact doing more damage than he realized. Had she screwed him up. Or was it everybody else he'd dated. Or was it just him. He didn't know. He was trying to get over Dewey now. Like her a little less. Really he hadn't realized just how much she'd affected him but how was that even possible he barely knew a thing about her. He knew she had two majors and one was music but was the other theater or English—how could he not know this—and she was going to pharmacy school in Madison in the fall. He knew that but where did she live. He sort of knew that but not because she'd told him. She carried her notebooks in a cloth tote bag instead of a backpack. She liked pens. She checked her email sometimes three times in a day sometimes not at all sometimes early Sunday morning sometimes late at night sometimes through the web and sometimes through Unix. Basically he knew nothing about her. She had two brothers and a sister married parents was right handed looked like Jane when she pulled her head through a sweater spoke without looking at him sometimes but other times looking directly at him had drunk something called a grasshopper once. Most of what he wanted to believe about her he'd imagined. He envisioned some things that were real. She knew what an antecedent was knew something about signifiers and how they were arbitrary liked pens seemed to like Hunter but for some reason didn't want to spend time with him.

    Face it he told himself you wouldn't know the first thing about what to do with her if she were available. It was true. What would he do. No place to go nothing to offer her of himself but superficiality. Restaurants. All he knew was restaurants. Maybe this time things would be different. Maybe they could talk about writing but he was basically a writing introvert. He didn't like sharing especially with someone he was screwing.

    Do you think Frida's a virgin he asked Jimmy P.

    Nah he said not with the boyfriend down the block.

    She's been dating him since high school.

Well in that case definitely not.
I can't picture it.
Why not.
I just can't.
She doesn't exactly seem like Oh I'm too innocent to fuck.
No she doesn't but well I guess it's just weird trying to imagine that.
Hunter also told him about Kate how he couldn't lose her. I guess I like her because she pays attention to me he said. I feel like I don't have to be careful about what I say or do. She doesn't expect very much from me.
But you're not that attracted to her.
No and she kind of scares me.
He laughed. I'd be scared too.
Hunter checked his email when he got home after taking a piss. His head buzzed. He was very tired. Nothing from Dewey. He expected that. Some other crap and a note from Angela. She was concerned about a magazine and if they'd buy a story she wrote about a sister whose brother is getting married that takes place in a kitchen appliance store. Hunter had read it. She sent it to him to critique. He really liked it hoped that the magazine would buy it so she'd be happy. He didn't like to hear about disappointments sadnesses in her life. He tried to keep a positive tenor in their exchanges. Lately he'd been whining a lot about the girl situation Angela more or less remaining open minded about Dewey had yet to brand her unredeemable though Hunter knew he didn't need Angela's verdict to know that it certainly felt like he was wasting his time. Lila seemed to be emitting some strange and hard to ignore signals this inviting him to her sorority formal in two weeks not rushing off to her class the other day when they saw each other. This was strange. Hunter was actually trying to get rid of her and it wasn't working. She was beautiful. It didn't make much sense why she'd be interested but maybe she wasn't and just liked him as a friend and wanted to spend time with him as many twenty-year-olds often seem to want and think

unproblematic. God he needed some time away from all of it. It was hard to stay focused. He still had these papers due next week. He hadn't even started yet. This weekend was going to be ridiculous and he already said he'd babysit Maya on Friday night. He did that in part because he wanted to see her but also so that if in the remote chance possibility that Dewey might write and say Let's have dinner that he could regrettably say that he already had plans. Of course she wasn't writing she wasn't suggesting she wasn't regretting. She was doing nothing and Hunter felt that nothing.

## 40

After exercising Hunter Flanagan went to the C-Shop found a table set his things in the empty chair bought a sandwich and a cup of coffee and wondered if he had been overreacting. Maybe Dewey's tacit strange apparently unprovoked quasi dumping was a good thing. As he saw it he was overextended. Papers. Readings. Tonight Eve Sedgwick. He wondered what she'd say. Certainly she'd have something to say. Same with Cixous. The theorists didn't pass up an opportunity to pick him apart. People take themselves way too seriously sometimes or not enough. He was certainly guilty of the former. Or maybe some people were simply not intended to be taken seriously. Take odd girl in the white turtleneck for example. Mannered posture arch of her back the way she touched her chin the grating way she laughed these deep wheezing low to high sounding guffaws. It sounded like she was gasping perhaps choking on her ridiculousness and he could hear it from three tables away. Yes definitely guilty of taking herself way too seriously. See they were everywhere.

    Dewey made him feel like a goofy heady insouciant adolescent but not in a bad way. The way he thought about her half fearing half longing to run into her a chance meeting in the Writing Center the cafeteria in BSB—did she even go there—somewhere some Oh hi well this is weird sort of meeting. Maybe then Dewey would apologize to Hunter Flanagan for not writing. Oh that's no big deal he'd say if she mentioned anything but maybe she'd just not even broach the subject. He wanted to say something coy and cutting like Oh so you do still exist and she'd smile guiltily. He'd add Because I was starting to wonder. Yes Hunter I do still exist. It's just _____ and then I really was starting to feel like I was beginning to neglect _____ and so you know how it is. Yeah he'd say not wanting there to be tension between them. He already having forgiven her the minute they stopped moving close to each other. But then what would happen. Would he mention the Windy City Gay Men's chorus that had already come and gone. There was a show at Rockefeller. He had read about it written in chalk on the sidewalk in front of the Reynolds Club and thought about asking her to go to it with him but that was Monday. There were movies he also thought about seeing with her. He barely saw new films—most of them he found utterly unappealing—but the thought of going with her interested him. Maybe he didn't have time for the cinema.

 He didn't feel angry—as angry—about things the next morning. Tea and yogurt before him Hunter Flanagan thought maybe separation was part of their relationship already hard-wired into the coding of this potential union a necessary and functional cornerstone of distance. He thought about the first times he became aware of her. He guessed she had no idea who he was probably never really wondered or made any connections prior to that Friday when they actually spoke but there were these large gaps of time and space where they didn't speak to each other didn't think about each other and so maybe he was supposed to expect that now. He vowed this would be the last weekend he'd hold open but what about the meantime. The backup choices didn't have much promise. Miriam still emailed though Hunter Flanagan had barely noticed had been ignoring about 90 percent of them. The ones he replied to he only wrote a sentence at the most two sometimes only a word usually derisive comments which either she didn't pick up on or simply had so little respect for herself if that she chose to ignore it in exchange for the brief self-induced euphoria over Hunter Flanagan actually stopping to think about her. More likely the latter. It saddened him that someone would not want more out of her life than that. More Than This was on XRT while he combed his hair dried his body with a blue towel that morning and he couldn't help thinking about her and then wanted to throw the radio through the mirror.

# 41

Kate certainly should have wanted more than this. He gave in and called her last night. He didn't want to but her chasing was so pathetic so obvious. Though what did he expect. This was someone who did online dating. No matter what people said you pretty much have to reach a considerable low to sign up and pursue something like that. They talked about art. He half listened. She mentioned liking Hopper. He sort of did too. They discussed the Starbucks version of Nighthawks. He liked it not seriously of course but thought it was cute. She thought it was wrong.

He sat in front of the iMac while they talked checked his email nothing from Dewey and and and she had been in her mail file the time stamp 21:47. He asked Kate distractedly what time it was. Nine-forty-seven right.

No it's 10 she said.

No I mean 21:47. That's 9 right.

Yeah she said I think so.

Okay just wondering.

That sucked. He really didn't understand. He downloaded a jpg of Nighthawks and made it his background. It filled the screen rather impressively no pixel squares jagged edges everything smooth as though it had been designed painted conceived of for his screen even though it wasn't. How did it do that. The color overtook him. He felt like he stood on that empty street. Not so much at the counter though he imagined being there briefly but more of him outside alone wandering itinerant.

She asked when the last time he'd been to the Art Institute was.

November he said.

Now it was officially a week later. Sometime a few days earlier maybe Monday or Tuesday Hunter worried about it getting closer to being a week later. Of course he had to qualify a week since the date was not a week since he'd last written her—that was still several days away—but a week since their coffee. He had iced tea that day. He ordered one before she got there and ran out well before they left. Colleen the waitress from his writing class curiously stopped visiting the table after Dewey arrived maybe came once to deliver her mocha but he wasn't certain of that. At that point he was definitely enraptured not quite aware of any elements seeking to constitute the outside world only knew Dewey. Her presence was the only presence. That and their drinks hand gestures movements. She spooned off the frothy top and ate it before drinking anything beneath. He thought that cute. He liked the slowness with which she approached this drink like she somehow wanted to prolong things at the same time knowing she was only going to drink one mocha during her visit. Whereas Hunter had thought no doubt initially that he'd end up having several things to drink and that was why he ordered from Colleen so soon after arriving.

Three different women had three different reactions to the situation. The one good date seemingly really great date followed by sudden and unprovoked unexpected abandonment conundrum. He realized he'd involved these three other women from the start of this. They were the only ones really who knew he even had a date the only ones he knew who knew he currently liked a girl named Dewey and they had opinions.

He spoke to Nicole first. She was the girl he worked with the girl he sort of briefly liked during the week of computer consultant orientation. She said he wrote her—Dewey—too quickly that that had not been a good move. He sensed that was true. That was basically the last of the communication. Earlier he checked his sent mail. He had to go back to March. They hadn't spoken at all in April. He had read what he wrote to her the last time. He'd forgotten that comment he'd made about her being a *Rules* girl. Maybe that was what made her stop. Maybe that comment which he framed of course as a joke but still maybe that was what made her go away. Maybe it didn't have as much to do with the fact that he wrote her so quickly after the date as that comment but why would she read the email so closely. Only he read email so closely. Maybe it triggered something acrid something repulsive something utterly repugnant in her mind the same way he felt when Kate said she planned to stop going on dates with guys from the service when they were kissing—what passed for kissing anyway. Or how during one of his pull aways at first to gauge then to protect himself at least temporarily from what was happening—what was happening he absolutely could not control anyway—she mumbled something he couldn't hear but suspected. Maybe it wasn't even words maybe just an exhale. He thought he heard her say something completely ridiculous. She must have just sighed or something suppressed a yawn. He thought she said I love you and it was like Okay what the fuck are you thinking we just met. That was weird weird weird made him even more eager to get the hell out of there.

    Maybe the *Rules* comment was as though he were suggesting they were now or about to start dating in an implicit way and by saying that made the situation much more unwieldy made her say okay wait I can't or don't want to or never wanted to handle this forget it and Hunter hoped that hadn't been what happened. Christ he was only joking. Obviously he didn't want to be withholding on whether he wanted this just casual friends or if he were really interested. He felt like it had been okay to be a bit forward that way. How coy did one have to be. He couldn't get over how utterly pedantic the whole thing could be how these otherwise forthcoming individuals resorted to this silly punctilious pageantry. It was so dumb but it may have fucked everything up.

He wanted to write her find her in person hell call her house. He so easily could have gotten her number at work. He could get any campus employee's name address phone birthday everything short of income and astrological sign though he could theoretically compute that with the person's birthday. He didn't do this or really consider it because that would have certainly freaked her out. No he hadn't gotten so distraught by this that he was starting to consider stalking.

Angela didn't think this was the end of the world. In fact she still remained quite optimistic upbeat even in her email and maybe he was just reading it that way the way he wanted to but she said maybe Dewey was just busy why not send a follow up note in a week. Fuck. The whole *Rules* thing was Angela's thought her initial droll reaction to the report of Hunter's impetuous Let's have dinner email. She said Maybe Dewey is a *Rules* girl and wouldn't accept a date after Wednesday. He thought that was funny when he read it cute flirtatious and appropriated the line used it when he wrote Dewey last the last ignored email. He would have never even thought about it thought to say anything about it had it not been for Angela's remark. Fuck. That's what he got for stealing material. So now he didn't feel too inclined to believe her and felt like siding with Nicole even though her advice seemed extreme. She proposed waiting and planning a chance encounter. She was more renegade and definitely more vociferous in her admonishing Hunter for writing too soon.

And last night he heard from Peanut. She didn't think things were completely doomed. You have to expect this sort of thing from Virgos she wrote. It takes them quite some time to let you in. Maybe he thought.

At 3:10 he was still thinking lacing up his white Nikes in the locker room at the gym. One week ago at exactly this moment it all started he thought remembering her early entrance. He might have finally begun to think of something other than her at that moment the Irigaray article finally managing to distract him long enough to read maybe a paragraph and then he looked up and she was walking to him to the table and sat in the chair perpendicular to his the one he wanted her to sit in her back to the front door and the rest of the mélange of café business. Now certain details were becoming uncertain maybe these things he was never aware of should have paid attention to but didn't like her eye color. He guessed brown but it could have been hazel. Would he have been able to tell the difference. He missed her face. He was uncomfortable with how simple it was for them to return to how things had been previously the way of life before the party. That afternoon they basically didn't know each other and their lives functioned basically he guessed okay but he didn't want to simply efface her from his memory work her out of his day to day life. She'd happened and he thought that should mean something.

At this point she basically was gone. He only half seriously expected to find email from her didn't even slightly anticipate a phone call and while he hoped when he did look that there would be something a sort of apologetic but promising message such as I'm sure you already have plans or if she were in a jocular mood So if you're not a *Rules* boy I'm not doing anything Saturday night and he'd think Fuck babysitting but would work something out. He really didn't give that scenario much serious consideration not because it wasn't just a You didn't write issue but it was becoming a We really didn't know each other at all and probably just invented this whole thing imagined any possibility because we're fools sort of an issue.

After he exercised and got dressed he went to his car and found a white Ford Explorer parked in the adjacent space. There was a girl whom Hunter always watched closely on the elliptical machine before she disappeared quite suddenly stopped coming to the gym or at least was never there when Hunter was. One night months later he saw her again—an event almost coinciding perfectly with Hunter's rejection from B— almost coinciding perfectly with Hunter's first and worst blind date hours after receiving the news in the mail. Did he really want to give that in retrospect almost painless encounter the distinction of worst blind date with the much longer and disconcerting entanglement with Kate unbeknownst to him at the time that he was to find himself embroiled in soon after that. Maybe he should reconsider the rankings.

That terrible night Hunter felt a surge of relief that he hadn't asked her out or worse made a fool of himself in front of her at the gym. He did want to find out why she stopped going—he was somewhat curious about that. He had finished his dinner babysitting date with Christine and left almost mortified but more so numb. He really was outside himself that night playing with the kids Elena—Maya's friend Hyde Park Elena—and a classmate of hers Robbie. They played a game without title and they banished him to the closet locked the door peeked their heads in to taunt him. He reacted with exaggerated gasps and sighs and muffled shouts but really only could think about how disappointed he was both with Christine's blandness her smallness how unattracted he was to her and with the bad news in the letter he'd read. He didn't say anything to her about it. He wouldn't have. He couldn't even imagine telling anybody else let alone somebody he'd only known for half an hour. Everything had changed. B— had rejected him. There was no way around that. His life was fucked or so he thought. He didn't want to be where he was but had no way out. They ate pizza. She eventually let him go. He was thankful relieved it was only eight-thirty. He drove to the Co-op and bought a bottle of wine. Driving home he saw a white Explorer. He pushed forward close to the car's bumper and at a stop sign on Fifty-seventh squinted to read the license plate. It was her dealer's frame. It was three letters and three numbers. He knew it was the elliptical machine blonde girl's car. He knew it was. He followed it down Dorchester turned onto Fifty-eighth so she wouldn't see him when she braked in front of space which was too small for her to park in or maybe it was big enough and she didn't know how to parallel park. Then she gave up on it and turned down Fifty-eighth. Hunter freaked began driving turned onto Kenwood sped down the block back down Fifty-seventh circled around. When he got back she wasn't there. Her car was parked. She was nowhere. During the chase he offhandedly imagined pulling up saying something like Hi and of course she'd remember him. They looked at each other for at least forty minutes on and off twice a week for—what—two months. There would be no conceivable way for her not to know who he was so he wouldn't bother introducing himself. He'd then say I didn't know you lived on this block. I live down there. I bought this wine. Do you want to drink it with me. Strangely enough he felt emboldened then willing to take a chance somehow more powerful because of his defeat. The feeling of total and complete destruction that would render him utterly insentient for eternity actually might give him confidence when approaching a girl whom he'd had more than ample opportunity to talk to. Occasionally they even ran on the treadmill side by side but he had consistently and routinely not found the requisite courage to ask her out not even to say hi. What a dork he could be at times.

But then that night she was gone and would never return again. She had slipped into a house. Did she live on his block. Wouldn't that be quaint. He couldn't avoid observing the inherent erotic possibilities in such an association—two treadmill running neighbors—a short distance to travel for sex always an attractive premise—a situation he'd really not experienced since high school when he was fucking Dewey. Since then it had been nothing but travel geographical distances all the fucking driving. He liked that Lila lived in the dorms.

Sometimes after he lost her he would see white Explorers in the Bally's lot or think he saw white Explorers—some of them turned out to be Expeditions or Broncos or weren't even white were actually tan or beige. Well this went to show how totally ridiculous he'd been. What was he thinking. Did he have an alternate view of people the world girls he lusted after a way of visualizing them which made them larger more impressive more beautiful then they actually were or was it the opposite. When he stopped seeing her stopped lusting. Was he more attuned now to imperfection the frizz of hair which once seemed to have all this luster and sheen the unmistakable droop of a once well-supported breast. This was sort of depressing to have seen her then so young and inspiring and now feel nothing. He wished he hadn't seen the car and had to think of her.

# 42

He started thinking about how awkward it was—sometimes was—resuming a relationship after some sort of interstitial gap. Weeks months sometimes even years of not speaking. When Trey wanted Hunter to contact Julianne after their almost two years of not being friends he was reluctant at first but within minutes of speaking to her felt like things could be as they once had been again. He hated awkwardness things that brought attention to themselves moments where he or someone felt uncomfortable and that feeling was palpable.

So in the shower he started wondering if maybe that was what Dewey had been feeling. Like she wanted to write Hunter but wasn't looking forward to having to explain. Gaps almost certainly required explanation. Hunter didn't tell Julianne why it was he'd gone without returning her calls bitter exhortations tearful voice mail messages. Stolidly they didn't discuss it. They just resumed like nothing had happened or in as close an approximation as was possible for either of them he guessed at the time.

He wanted Dewey to know he wasn't angry. He felt like he'd really screwed things up somehow or maybe it was just quite bad timing perhaps for both of them. His rage or maybe passion had definitely managed to subside. It wasn't that he was indifferent exactly. It was more like he'd finally realized that it didn't have to always be about so much drama. He wrote a small email following Angela's suggestions and in some small way maybe Nicole's advice too. He'd waited fully a week. Nicole said two—could they split the difference—and Peanut of course said Astrology so maybe unconsciously he was writing with a better understanding of whose moon was in whose Jupiter or whatever. He wrote simply and looked it over a couple of times but definitely only one draft one basic one anyway. *I just wanted to see if you were okay. Eliot said April was the cruelest month and I think he was right. Write me sometime. Hunter.* He thought Simple she doesn't have to think about how to reply with the big gap because now that's in the past basically forgotten about and now she could reply or not but at least he'd given her the chance. It was the least he could do.

On Friday Kate went home to Cincinnati. Hunter thought at first she was going for a week but then found out no only for the weekend. She wrote him asked what he was doing Sunday night. Sunday night was dinner at his father's house his time to see Maya all in giggles Maya excited about her birthday party next month Maya who liked to play Barbies with Hunter. He was always Ken of course. Hunter didn't obviously want to disturb that ritual. He'd pretty much deified Sundays. They were sacrosanct inviolable and he was glad when she asked he had a ready-made excuse. She kept calling him and too much. He half jokingly entertained the obvious have a relationship with her but he could never force himself into it. He just wasn't attracted to her. It wasn't that she was physically undesirable—who was he to talk he felt like shit most of the time and probably looked worse—but regardless he just didn't want to think he was that desperate. Maybe it had been so long since he'd had an orgasm on top of or inside someone during the Hilary imbroglio that he was willing to say or do anything and that was how that aberration came to exist: his desperation. Now he definitely didn't feel that way. He felt like his libido was purely if not predominately academic intellectual. He wanted—here was what he wanted—he wanted to feel an intense and immediate physical somatic fiery reaction to someone and to also desire to hear her speak. Crude and deconstructionist yes but that was basically it. Maybe he was back to not being ready for a relationship. He could always have idle worthless sex with Miriam even though the thought of ever doing that again sickened and depressed him. What if Dewey did write back. Would everything change suddenly return or had the interstice really marked the beginning and end of something irretrievable.

# 43

He really hadn't expected her to write back. She did and was very apologetic said Oh god Hunter. I'm so sorry. They didn't seem like ersatz excuses maybe because he didn't care about the whys just that they were talking again. Those vacillating Virgos definitely. So not only did she write but she changed the preexisting terms. He got bumped up to dinner. A meal. She wrote What's a good place we can go eat. He quickly thought of two restaurants he'd been contemplating going to if of course he had someone to go with. He didn't respond immediately so he could consider the choices intelligently. It was part of his new philosophy. The I am calm and rational approach. Maybe it was working. Maybe that was why she subtly elevated their status. Not that dinner suggested more than coffee but dinner probably meant off-campus. He didn't ask just figured that's what she meant when he wrote back. There was Hi Ricky. He wondered if that was a bad choice since it had almost become anathema—it was the place he had suggested in more impetuous fervor—but he offered it. Anyway it was a cute place and seemed kind of romantic. The food was good. Then he added Heaven on Seven. Maybe he should have skipped that one. After all he never thought of the place independently always had Jessica Emerson echoing circumscribing the suggestion. When he liked a girl and she was coy she was Jessica Emerson that summer when they went everywhere together and even after a year later almost when he took her to see *Rent*.

Their relationship was all suggestion. Everything about her intentions had always been ambiguous. Maybe she gave him cause subconsciously to fall for her in the first place nine years ago when he first met her. Maybe something in her eyes her words implied possibility. They'd never really talked about it.

Dewey's email had that certain sense of renewed possibility but he didn't want to think about it too much. This was a second chance but not to bombard her not to be ingratiating to no end like Kate—and he was genuinely sorry that he didn't regard her more. It just wasn't the right time. Gag what a hollow cliché but it was true. Dewey's email pretty much decided the fate of that Deanna person. She probably had forgotten all about him anyway. This talking to five girls concomitantly was ridiculous. He never was the sort to be able to manage all of that but it wasn't strictly speaking an administrative issue why he knew that was a bad idea plus he was thinking about Dewey again and didn't want to diffuse his emotions and become distracted. He'd planned to see Kate on Friday but only felt mildly guilty control-x send and quickly returned to Dewey's paragraphs. There were three of them. They were thick ones. He smiled. He liked her words. He liked her. He wanted to have dinner with her. He wanted to know maybe where this was going to go.

# 44

It was Tuesday Hunter's last exchange with Dewey Sunday. The issue: dinner and what day. He was holding basically the entire week open for her and of course for his papers remotely. He was going to have to really start doing something about those. They were due next week. Waldman wasn't an easy grader very critical and specific like Hunter himself or like Hunter wished he were. There was only one more week left. That was hard to believe. One more week of undergrad. One more week. He of course wished he could be less concerned about Dewey but it wasn't concern really. He just wished he were satisfied with the amount of written correspondence between them. When she didn't write he remembered the phone and how he couldn't call her. Would he call her if she allowed him to. He told Lila rather emphatically before class the other day that he'd call her that night. He didn't. He thought about doing it but was suddenly very tired actually lay down closed his eyes for twenty minutes. He thought about their last conversation on the phone. It went on for too long and became really tedious. Hunter called her after returning from the gym buzzed from a thoroughly satisfying run and climb bet that the energy would fortify his conversation make him more interesting. He at that point still at the gym planned on calling when he got home. It worked somewhat at the beginning anyway. The first half hour she didn't ever seem to want to get off the phone. They'd only talked a couple of times really both in person and on the phone so what sort of a reference point did that make. Her lingering only added to the confusion over what she really wanted from Hunter. Maybe that was the element he liked the most in relationships situations arrangements initial trial couplings: he could never be certain what the other person wanted. Maybe he liked trying to find out which always inevitably ended up meaning a game a stratagem a smoke screen. That was the core of flirting of romantic inclination the most animated most vital part: the trying to in the beginning crack the code decipher these intentions through a series of emails coffees maybe dinners and you will then be allowed to find out what she really thinks of you because simply the fact that she's near you or maybe writes emails to you occasionally cuts a class for you laughs at your jokes trains cow eyes on you that doesn't mean she likes you. So many ambiguous uncertain motives both in Hunter at any given moment and in the women he had about him since probably birth made this a grand jury proceeding. His life as it had been the situations burned into his consciousness the images which stood impassively those with which he had formed opinions perspectives likes dislikes expectations those had led him to this point and made necessary the enervating seemingly superfluous routines and dances which of course he secretly enjoyed which of course secretly kept him going regardless of ethical considerations regardless of future impact on the long term regardless this was how it worked for Hunter and all he could do was just deal with it hope it wouldn't eventually do him in really fuck him and just hope to gradually be able to better understand what it really all meant. He wanted to better appreciate this the current situation because it could only become more confusing was certain to become more problematic though not in the same way. Actually in this context things could only become simpler. Dewey could make it clear one way or the other how she felt and what she wanted from Hunter that she desired a real committed thing eat in restaurants together make out in cars on park benches in movie theaters since really neither of them had private space to bring someone into. And he definitely didn't. He was too embarrassed about his living situation occasionally pulled down phone numbers from sublet ads but never called. It would be ridiculous to take one of them at this point especially since he was now definitely moving at the end of the summer. He knew even with the tuition waiver moving and living in Boulder couldn't be cheap so he saved what little money he had instead. So now as far as liaisons were concerned he could only hope to meet girls with apartments. Miriam fit into this category albeit with roommate but he really had no interest in returning to her tiny rusty place and Kate's apartment was nice clean but dander infested so either it was to be a summer of nosebleeds and drowsiness from Nasalcrom blasts and temperance or itching and bitching or celibacy but of course obstacles heightened awarenesses and furthered the drama. The unknowing part—the ingrained *Romeo and Juliet* imagery—maybe was the best part or the part most interesting. So possibly it was better not to rush through things with Dewey impetuously like he did everything else.

Angela wrote She just sounds flighty. I'm sure she likes you. You just have to relax chill out don't think about it. Hunter tried—he did—it just felt so nebulous so irritatingly uncertain.

Nicole said that morning when they worked walk-ins Sometimes people want to play games. Mixed signals are the worst.

That's what this was a big mixed up ambiguous signal. Last Friday Hunter felt like maybe things were going to start happening—of course what start happening meant he couldn't quite say. This morning still no email no word on Friday or the weekend only two more days away. She wasn't going to write him. It wasn't going to happen.

He drank coffee with skim milk felt reaffirmed by its implacability also by Nicole's advice that he definitely shouldn't write Dewey again. That it was her move. It was so much easier to navigate make decisions for someone else to live when the living was all academic hypothetical advances no consequences except only living vicariously no first hand experience but were we all just entrenched in this belief in empiricism. Was that the only thing viable. Nevertheless he wasn't at this point counting on anything happening.

What's going on with the blind date girl Nicole asked. Hunter sighed and covered his eyes. Is she still stalking you.

He told Nicole about the phone calls and the Sunday rescheduled Friday plans but left out the part about the kissing.

She probably thinks she's your girlfriend. What's her name again.

Kate.

Mrs. Kate Flanagan.

Yeah right like that could happen.

This girl has no life she said.

Yeah I'm starting to get the feeling.

Yet he sort of wanted to go back and make out with Kate some more though felt completely guilty about it. He wasn't the provocateur here. He wasn't making her call making her lean into him and start things as she had been doing. This was all external to him. He kept going along with it though.

He wanted to organize a symposium. The topic: What was wrong with Hunter Flanagan. A long panel discussion or maybe several nights at a round table old girlfriends momentary distractions and newer interests badges with names scrawled in Sharpie translucent cups of water microphones stationed every other seat Eileen would say he got too clingy too fast too overwhelming but she knew him when he was so young could that be his excuse for falling in love so quickly so recklessly next up the first Dewey she would say Hunter Flanagan just wanted me when it was convenient for him he couldn't disagree though he felt bad for how he treated her she was so naïve didn't deserve to have her first experiences be so unpleasant he was sorry he'd handled her so roughly what would Hilary say she would say he wasn't serious enough or too serious pretended to love her when he didn't really stayed with her when he didn't want to be with her just because he didn't want to hurt her but wasn't it worse for her in the end than if he had just gone away when he first had the chance why did he fuck with her head like that Kate would say Hunter is great everything I've ever wanted in a guy he reads he appreciates art he's not obsessed with cars or fashion I could see myself spending the rest of my life with him she was like that such a fatalist it wasn't what he wanted but had he learned any more since Hilary about how to say what he really was thinking to a girl he was seeing not really some guest appearances by girls he made out with in high school they'd say he was a good kisser but never returned phone calls Simona what would she say he wondered if she ever thought about him these days was probably so mired in tattoos and pot or maybe she'd returned to heroin maybe she'd forgotten all about him. They'd hypothesize and argue but eventually realize they'd gotten nowhere that they'd never get anywhere and have to go home agree to disagree plan to fight it out the next year and return to their hotel rooms take a swim at the pool and go home. He knew even less than they ever did about why he behaved as he did.

    He of course could never really believe Dewey was trying to hurt him intentionally. He didn't make a habit of falling for mean vindictive types or was it maybe he fell for them but didn't go about getting involved with them. He had no trouble imagining a dozen reasons why she might not have written. He kept reminding himself of how annoying Kate had been to his situation the parts he shared of it anyway. She called him last night left a message on his voice mail said I'm calling since I haven't heard from you and you didn't send me an email today. Okay this really was getting ridiculous. Since when did he have to intentionally or not check in with her. She was clearly delusional. He had been thinking about calling her just to say hi see how she was laugh a little but after hearing that he decided absolutely not to call her. He could of course go see Dewey today run into her accidentally but he didn't want to. He of course wanted to see her be apologized to hear about whatever test whatever paper whatever grandmother emergency made it such that she couldn't write or couldn't call even for five minutes. He wanted to hear that because it could make him forget. It would make him okay for the moment because she was focused on him paying attention concerned even if just a pretense even if just to try to make herself feel better about ignoring him and not just ignoring but this mind fucking. Of course how much of a hypocrite was he being now. How sanctimonious was it to say The way she's treating me the way she's not being forthright not being honest with me that's what wrong when Kate probably very likely in fact felt the exact same way if not more so since she lacked irony. It was just not a very nice thing to do. Maybe it made for bad karma. Maybe Dewey existed merely and for the sole purpose of taunting him reminding him of his mortality which he still despite all of this was not immutably convinced of. He never seemed to have a clue never even suspected outcomes like these yet somehow became defenseless porous when they came along. What was it about her. Was it that she was unavailable. Was it that she was actually intelligent. Surely there were other intelligent girls out there yet for some reason those weren't the ones he ended up with. Could the intelligent girls have been intimidated by his demeanor or did they just know better were equipped with some sort of technology for seeing through artifice. He really wanted to and especially if things were to progress with Lila needed to tell Kate the truth or at least be unequivocal about what the not calling meant. Otherwise it was just going to get worse. She'd keep calling making him feel like shit emailing and he did sort of like her after all so there wasn't any sort of pressing need to be a bastard like say in the Miriam situation. He was taking pleasure in having not emailed her in a few days maybe not since Monday and watching her meaningless and cliché riddled prose get more and more riled up and frantic. It was sick. It was mean. He knew that but it was slightly satisfying and more or less harmless.

 The next morning he felt more anger than hurt. He recalled the night before. He had babysat for Maya. He didn't fancy himself the babysitting type but for her he'd make exceptions to any of his illogical rules. They sat on the back porch together and ate Passover matzo.

Maya hugged him standing beside where he sat and said in a lilt Everything's starting to bloom.

Her hair was damp from a bath her eyes glinting with the light and exuberance pink shorts and a pink tank top. They went inside and ate pasta Linda prepared and left for them on the stove. Hunter poured orange juice. She drank some from his glass.

This is really good juice he said.

Pulpy she said.

They watched *Rugrats in Paris*. She didn't seem to notice when he fell asleep because his head faced the screen. He was tired. The day had been taxing. After he put her to bed he checked his email. Nothing good. Miriam said something he barely read something like Well maybe I do make a lot of excuses and am lazy and procrastinate but you never want to talk about anything serious so we're even. D delete. He hated cluttering his folders with Miriam. What a dim clueless waste of his energy. Not that he spent much of anything on her but still.

Maya was already asleep when his parents returned from the opera. He didn't feel ready to leave as they thanked him ushered him out. On the expressway he drove and thought about her. What would she be like at fifteen. What sort of person would she become was already becoming. Would she be like him. Would she have ideas and desires and an acute awareness of the inadequacies of people and democracies and life and love. Would she date guys that would be attractive but end up hurting her. Or maybe it would be the guys who weren't that attractive but were articulate and seemingly sensitive and aware who would break her heart. How could Hunter protect her how could he keep her from turning into himself how could he keep her away from guys like him. He couldn't keep her young and optimistic and happy forever. They'd watch videos now and drink orange juice but someday she wouldn't need him she'd be consumed with things other than his Sunday visits and dumb jokes and piggyback rides around the house. All he could do was accept that he could never be enough and just try to be what he was. People can't be more than they are no matter how many degrees or books or girlfriends you throw at them he reminded himself.

# 45

The bathroom smelled like paint. Fresh paint. Gray paint. Did it actually smell gray or did it just look gray. It wasn't quite the end of the semester. Why were they already repainting bathrooms. It didn't seem to make sense. He'd been beginning to sense the walls of the semester close in around him the knowledge that soon he'd no longer be an undergraduate unequivocal. So what was he supposed to do with himself in the meantime.

Five years of college and he still could not write a paper—whether it was about Cimino's profligate ways or Steven Bach's ineptitude or The Mirror Stage or Derrida or Aphasia and the Sublime—without starting three weeks before it was due outlining several times producing numerous drafts. He railed others for what he considered to be their laziness found it perturbing to hear Miriam's accounts of her own half-assed lame attempts at academic work. Obviously what he did when he wasn't doing schoolwork was always—most of the time—important. He wrote books after all. He concerned him self with his fiction developments in characters often awakened in the middle of the night by them quickly reaching for a pen or while driving scribbling lines of dialogue on the back of a gum wrapper or a receipt from the gas station. He slept with a dictionary in his bed. Well no one else was sleeping in it. He submitted stories to magazines queried publishers about his other book the act of which he was definitely starting to consider pointless. He wasn't as confident in it because he liked his new work better saw more possibilities in it. Of course it would need work revision definitely. Maybe a lot of it was redundant but he wasn't convinced that was a flaw. Sure if he took parts of it to his grad school workshops people were sure to find the things he considered valuable problematic. That's just how workshops operated. Who would be in this program at C— anyway. He still didn't even know how many other students were there. He said twenty when others asked but that was just a guess. Maybe more like a hope. It couldn't be very large could it. Even at his university he didn't think there were a ton of creative writers. He knew some of them. Would these people at C— have any talent. Would they be diligent dedicated or snobby and superfluous. Obviously things would be different. He'd probably get more respect from the professors a chance to begin again. The professors he couldn't stand at UIC venerated their grads and didn't seem to have much patience for the undergrads though maybe only Hunter Flanagan they didn't like because of his confidence because of his unwillingness to be the typical ascetic undergraduate writer. Well this was soon to change. Soon he wouldn't have any of that stigma attached to him or his work. He could begin again. He hoped he would develop relationships with the people in his workshops hoped they wouldn't be forty-year-old pikers delusional confessional looking for group therapy I-write-to-feel-better-about-my-life dolts but instead young dynamic people like him—no like Angela. She was the only one who wrote and felt like he did the only one he really knew who did anything the way he did and wasn't just all about ease and vapidity.

But how could he say his life wasn't about ease. How often did he opt for lying around instead of reading when he should or sleeping when he felt tired. Hilary always used to say that he should force himself to stay awake to finish papers do things that he didn't feel like doing. He ridiculed the idea.

Why would I stay awake he had asked her. I probably wouldn't be able to do anything worthwhile so why pretend.

She said these things to him that summer two years ago when they took anthropology together. He was tired a lot that summer worked at Market Facts still full time and the class hours were long. It met on Tuesdays and Thursdays and there were lectures lab sections and field trips. It was his last science course to take and her last five hours of college. She was already graduated but not technically until the end of that summer. He was also working on his book then twisting around the words occasionally. He could now barely look at what he wrote then. It sucked. It wasn't any good at all. It was the hollowest shallowest crap he'd ever seen. Whom did he think would feel otherwise about it. It didn't just have to do with not having a plot though he wasn't entirely sure it didn't things happened there was a trajectory the action took place along but it didn't have much feeling emotion just events no thoughts really reacting to a lot but superficially. This probably reflected how he was thinking at the time. His relationship with Hilary was similarly superficial his participation in the anthropology class barely a murmur his life a corridor glancing off the walls but never reaching any sort of door any sort of destination.

They fought a lot about his job. She wanted him to quit to become a serious student more or less what he ended up doing after they broke up but he didn't want to then. He didn't want to because she said to. He said he would eventually leave Market Facts that he wasn't going to spend his entire life in the place and she just had to trust that things would work out.

She kept insisting demanding he do something now now now she would say and he said It's not the right time I'll do it when I'm ready but that didn't seem enough. She would just sigh or cry and make him feel like shit which she was definitely good at doing and he guessed it was sort of ironic that when he finally did scale back his hours in Evanston and began to take a full load of classes and wanted to do the reading—to actually do it instead of pretending—that Hilary's response to that was to put more demands on him to be less supportive to bitch and moan and he would say But I thought you wanted this I thought you wanted me to take things seriously and here I am doing just that and you're complaining but she didn't get it pretended she didn't remember made up more excuses to try to shift the focus from what he was saying to some other irrelevant minutiae. Anyway that was done with and he did do all his reading this semester that he could do and fairly well better when he took notes but he always highlighted things looked up key terms tried as best he could to stay focused to not waste time and he did but now trying to write a paper going through a charade of good intentions slacking self-flagellation before finally doing it—it all was so stupid. All of these things going on now made him act like a fool like he hadn't learned anything at all in all this time.

# 46

Hunter volunteered to bring the envelope of Critical Theory course evaluations to Douglas Hall. He volunteered because he thought I'll see Dewey there she'll be leaving the Writing Center and I'll see her. This line of thinking of course counter plan—the plan to not see her talk to her—but he didn't care. He left the classroom a few minutes after eleven. He was sort of relieved. He didn't want to see her he realized then and was glad that she'd be off already in Anthropology or wherever. He wasn't ready to see her. Though he was somewhat curious to see what her excuse would be this time he didn't want to deal with it.

He dropped the envelope in the office's slot and then stepped into the Writing Center said hello to a few people. He didn't see her. That was good. He wandered back into the hall and into the vestibule. He had passed the first door and was about to reach the second when he saw her. She was walking toward the building. He was uncomfortable and happy. She opened the door and stepped inside.

Hi Hunter she said.
Hi he said back.
I thought you had class now.
I did—I do—but it was cancelled.
Oh.
It's been so crazy she said. Okay here she goes he thought smiling nodding thoughtfully. I have to do this presentation in

Greek it has to be ten minutes I have these physics reports everything is due Monday I'm so fucked I'm so screwed.

She smiled and relayed this information rather indifferently. It wasn't like she was really upset. She looked different than from when Hunter had seen her last. She wore a black sweater with some sort of blue shirt underneath that kind of sparkled. People walked in and out clicking the door letting the door open and then close locking and unlocking of the lock mechanism.

Well what are you doing now. She held a book from the library. She held it tightly like she was trying to send a message with it held it between her and him. It was this stupid thing between them and it didn't go away.

Not only that she continued sort of ignoring his question but I have this music stuff. Apparently I need to make a tape of scales that I should have done a long time ago.

Well you could just buy one.

Buy one.

A tape of somebody else singing and just blot out the name write in Dewey.

Yeah I think my professor would spot that one.

Yeah you're probably right.

He touched her shoulder. It seemed not to matter that she had gone yet another week basically without writing him.

I'm just so busy right now it's crazy.

Well this is sort of that time I guess.

Everything is literally due Monday she said.

I have stuff due too. This weekend is going to be a nightmare.

I don't even know what I'm going to write about for this Greek presentation.

You could write about quotation marks the Greek kind.

I couldn't fill up ten minutes with that.

Why don't you just do it in English.

It's supposed to be in Greek. I don't think I can go into Greek 104 with a monologue in English. I don't think it works that way.

You can say you're doing it just as a test you know to see if anyone's paying attention.

But it's for my professor. I'm sure she'll be paying attention since she has to grade me.

I think it would be unique all these people in your class are going to do presentations in Greek.

Well it is a Greek class.

Still you can do yours in English break from the crowd be a leader.

He didn't know what he was really talking about. He felt nervous in her presence started to like her like he had before all the absence. Maybe he was attracted to her in his head. The way he remembered her looking changed. He guessed they didn't see each other enough for her to have made one specific mind print. He still relied on scattered images to conceive of her clearly. Inside his mind when he did see her like when she was walking up to the door it was as if it were someone else even though he knew it was her right away but if he really thought about it he hadn't seen that much of her like at all.

Maybe you could write in English about how language shouldn't have borders it shouldn't be all about Greek this or English that we should work toward having dialectic unity.

She laughed at that. I really don't think my professor would see much merit in that but I see what you mean. Southern Greek is different from Northern.

Yeah he said you could talk about how Midwestern Greek people say weird things like pop and like expressways.

She laughed again. As opposed to soda in Southern California Greece.

Yeah exactly. Hey speaking of which do you want to go get a soda.

She said No loudly not shouting but in a weird sort of frustrated punctuated way.

Okay he said.

It's too early in the morning for caffeine.

Well we could get something else.

I am just so totally fucked with all this stuff she said. Okay now she was avoiding for some reason but why. I hate getting fucked.

He looked at her for a second. They paused. I didn't mean... That sounded very weird.

No it's okay I know the context so it's not as if I had just walked in here and heard that well—

It's a mess a disaster she said. I hate having to do all this crap at the end.

He said I guess once it's all over—the semester and everything—things will be normal again.

Yeah I hope so she said and sighed looking at the book in her hand.

So you didn't forget about me Hunter said.

No she said. Her shoulders moved up slightly her eyes apologetic. I didn't forget about you.

Well that's good to know he said.

Yeah it's just you know right now everything is so crazy.

Well I hope you know he said once we're done then we could I don't know have more time I remember something about a dinner.

Listen she said I wanted to sort of talk to you about that.

They were standing now in a corner of the entranceway. They had moved over to the side probably without noticing it stepping out of the way of moving people people coming and going through the doors now. They were in a corner her back to the glass door Hunter standing close in front of her. He could see people coming in or near the glass doors. He kept looking when he would sense motion wanted to know if it was anyone from the Writing Center. The director had already passed them nodded briefly before walking through. He expected to see someone else come knew it inevitable people would disturb them.

She started to speak again. I've been meaning to talk to you about well this is sort of hard to say it's just that... Well I wanted to say well I'm not really looking for—it's just that I don't want you to think—look it's like this: you know sometimes people—well—get... I didn't want you to get the wrong idea you know to think things were a certain way. I just thought it would be better to tell you this so you didn't think I was... That I... It's not that I don't like you but I just wanted us to be on the same—

He was listening to this he was hearing the words he knew the conversation he had heard all these things before but not from her. He was shocked. It wasn't that shocking. He could have expected this. Now the absences made sense when you looked at it like this. He of course had many times before just not today felt like her absences meant something more than she was just busy but then it didn't make sense then it must have been that she really didn't mean for that and she didn't know what else to do because he had—well basically up to this point—been working from the assumption that she was at least interested in his being interested that she wasn't completely opposed to any of this that she just needed some time to warm to the suggestion to let him in. She was a Virgo. Virgos were like that sometimes—that was Peanut's advice from some time ago—that he should handle the situation with delicacy since Dewey was a Virgo.

Then there was a lull. He felt like he was supposed to speak next. Oh well no I understand I mean clearly yeah no seriously.

Do you know what I mean she asked still not far from where he stood. Maybe he'd stepped back a little. He didn't feel like they stood as close to each other as before but they were still jammed into this corner. He started to think specifically about that fact then: now when people come in they're going to know what she said what this conversation means. Of course it was empty in the corridor until Ricki came from outside. In she walked almost passing them but she stopped.

What are you doing out here.

Writing Center annex Hunter said quickly.

Dewey spoke too. Just hanging out.

That's weird Ricki said walking through and away.

Great Hunter thought of course she would have to see this. Did she know anything about his liking Dewey. Maybe she didn't know but maybe the proximity with which they stood gave something away. Hunter felt like his feet were tired. He was suddenly aware of his clothes wondered what his face looked like but from somebody else's perspective if when she smiled or spoke he looked like an idiot maybe unattractive. Undesirable. That's what she was saying. She said other things of course but he wasn't listening still thinking back to the first things she said before she started repeating before it was over and finished with.

There were these bifurcated sections of the conversation. The first part where he was sort of forgiving and didn't want to think about what had happened or what hadn't happened when she was ignoring him as he was wont to do in these situations and had done with her previously. The second part was now. Last Friday one week ago was their serendipitous meeting when they sat on the bench in the quad. Now this happens. He thought in a way while she spoke and repeated and tried—what—to convince him of the necessity of this she didn't quite say directly it was because she wasn't attracted to him but he felt like that's what it meant which was reductive sad made him feel self-conscious conspicuous. He again wondered if he looked like an idiot if he were physically unappealing and especially now. This would have been the time for her to say to herself that she was wrong that she wanted him regardless of how much sense it made or didn't make.

He heard something she said that stood out from the rest: I guess I felt like you—I don't know—you came on too strong inflected up like a question. I don't know maybe I'm just well... She looked away down and then at him again. Maybe I'm shy.

He stopped her from speaking by speaking. I'm shy too. She looked at him like she found that hard to believe. Don't you know I don't do this a lot. I hope you don't think I go around acting like this because I don't. I just felt a certain way. When people feel a certain way well—you know. I'm sure there are different ways to handle whatever and people told me I read manuals you know got advice about what to do and I guess I didn't listen and maybe that's my problem but I like to show I guess and tell people more or less what I'm really thinking and I'm sure some people will feel a certain way and just not say or do anything about it but I'm not like that. I don't feel like I shouldn't say or do.

Maybe it's just too much for me or right now I don't know. It just felt like you were—

I know but I just didn't well I didn't want you to think I didn't care because I did care about you I did and so well I'm sorry I really am if I if I you know was overwhelming because it's just how I felt.

Why did he say felt. Was he supposed to make an impassioned plea here. He didn't really want to. It sounded like it was over.

I still want to be friends with you she said.

I want to get to know you because I really do he said. I just felt like we connected.

And that's why I just didn't want to have you having the wrong impression. Some people just ignore things and hope that they go away but I didn't want to do that. I didn't want to tell you something like this in an email either. I didn't think that would work at all.

Yeah he said but you know I did whatever I did because— he stopped. You know I really appreciate you doing that. I don't know if a lot of people think about this or care but to me attraction desire whatever it's when you see certain qualities in the other person that you admire about yourself or you wish you had more of or that you wanted to be like. I guess I really appreciate you telling me because yeah a lot of people wouldn't. Maybe even I wouldn't but I have to give you points for that you know like three points. Maybe two.

She laughed. I'm sorry Hunter you know that don't you.

I am too.

It's just that even if I wanted... I just have so much going on right now and so do you.

Yeah I know.

It just probably wouldn't even work out so I didn't want to make an appointment to have dinner with you.

He laughed at that. An appointment.

She smiled too. Well you know sit down with you and be in some place like that and say this stuff so that's why I didn't say anything. I didn't want to hurt you.

It's okay he said.

It was stunning. He felt stunned still aware of the bifurcated parts and replaying parts of the beginning the way he touched her shoulder maybe too assertively like he already possessed some part of her that would allow touching of the shoulder without really even thinking about it which obviously by what she said wasn't the case at all. Things had changed over the course of that conversation in the hall.

We should still talk to each other. I know this sounds completely eighth grade of me but I want to stay friends.

Yeah me too he said and for some reason it didn't feel like a total lie either when he said it. For some reason he imagined spending time with her having a better relationship now that this was out of the way. It was like the courting. His pursuing her was just a big lie a fabrication and now they could talk to each other openly. He knew what she was thinking that she didn't want to like him and he got to admit that he liked her which obviously she knew though she could have been just assuming. He could have pretended like she in fact was the one who had misunderstood but that would have been a lie. He didn't feel like lying. Her honesty made him want to tell the truth.

I'm glad we had this conversation he said. I feel strangely enough like it's been sort of empowering I don't know I mean I feel like shit obviously it's still kind of shocking but I guess I'm glad.

She said Me too. I know I keep repeating the same three

things but I didn't want you to have... Because it wouldn't be fair to you not to tell you and for things to get more... And so I just wanted you to know where I was at with all of this.

Hunter thought So okay now what. This was definitely a sort of closure which he did appreciate. It made things less confusing to be sure. He'd stop checking to see if she'd checked her email the same way he did when he stopped looking for Helaine or waiting for replies from Iris all the times before. Of course Iris told Hunter she was married. He asked her several times indirectly to spend time with him have coffee with him go to the library with him and she always tacitly refused. He stopped thinking about her constantly at one point. He'd do the same now with Dewey. It was like a death. A breaking up without the relationship. He already felt like things were different besides the bifurcated conversation. Other elements—she didn't look the same he didn't feel like smiling as much. He sort of wanted to leave but didn't. He didn't want to plead for her to let him like her. That would be ridiculous. What good could come out of that. No what he wanted to know was did he ever really like her or did he just want to like her. He did feel like they'd connected but whom couldn't he connect with really. They weren't astrologically compatible and had a very low love match score. He barely saw her. They'd both be moving away in a few months. Why did he care so much or want to care so much. He had no control of his desire. His desire moved him in directions even he felt unwarranted but went along with it regardless waited for it to run its course to do what it needed to do just to fill space and gaps in time and then be done with it. So this moment became a sort of relief. Dewey did what Hunter probably wouldn't have had the balls to do to decide that he was going to move on or just move away. Frankly he didn't feel like dating anyone really. He didn't really want sex. Maybe he was depressed. What did he really want.

He walked down a different street. He was now late. It was eleven thirty. So much of his life had changed in the brief space of a half hour. He walked down a side street Vernon Park instead of Harrison which he normally took to the computer lab in SSB where he worked in that hour. Everything was strangely quiet around him. He noticed cars parked along the curb some at odd angles like their drivers had tried to squeeze them into spaces the cars were probably too big to fit into comfortably but now there was no car in front or behind so it just looked strange. He saw a TA this guy named Dan walking with a stroller and a woman. Hunter took Dan's section of Philosophy discussion maybe three or four years ago. He saw Dan periodically and sometimes said hi to him. He waved and Hunter waved back. Dan probably had no idea who Hunter was only was vaguely cognizant of their relationship. Child in stroller wife pushing and Dan walking a step behind them on the south side of the street Hunter on the north. He walked alone and looked at cars and thought about being stunned by the news and thought about Lila and thought about Kate and felt kind of sad that he was left with those two. It was like an army that had been fired at-some down some still standing but barely. He was trying to regroup figure out where he walked to now where he'd go. She said she wanted to still talk to him but he knew that was probably bullshit. He was losing interest in her long before today. He'd let himself forget about that bolstered by the interspersed attention relying on that to carry him but no longer. Things were out in the open. She'd said things she couldn't take back. Well maybe she could. She could write him call him up say I was wrong I was scared I am scared I don't know how to relate to men I'm scared of men I'm scared of you and how I might feel about you and I said things I didn't mean. But would that really mean anything to him. He wanted Dewey to be something. He had for quite some time now before spring break the last month at least. He'd been thinking about her wanting to see her. Why did she do the things she did say the things she said. He should have known. Is that what the no calling shit was about. Did she know even then that she wanted Hunter to remain at a specific and certain distance at all times that she might on occasion stand near him but always from behind a specific and certain

THE WEEK YOU WEREN'T HERE 199

line a line he would always be dimly aware of and forever want to cross. God how could he have been so foolish to let himself become victim to all of this.

Had he though. He again felt remarkably calm. He was never the sort to cry over a woman. He wouldn't have say as some do smash in windows or shout at people. That wasn't like Hunter in the slightest. He was a writer after all. He was used to rejections. He'd learned to take them in stride keep on moving keep on submitting keep on writing. Why would he fall victim now. Why would he become debilitated and a babbling lachrymose idiot. He was a writer god damn it. Plus he wasn't alone. He was going to have a date Lila next week and then go to that formal with her. Maybe that would work out. Yet he felt so dispassionately about everything so numb. He needed to snap out of this. This weekend he'd immerse himself in his papers and not think about sadnesses and losses and just get the fuck on with his life from here. Fuck Dewey. She wasn't worth it. She didn't mean much to him. He didn't know much about her. She was attractive but not enough to warrant jumping from high buildings. She didn't know what she was losing out on. Hunter Flanagan didn't choose to like girls freely. He really didn't. He had to be inspired to do so and maybe she wouldn't have the chance to know someone like him again and experience all that he wanted to do with her. Let her live in her small insignificant life. Let her be alone and without him and with dumb men who don't feel things who don't know about love who can't feel love who can't feel anything who only want sex and banality. Let her have that. Why should Hunter Flanagan who wrote books why should Hunter Flanagan who was going to graduate school Hunter Flanagan who was moving to Boulder to teach and learn and become a new person why should he fall victim and die because of her and her hang-ups and her unwillingness to be willing. And it wasn't as though he were asking for so fucking much. It wasn't as if he were calling her every fucking night saying do this with me do that. It wasn't as though he weren't being reasonable. All he wanted was a fucking chance.

Well that's what he got. He had a chance. It didn't work. She was the wrong sign. He was too much or she was too little or she was a sadist or she didn't like men or she was just a fucking bitch. Any of those things.

That wasn't how he felt. He didn't think those things. He was hurt. He was angry. Her announcement made him feel like everything else was shit. It made him look at things differently. He gave in and wrote to Miriam—nothing significant—pretended he'd been in New York—she believed it—wrote to Kate told her to call him in the lab. She did. They talked briefly. He apologized about having not called to her in a couple of days. He thought two but from what she described it sounded more like three. Maybe he hadn't spoken to her in person since last Sunday. Maybe he'd start paying more attention to her. He didn't want to do that just because he was moving down the line and it was time to go to the next choice on the list and find out what happened there but maybe he didn't want to treat her like shit behave the way Dewey had. He was better than that. Fuck her. Just because she told him that didn't make what she did right. Did it. She made it sound like it was all Hunter Flanagan's fault like he had twisted and contorted and reified that which didn't even exist theoretically. He hadn't. He hadn't done that god damn it. She had made certain things abundantly clear and then reneged on those certain things. He wasn't making this up. He was there. He watched her say certain things and want to sit next to him. So what happened. What changed from one week to the next only one hundred and sixty-eight hours only ten thousand eighty minutes really only six hundred four thousand eight hundred seconds. That was all the time that had passed from one event to the next give or take ten minutes and now Hunter was alone without wondering alone unequivocally alone alone alone. He felt shitty enough to want to go see Miriam. That's what usually made something like this a little more tolerable: sex. Fucking precisely what he told Dewey circuitously of course he wasn't after and that wasn't a lie. He wanted to spend quality time with Dewey get to know her relate to her drink tea with her and he wanted to fuck Miriam like it didn't matter like passing through a turnstile like sitting in an el car riding the red line downtown. That's what he wanted. He didn't want to talk to her he didn't want to make out with her he just wanted to plug her up and come when he felt like it and the hell with her and everyone else.

    He of course wasn't going to go see Miriam not this week anyway. He had too much to do and knew that in all likelihood he'd end up feeling worse about himself and the situation if he did. Besides he needed to work on his papers. He was really screwed waiting this long to start them. He had basically until Wednesday for the Film and Authorship class and Friday for his critical theory but he wanted to have drafts by the end of the weekend. He was going to sequester himself in the library tomorrow and not think about anything and not check email just be alone and write and try to get through this week. And what he said before was still true. All of this was going to be over in another week. He was going to graduate college and be done with Chicago and start over and meet new people and he hoped find new inspiration and new writing and he still had things. He would have a good summer. He didn't need a girlfriend apart from the several who already seemed to perceive some sort of claim on Hunter Flanagan's attention mistaken or not and he wanted to start thinking about that let himself move ahead and all of this would soon enough just seem like the silliest things as they always seemed to once you got far enough away from it all.

# 47

Did she wonder what he did after they parted the last time outside the Writing Center if he were perhaps more upset than he let on being. Did she even think about what she'd done or was it just another annoying item to take care of on a long list of stupidity. She didn't write. He wasn't really expecting her to. He looked at his cell phone. Of course she wouldn't call. But maybe she was having second thoughts. As he drove to the house he had second thoughts but a different sort. His had to do with how he handled himself during the confrontation. It was a surprise attack. He wasn't prepared. How long had she been planning her words couching her intentions to let him go. For how long had she known she wasn't interested. Maybe from the first conversation they had at that Writing Center party. Maybe even before that. Anyway there were things he felt and wanted her to know but the way she did what she did making it all her decision seemed to vitiate any argument he might have wanted to present. That wasn't fair. What if now he wanted to say So that's the game you play. You were fucking with me. It's simply not possible that I created all of this and you are not the least bit complicit. I'm sorry it just doesn't work that way. How about if I give you a list. I will cite examples from the text where you said things that somebody completely uninterested as you purport being would not have said done planned on doing. I have the emails. You want dates times subject headings. But of course the fact that she had done the pushing away and the fact that she got to say I think you've misunderstood made anything he had to say completely irrelevant and probably would seem like just vindictive lashing out dumpee vitriol but that wasn't fair. She did lead him on and he just pretended he was unfazed by what she said and by default the accompanying behavior and a month or two of mixed signals and felt like he should have gotten angry maybe even shouted or paced or at least walked away because what she did and not just the dumping part did hurt and did piss him off and maybe she was happy now and relieved and could think about things in Greek peacefully but he certainly wasn't happy.

Kate was surprised he called. She said something derisive but playfully about this being a first. He didn't know why he was calling. He sort of got excited in a perverse way when he thought about her that he wanted to get back in bed with her and make out some more. This didn't help to make him not think of Dewey as much as it just made it seem as though there were two Hunter Flanagans living in parallel planes. Most situations characters events in both Hunter planes were more or less identical but some things were so incongruous outré not easily explained or rationalized in the other plane that it made sense that there would have to be two. Here she was Kate so amused and fucking giddy that Hunter condescended to call her that she practically invited him over just to sleep. Though tempting he had no interest in sleeping all night in her bed or really anyone's besides his own. He didn't like seeing her so willing—he never had—but that was who she was. Maybe he needed to try to realize that and know that was simply the way some things were.

# 48

He thought about Colleen O'Rourke—the girl who went to B— and died before she could graduate the girl whose place Hunter was to take her role he wanted to assume—again for some reason. Maybe it was because he hadn't thought about her in quite some time. It had been more than a month ago that they found her body in the apartment more than a month since he found out that he wouldn't be attending B— in the fall. He'd fallen out of the habit of reading the daily news headlines. At first it was too painful now he just sort of ignored them didn't open them didn't delete them didn't move them unopened to the Hotmail folder he'd created to store them just in case he'd want to look later. He wished he hadn't subscribed to the daily headline service or the writing listserv. He supposed he could unsubscribe himself but he never felt like it. He always imagined at some point stopping using the fake Hotmail account losing interest in it and it would just continue to amass messages until exploding or until Hotmail would shut it off and then maybe the emails would just bounce back and forth against walls of nothing until he didn't know what.

What would she have been doing at this very moment he wondered had she lived. Maybe writing a paper anticipating her graduation. Why did Hunter Flanagan feel connected to the dead girl. He never knew her only really conceived of her for a short period of time when he was trying to figure out the answer to a question a quandary that perplexed him. He knew the answer now had spent time recovering from the shock and that was a shock not like when Dewey said she didn't want to have a relationship that was less of a shock obviously the investment not as significant as he thought it had been in B—. He wasn't prepared for that news but maybe having to deal with it think about it begin damage control begin to think realistically about other options maybe the experience of that prepared him for Dewey.

The day he found out about B— was the day after probably not even twenty-four hours after his conversation with Dewey in the Writing Center when they stood in front of the coffee table and talked. Hunter hungry for pizza but intrigued wanted to hear more what this girl had to say this girl who up to that point had barely even if ever looked at Hunter this girl whom now he had the full attention of somehow. She looked at him deeply nodded smiled held close her Styrofoam cup previously full of soda then empty. She held it close to her like a shield or maybe she held it close like a gift she thought about giving but hadn't yet decided what to do with. It was all he could do not to tell her then ask her out then of course how could he have known. Did instant attractions exist. He was not drunk but slightly smitten by a sip or two of alcohol an assistant director had smuggled in—a bottle of vodka—but he'd forgotten a mixer. Hunter watched Peanut give Dewey ten bucks and send her out in search of orange juice and he didn't think to ask to come with or just go along with her. She couldn't get any juice and came back with bottles of Sunny Delight instead but no one seemed to mind. At the time Hunter didn't like her. At that point—at that point before he liked her—she was just that girl Dewey though he didn't actually know her name at all that afternoon. It wasn't until he went home and looked up her picture on the Writing Center website that he knew she was called Dewey. He had always meant to ask someone before because he did wonder who she was. At the orientation in January he wondered who she was. He tried talking to her at one point several small group conversations unimportant chatter. Hunter tried saying something to Dewey but she literally didn't notice didn't hear him or maybe assumed he was talking to someone else. Maybe others were standing too close throwing off her sensory perception. He didn't know why he thought of that day or the day of the party. Perhaps in search of some kind of answers he was backtracking to try and decipher meanings understand better mistakes he could have avoided. What the fuck did come on too strong mean. All he did was send her a fucking couple of emails. He wasn't doing anything to her that was that out of the ordinary. He really wished he could ask when the last time she dated someone was anyway because if she considered this to be coming on too strong he could only imagine how passive the rest of the guys who had chased her had been. Maybe nobody had. She mentioned boyfriends. Did she even. Who knows. The only thing he remembered clearly was something she said that day when they had coffee.

She said I dated this guy for two weeks and he drank milk when he ate pizza. She found this abhorrent.

Did you break up with him because of that Hunter asked sort of playfully at the time caught up so profoundly in her and what she was saying it was hard to think.

Well that definitely had something to do with it she said.

Now of course in retrospect that looked like a warning sign seemed benign enough at the time whimsical adorable in a way charming but now foreshadowing of her certain and ineluctable turn for the destructive her tearing Hunter apart like a sheet of paper and balling him up before tossing him out the window. He should have paid closer attention maybe or maybe he couldn't have known for she was just evil and demented and bent on destruction and he perilous to escape.

# 49

There was a gigantic spider in his kitchen. This spider was spinning a tremendous invisible web and rode it up from half way between lamp and floor to the top of the lamp all the while appearing to be floating. This spider was maybe a black widow but he didn't spot any red. He felt like an idiot for having not finished at least a draft of a paper no more confident than when he printed out those jokes he produced blindly and turned in three years ago when he didn't do any reading and just wrote papers because he had to. Who the fuck was he kidding. He was no different. He enjoyed the reading but why was it so hard to organize some thoughts and write something. His fingers hurt. It was too hot in the room or everywhere. He felt lackluster. He wasn't well prepared. He didn't have enough material. He was tired and then of course his excuse followed: Maybe I'll just go to sleep and pick this all up in the morning. That was the usual game he played with himself. He was annoyed but it would have to do. It was what he'd done and what else could he do.

    He had a strange dream that night. Several in fact. First Dewey again. This time she was very mad angry at him. They were talking on the phone. He didn't seem to find that peculiar at the time. He had called her and was saying something. Her responses were perfunctory stolid.

    He asked her why she was acting that way. She responded basically saying nothing.

Do you not want me to call you he asked.

Do what you want to do she said.

The only reason I'm doing this is because you said we should still try to be friends he said but it didn't seem to matter. She acted like all of this was a burden an inconvenience and he felt that maybe in the dream his sense perceptions were heightened. Maybe this dream was trying to say that he wasn't capable of being duped again. Or maybe it said that Dewey actually was a bitch who had no interest in being friends. But then again did he really care that much about being friends with her. He had plenty of other people to talk to without the issue of rejection looming in the background. Besides they weren't really even friends to start with.

She did say the other day in the corridor I still want to get to know you but that was probably a lie. Earlier in the night he dreamt of Angela. She was older prettier. He hugged her a lot kissed her neck standing behind her but she pushed him away. Hunter wait she kept saying. She was in Chicago for some reason or maybe he was in New York because he didn't recognize the apartment. Then she left. She was beautiful though she looked very different from what he remembered. He kept touching her. She must have let him get away with it earlier in the dream or off-camera because why did he persist. They circled the apartment. They were walking. Angela kept saying Hunter in a warning sort of voice one you would use to reprimand a child. He wanted her though.

Why were these women plaguing his dreams. The Angela dream wasn't as unpleasant as the Dewey dream. Angela while rejecting him wasn't as hostile and abusive about it as Dewey was in real life. Years ago he would try to convince Angela to come to Chicago and see him. She was reluctant said he should come see her in New York. He did go to New York once after they met but they didn't meet. It was in 1994 a weekend with his father and he thought about calling her but didn't. It was during a lull in their relationship a point where they had fallen out of touch but maybe that's just how it was back then. They didn't always have email which allowed them daily interaction in a certain sense anyway. He didn't call her that weekend but told her about it later. She said You should have called me. She still lived in New Jersey then. They were both still in high school. He carried a manuscript with him on the plane and read parts of it then and in the loft in his uncle's building in the Village. His father wanted to read some of it find out what he was working on. Basically it was a book about Eileen. He flipped through the pages trying to find something that wasn't stupid something intelligent and sophisticated well-constructed. He finally picked out a chapter and removed it from its place in the pages gave it to his father at the end of the weekend. Hunter's father never at least as far as Hunter thought read it. Hunter later found the pages in a copy of *Chicago* magazine in a wicker basket they kept magazines in at the house. It embarrassed Hunter. Later he confiscated the pages took them back. His father never mentioned it again. Did he even remember Hunter giving the chapter to him. Years after his father would always say things like You never let me read anything you write you say you write but I never see any evidence of that.

# 50

Hunter didn't really feel like thinking about it but deemed it apropos to reflect for a moment anyway. This was the last week though he wasn't going to disappear from the campus for some time. He decided to stick around keep his jobs until he had to move away. This way he'd still be able to work on his novel use the lab printers. He probably would soon have something which resembled a draft the story of his young author in search of everything and nothing very much his own story.

 Suppose he wanted Dewey only for dramatic exploitation. Suppose he wasn't really in love with her. Suppose the pursuit had been enough for him—not just an outcome he simply had to tolerate but rather the thing he'd desired all along. Suppose he was only looking for dramatic distraction something to shift his focus from all these endings all these transitions to other things. Suppose he just wanted a buffer a diversion. If all or any of this were true which he supposed to some extent it was how did that bode on future events. As far as he was concerned he was not going to make any sudden moves. He was to remain at an appropriate distance from romance for the time being. He was seeing that screening of *Amelie* with Lila on Tuesday and that would probably follow a dinner of some sort. Would his newfound sense of equanimity make for a better time less nervous impulsivity less tacit demanding less as Dewey so eloquently deemed it coming on strong. He didn't feel like coming on to anything. He could no longer unequivocally ascertain how he considered Kate. In a moment of randomness that morning he called her and spent longer than he'd expected on the phone with her. He wasn't even really returning a call she'd initiated. What the fuck was he thinking. Things had definitely changed since last week when they made out in her bed. It was almost as though he'd started to become a bit attracted to her but maybe he was just getting used to her obviously basic willingness to let him make all the decisions choose what he wanted and how much when where and if even at all. Did she think this was the way to effect a real relationship. Could she have been that blind. Anyway it wasn't inconceivable that they could have a purely physical relationship. He wouldn't have sex with her if she were still a virgin but if by some strange and clearly out of character turn of events she weren't well then they could have exactly what he and Miriam had had before he grew to hate her and the conditions. But he still hadn't told Kate he was leaving and figured he'd have to sooner or later.

Hunter and Hilary had only been dating a few weeks when his father and stepmother began to plan for Thanksgiving a trip to spend the holiday with Hunter Flanagan's grandmother who was very old and very cross and living in a condo in a very tall building that overlooked the ocean with a live-in caretaker the estate paid eighty-five thousand a year to be his grandmother's only full-time companion. Hunter wanted to go swim in his grandmother's pool with Maya see his uncles fly in a plane. He thought the trip would be good for material a short story on tenuous family ties. The more precarious the connections the better the fiction he always said. So Linda ordered tickets on-line maybe in August and he really didn't think much about the trip after that. It wasn't as though he had much to plan. A day or two beforehand he'd begin assembling his belongings some clothes toothbrush facial products a hairbrush a notebook and begin packing them into a suitable duffel—no big deal—and decide on a Faulkner novel to carry with him. That would be the extent of it.

He began seeing Hilary in May so it had been three or four

months. He was happy with things more or less. He missed sex she wouldn't sleep with him and missed his friends he wasn't allowed to see them. He had barely spoken to Julianne at all by that point maybe only a couple of times and he hadn't even seen her in person since the summer. Hilary had already proclaimed Julianne anathema and Hunter maybe even believed in his new relationship's supremacy enough to believe this too or just went along with it anyway. He didn't complain hoped things would resolve themselves. Everything makes sense in so much time. He spoke about the trip with his parents when he'd have dinner with them but didn't tell Hilary about it. At first he avoided mentioning it because it seemed so far in the future. Who could think about Thanksgiving and November when people were still wearing shorts. He was still getting used to his new semester this new relationship why think about things so far away.

Then he started to think that he and Hilary would probably break up by November and that made him not want to tell her about the trip even more. First it saddened him but then it felt inevitable like it was just the sort of thing that usually happened so why bother planning their relationship so far in advance when his going away wouldn't be shared experience by November but his alone. He began to use Thanksgiving as this tangible boundary this point before which there was a relationship and after which there wouldn't be one. He didn't want to talk about Christmas or New Year's. Everything beyond November 26th was just quixotic foolishness. He didn't tell Hilary about any of this. What would be the point of that. This was just knowledge only for him knowledge that could help him make rational practical decisions about the relationship and his participation in it. He'd be pragmatic for once instead of always allowing romantic drunkenness to overtake him. But things moved contrary to this plan began to become more serious and then she began to ask him about his Thanksgiving plans.

Maybe a month or three weeks before the trip—it was the beginning of November and was cold enough for honesty—they were inside a Sportmart. He was testing out different varieties and calibrations of children's basketballs a gift for Maya he planned to give her for Christmas to go along with the inauguration of the new regulation garage hoop. He took free throws at a small enough net situated less than regulation distance from where he stood. He missed every one of them. A display of ineptitude and opprobrium a three-year-old would have no trouble spotting the irony in.

So I guess you'll come to my house for Thanksgiving she said.

He decided at that point to tell her. Well you know I'm going to Florida.

What.

Yeah I thought I told you.

No you never told me.

Oh that's strange. Are you sure.

No Hunter. You didn't tell me.

The ensuing fights. Hilary really was pissed off about this. It was the angriest he'd managed to make her. She actually broke up with him for a week over it which made sense. He wanted to move on but he began to think he'd miss her too much if things just ended this way that the trip wasn't worth it and that he wanted her back. Later when they got back together he resented her for making him abbreviate his trip and he wished they hadn't reconciled. He'd only spend roughly twenty-four hours away after adjusting his ticket so he could return to Chicago in enough time to attend one of Hilary's high school friends' sister's last-minute wedding—probably the real reason she had become so angry about his having not told her. If Hunter left she'd be dateless and they couldn't possibly allow that.

They spent another fourteen months together the fact of which he regretted later on even more because his calculations had been off. He got trapped after only a fleeting release and still could not no matter how hard he tried no matter the location no matter the calibration sink a free throw from any further than five feet from the basket. Maybe he was doomed.

# 51

Lila said between four and four fifteen. It was only five after four when Hunter walked outside. He had tutored twice. The first session only lasted about half an hour. The second was longer. He felt kind of ineffectual in both maybe a little more confident about the second one. The students didn't seem interested in what he had to say. The girl the first session a Chinese girl didn't speak much English. She just nodded a lot when Hunter made suggestions giggled or smiled. Her face was odd. Her lips turgid. Her features oblique lines obtuse angles. Anyway Hunter tried to usher her to some sort of conclusion before their time was up. Finished he looked outside Douglas Hall for Lila not missing the chance while there to remind himself of the now famous event: the conversation that took place in that very doorway. She wasn't there yet. He took the opportunity to go back into the building and into the bathroom looked at his face in the mirror. He had developed a giant blemish the day before. It was going away but he kept scratching and touching the scab. It wasn't pleasant. Fuck. Why today of all days he thought. All the Acutane for what. Why. It was irony. When they talked on the phone the week before when she invited him to the formal he joked about being in high school getting nervous before dates getting zits and now this. He didn't feel nervous exactly. He didn't expect much just wanted really to get it over with. Maybe he was a little tired. He stood outside and waited and he called Karen on his cell phone the girl in Film and Authorship. She had a question about the final paper. She'd left him several messages. He figured he'd better call back before meeting Lila as he probably wouldn't have much of a chance to do so during the date or after. The movie was at ten. That meant he wouldn't be finished until late. So he called her. She was home. She asked dumb questions. She rarely went to class and Hunter couldn't figure out why she thought he was so knowledgeable. He did go to class and probably sounded fairly intelligent familiar with the material which he was and maybe it made sense why she would think about him.

Several seconds into his conversation with Karen Lila showed up. It was about time. He waved and whispered Telemarketer which she actually appeared to believe even though he was talking about auteur theory and the studio system and post structuralism. She was wearing a red sweater and a thin brown jacket. Was that lipstick. Hunter was impressed. He didn't think he'd ever seen her in lipstick before. She looked pretty happy to see him. Maybe she thought this really was a date. Hunter was happy with that. He wanted to think it was a date too. It wasn't quite clear to him the context in which they proceeded. They were seeing a movie but was it as friends just like how she asked him to the formal.

He finally got Karen off the phone lied said he was entering a building and losing reception closed the phone. Lila thought that was funny.

What. You know sometimes when you go inside the phone doesn't work. Anyway sorry about that.

It's okay she said.

He threw an arm around her said Hi it's nice to see you.

It's nice to see you too she said. She reached around him briefly before retracting her hand. He pulled his off her too. They walked out through the building and across the street to Hunter's parking lot.

He unlocked her door first let her in closed the door and unlocked his own.

Excuse the way the car looks he said inside noticing a thick layer of dust on the outside glass.

It still smells new in here she said. She was clearly being polite. He began to drive out of the lot and into the street and to the expressway rather urgently.

He didn't want to miss the tickets. They were handing out free passes at five. He had to make it. She talked about her job while he tried to drive precipitously yet without slamming into anything.

So I tried to call this woman Lila was saying because she wants me to start on Tuesday but I have a final on Tuesday but I can like go in there on Tuesday just not at ten o'clock so I don't know what to do. She didn't return my call.

Maybe that's just because she was out sick Monday.

That's what her assistant said I called her too so I don't know if she's avoiding me or if I should call again or what. It would be really great to work there but I don't need the shit you know.

Yeah of course. Well it's funny Hunter said I have a friend who is a bartender in New York and she started this job at a bar called Mexican Radio. I made fun of her calling it Sweet Dreams Are Made of This and Burning Down the House.

Oh eighties songs I get it.

Yeah so anyway like on her first night there this manager accuses her of stealing money.

Wow that's extreme.

I know I couldn't believe it I kept thinking this has to be a bad sign.

Was it.

Yeah she got fired for something else and in a really shitty way like a different manager called her up and said Uh I'm sorry you're not on the schedule.

That is really tacky she said. I can't honestly believe how tacky some people can be.

Well it's shitty management skills is what it is.

Wow. I guess so.

They picked up the vouchers. Two minutes before five. Now what were they going to do.

This is the Lab School. I went there Hunter said pointing across the street. They were in Hyde Park now. He'd been in such a hurry thinking so obstinately about his driving the time the sounds the car was making—he told Lila his plans to fix the fucking muffler once and for all—he had failed to point out significant landmarks. So he began doing so then. They had time now. There hadn't been many people in line and they barely had to wait maybe only a minute for the vouchers. The girl handing them out had a thick stack maybe five hundred of the things. It seemed ridiculous that Hunter had agonized over the time rearranging tutoring sessions and everything. Oh well. That was in the past.

They walked back to his car. Are you hungry he asked.

Not really she said. I had a granola bar before I went to the gym but if you want to go sit in a restaurant that's fine.

Well we could take a walk.

Yeah that would be good.

They got back into his car. He drove to his house and parked in his spot. He pointed out his neighbor's pop up camper secured in place with small cords of wood.

Isn't that tacky he said. My neighbors are very tacky.

Do they have a boat she asked.

No it's a camper that pops up he said.

Oh and they just leave it back here.

Yeah he said I don't know why my mother puts up with it. I think it's ridiculous. It was supposed to be two spaces for each house and that was the turn around or for a guest and now it's a trailer park back here.

Well it's not that bad. She wasn't getting his point.

They're just very well I don't know how to say this. She looked at him attentively. It's just that they're well I don't want to sound like an elitist for saying this but they have no art. Their walls are covered with pictures.

What like movie posters.

No not posters although that would be a little better. No they have all these family pictures. Hunter stopped for a moment while still talking realized maybe her parents had photos on the walls. He tried to couch this already unloaded statement a bit more diplomatically. I mean they have them all stuck together like no space just picture on top of picture. That's what's tacky. It's like they can't get enough of themselves.

Well I can understand wanting to have pictures up. I like photography. I'm taking this art class right now and we did caricatures. I'm waiting to see if I got an A on my portfolio or not. I hope I did.

Hunter pointed out bookstores Thai restaurants the Medici Rockefeller Chapel churches the Robie House. Lila said when they passed it That looks like a Frank Lloyd Wright.

Well Hunter said it's the Robie House.

Oh she said intrigued.

They passed students and ads for round tables written in chalk on the pavement in the quad. They looked at Botany Pond and Harper Library and buildings walked up and down stairs down University and Fifty-sixth and some of Fifty-fifth and Everett and Lake Park down a narrow stretch of sidewalk closed for Metra construction. They had to walk single file there. Hunter mentioned things here and there. They talked about her sorority sisters and how she didn't like many of them.

He said This is the building I used to live in.

By yourself or with your family she asked.

With my family when I was younger before we moved to the house before my parents got divorced.

I got the directions to the European Chalet.

Good. Hey let me ask you something. I keep forgetting to.

What.

Do you want me to wear a tux because I don't have a problem with it if you do. In fact I own one.

She smiled. No you don't need to. You'd be overdressed if

you wore a tux.

Okay because I just wanted to ask.

That's nice of you but I don't think it will be necessary.

He liked walking with Lila. They moved quickly. It didn't even feel like they were walking.

Hunter said when they were on Dorchester and Fifty-sixth I'm trying to think of—

She interrupted Things to talk about.

No he said quickly. Important landmarks to point out.

Why would she ask that. Did it seem like they didn't have anything to talk about. Hunter felt like that initially but not continually. It came in waves. He had a lot to say though hoped he didn't seem that way. People who always had an endless repository of things to say were those the people who had no or significantly reduced amounts of human contact. Did they save all sorts of pithy conversation quips for the few opportunities they had for interacting with others. But silences frightened him. He didn't want to walk he didn't want to move he didn't want to sit for a second without having conversation either speaking or listening even though sometimes that was hard and he appreciated those moments in which they could have silence without it reflecting negatively on him. It made sense that say if they were exploring a menu that that would be a time where they didn't have to talk but there was the rest of the time the time surrounding those events that didn't require talking. Why was it such a big deal. Probably because he didn't know her well but more than that probably because he didn't quite know what their being together right now meant. This moment they were yoked but what was the reason for it. He didn't know how to answer that because the truth was not only had he not been able to pick up any hints from Lila who was ambiguous as ever that afternoon but also because he didn't even feel like he had a fixed purpose a solidified reason of his own like before when it was I want to fuck you or kiss you. Now he didn't have that. So maybe he had to figure out what he wanted before he could start to pick up indications as to what someone else's proclivities were.

They decided on the Cafe Florian. He'd imagined them eating at the Medici but they were rounding the corner back onto Fifty-seventh from Lake Park so they were on the east end of the block and the Florian was there and Lila said I think I'm starting to get hungry now and so they went inside took a booth toward the front.

Smoking or non smoking the busboy who seated them said. Lila looked at Hunter.

Non smoking Hunter said of course. He looked at her strangely.

Well I didn't know.

You thought I smoked Hunter teased. She elbowed him and slid in. They looked at menus.

She said Have you had the soup here.

No but it looks good.

What about any of the appetizers.

Not really. It looks like they've changed the menu.

I think I'll have the nachos and a salad or maybe just a salad or should I get the soup.

So what do you think of this newspaper. A copy of the *Maroon* lay on the table.

She picked it up. It's okay.

Just okay. Look at how much better it is than the *Flame*.

Well they have more articles but that doesn't mean it's necessarily better.

He decided not to press it even though he wanted to ask how many articles from the AP do you see in this paper and just let it go. She seemed sensitive. She was into journalism wrote for the *UIC Daily* a paper even more desperate than the *Flame* if that were imaginable. Basically the UIC papers didn't compare to these. Nothing there compared to here. Lila was a little more reluctant Hunter supposed in seeing that truth but Hunter had had a bit of a head start. He'd lived in Hyde Park his entire life and had five years at UIC to observe the differences.

She said things like I could never go to a school like this. All these intellectuals they probably have no fun just spend day and night theorizing and doing long sets of calculus.

That didn't sound completely unappealing to Hunter. But it is a prettier campus he said. You have to admit that.

Well I am a bit taken by all the ivy and that all the buildings aren't parking lots or look like them.

She sounded like Hilary in her urban public school fascism. Hunter found it a bit attractive. It was kind of cute how she tried to be proud of UIC in the face of all this richness all this academic culture all the buildings that meant something the feeling of ideas and meaning abounding. How could she not see all of that. Hunter had been trying to learn to accept all of this as a resident outsider for five years. For five years or for at least two of them anyway he'd been wishing for more and maybe Lila was too young or just didn't know yet what it meant what it felt like to want things and see things know that they aren't yours and to try to figure out how to deal with that.

Could he be happy with Lila. She seemed pleasant enough attractive even. He went back and forth between being excited to go with her to the formal—some stupid end of the year thing for her sorority—and dreading it. He wanted to put on a suit—that would be nice—and it was only one night so if their being together was completely inconsequential then fine whatever forget about it after that night.

They were walking down Fifty-seventh Street past the Medici again past Edwardo's and University Market peering into windows. She said she thought the Fifty-seventh Street Bookstore looked romantic. They walked down Kimbark again and then up Fifty-eighth to Woodlawn.

Lila asked him if he'd heard from any graduate schools.

Yes in fact Hunter said—okay here it goes—I got into C—.

Wow she said. Where exactly—

Boulder.

Yeah wow that's so... Are you—

Yeah I think I will go. They want me to teach and they're basically letting me go for free so I think that will be fun.

That's so far away she said.

I know he said but that's one of the things I'm glad about.

When do you leave.

At the end of the summer.

I'd been thinking about going away too. There was this study abroad thing I was looking into she said to London and—

London. That would be great.

Yeah I know she said but I started thinking and I thought everything I want is here my family my friends my roommate and the apartment you know so I was just like I don't really want to leave all this behind.

Yeah I guess I know what you mean but here's what I've been thinking: I've been thinking I really need to challenge myself to do this Hunter said. All my life it's been basically a lot of the same stuff and Chicago and I'm too used to all of this. I want to—you know I think that part of the brain or wherever is a muscle and you have to condition it. My parents are both from the east and they picked up and moved here and I want to know what that's like too. I want to have to learn my way around a new city. I feel like I'm complacent and that that's affecting other things. I want—

He didn't say it but what he was thinking about was writing and then though not as much about relationships. He thought maybe if I knew more about life I would know what we were doing here or have the balls to make a move or not make a move but more importantly to want something one way or the other which at this point I really can't say that I do or don't.

Maybe Lila wasn't someone who challenged herself. She seemed so intimidated and hostile toward the University of Chicago campus. Was she jealous of it. Hilary sort of reacted in a similar way this embracing of the low brow the championing of the democratic ideology. Hunter was all for it in theory but he did find beauty in the campus in Hyde Park that he didn't see in the West Loop the academic culture and the students thinking reading important texts active desiring of knowledge wanting more just like Hunter. That excited him. He wasn't jealous. Well he was of course but not in a hostile way more of an envy that just provoked him to want more. Maybe he and Lila wouldn't work out for this reason that she couldn't see beyond her circumstances and that maybe she didn't want more out of her life than just what was laid out simply before her.

They went to the Reynolds Club. Lila looked around admiringly.

Hunter said That's where I sit and read Saussure a thumb toward the Reading Room. She nodded. They walked into the C-Shop.

This is where I read and get coffee. Did you want something to drink.

No that's okay. They picked a table beneath a light. There was supposed to be an open mic tonight. Hunter didn't plan on participating. He didn't have any material and besides maybe he wasn't ready to share that sort of an experience with Lila. It was a good way for her to get to know him if he wanted that to happen certainly but he didn't know. It was supposed to start at eight thirty but didn't get going until almost nine. In the meantime they talked about dumb things the computer labs printer quotas classes she was planning on taking or had taken. She was pretty enough. She yawned a couple of times which depressed him. She must be having a totally boring fucking time he thought and wished they could get to the movie and get this all over with.

I'm kind of tired she said. You look tired too.

I'm not he said. Must be the contacts.

Hunter grew very thirsty while she talked. A couple walked toward a table passing theirs both with tall mocha frozen drinks topped with a ridiculous amount of whipped cream. I don't know how no matter how good one of those could possibly be no matter how much I liked it I don't know how I could order one of those in public he said.

She laughed. A bit extreme.

Definitely. Hey do you want a latte or something.

Well she said as though really thinking. I actually would like some tea.

That's a good idea. Let's go get some.

Is it okay if we leave our stuff here.

Yeah of course.

They walked to the counter and examined the rack of tea packets. They had Tazo tea. The same stuff they served at Starbucks.

They sell this tea at the café in Borders she said.

Yeah what's your favorite one.

The Awake I think.

There were two packets left.

Mine too. It's really good.

But I don't know if I want one now. Maybe something without caffeine.

What was she trying to do. Make herself even more tired. She picked out a packet of Wild Sweet Orange. Hunter took from one called Spice. They took their teas back to the table.

I think you know someone in my sorority she said.

Oh yeah he asked.

Yeah. Do you know Molly. She's a computer consultant.

Yes I do.

He did know Molly. He knew Molly and Lila were in the sorority together this entire time but hadn't said anything about it. He learned that on the Internet but he never mentioned it didn't want to give away the fact he'd been looking for facts about her and uncovered that. He liked Molly. She was Iranian and desperately beautiful. She had the most difficult eyes the kind that could destroy your soul inside this wet clay body and he never could look at her head on for extended periods of time without turning into chewed up gum. Hunter had flirted with her at the beginning of the semester. She had been on leave during the fall but she clearly wasn't interested so whatever. That would be sort of weird being around her in a casual setting. Now they just said hi to each other at work he and Molly. He didn't try to flirt. Maybe she would want to dance with him. Would Lila allow that. Actually Molly would probably ignore him and he'd spend most of the evening trying to avert his eyes from her ass or chest and coax them back to his own date's ass and chest. Why was Hunter so obsessed with physical attraction. He became totally engulfed when it came to those arbitrary and superficial characteristics. He couldn't help himself. Just because he had ideas principles didn't mean he wasn't weak as far as sexual stimuli were concerned. Anyway that Molly-Hunter-Lila dynamic should prove interesting. He saw Molly the other day talked to her for a millisecond or two wondered if she knew whom Lila intended on bringing as her date. Date. He wanted to understand what he and Lila were doing together. Did she like him. He had his hands out on the table. She kept hers close to her cup. He picked up her bent swizzle stick started to poke at her cup and then at her fingers with it. She touched it back at points. He liked that. It was like they were connecting albeit through a thin bent up piece of red plastic but it was something. Maybe that meant she did like him. He seemed to be picking up more like signals than dislike ones but his sensors were in the shop for repairs so it was all just random now shooting in the dark grasping at straws no pun intended. He wanted to reach for her hand but didn't have the courage was afraid she'd not want it or he'd start sweating or something. He used to reach for girls' hands without trepidation. Flirting temerity where had that gone. Oh right he forgot that was part of the Coming On Too Strong routine which he was supposed to consider retiring. Fuck Dewey. He practically begged her to go out with him which she snubbed and here he asked Lila who was probably prettier to one thing and she said yes without even the slightest suggestion of indecision. Where was the logic in that.

The open mic finally began to happen. Some guys rolled in equipment big speakers a mixing board three microphones. Was

all that really necessary. Lila watched them set up at the table.
   Though she sat facing Hunter with her back to the stage she kept turning around and said I feel like they're doing something even when it was just the wind or a C-Shop employee moving from the storeroom through the tables to the front. She kept turning around to see what was happening as though involuntarily. Hunter was glad when the MC—a lanky undergraduate with glasses and bad skin and a worse personality—said I have Tourettes. Just kidding and spoke in a strange fake accent at first before switching to a normal voice to introduce the first act a woman who sang in a thick and not entirely terrible voice a gospel infused heady version of When You Were Mine a capella which gave Hunter the chills and then a song from *Anything Goes* Ain't She Sweet.
   It was nice not to have to talk. Hunter kept looking at the clock didn't know how many people would crowd into Max Palevsky. Maybe more people came for vouchers after he and Lila had left. He figured ten minutes at least. It was nine thirty and then nine forty and the gospel woman changed places with a tall wiry boy in a white t-shirt with a guitar who began a very long and silly song which had about twenty verses which he called a song about traveling and then later admitted was a Weird Al song. Hunter didn't like it but appreciated someone writing a song before he found out that the material was appropriated. From that point his admiration fell away.
   He whispered to Lila Do you think we should go.
   She said I don't know. How long will it take to get there.
   Probably two minutes.
   She hesitated looked at her watch and then at the stage. We could stay for one more song.
   Hunter couldn't tell if she was enjoying the performance or hating it. She looked at him several times during applause. He smiled and clapped. The boy played another Weird Al song a shorter one thankfully and then stepped down and Hunter thought that a good opportunity and he began to stand up and

Lila did too. He reached for her empty cup.

She said Thanks.

His still remained. He was trying to pull on his jacket with one hand. She took his cup before he could get to it. I'll throw out yours you throw out mine she said and laughed. They tossed out their garbage left through the side door walked through the courtyard. It was dark.

Hunter couldn't quite orient himself started leading her in one direction but wasn't sure if he were going the right way didn't want to turn around said I think we can get out this way.

She said You're leading the way. It worked. They were back on Woodlawn. They walked together to Ida Noyes laughed about the acts.

I thought there would be more spoken word Hunter said. Poetry or something. That's popular these days.

Those people were very weird she said. I didn't know what to think of that first girl.

Yeah well I liked the Prince but the other thing was well I don't know. I didn't like how she had the words in her hands. Don't singers usually memorize songs. That other guy didn't seem to have trouble remembering any of his fifty verses.

No he didn't. That was a Prince song. Which one.

When You Were Mine.

Oh. I didn't know that.

Cyndi Lauper covered it.

Oh really. No I don't think I've heard it before. But could you believe that guy covering Weird Al songs.

That is kind of weird. That's like saying Hi I'm a singer and my influences are Celine Dion and Colin Quinn or something.

She laughed some more. You should have read something.

Hunter smiled. Yeah you're probably right he said in a big voice. But it's funny every time I go to one of these it's never quite how I imagine it will be. Like tonight I thought people would have poems and well...

She said I've never even been to one.

Really.
Yeah I saw that one in *So I Married An Axe Murderer* though.
That's funny.
With the finger snapping.
What's the deal with that. That's very peculiar.
More civilized than clapping.
That must be it.

# 52

Well whatever he thought he was going to accomplish with Kate he didn't. That was fairly obvious because they'd left things with he'd call her later though she hadn't called him yet so maybe something did in fact get through. Now it was getting depressing. He wasn't getting attached but he'd started to feel somewhat responsible. She'd shown him an album of her college photos her in various states of pudginess. That was mean. It wasn't like she was fat now but she definitely looked heavier in those pictures. Roommates boys dates for dances sorority functions pictures with captions and dates embossed Screw Your Roommate February 1997. He hadn't been to any dances in college. Somehow he'd avoided going with other friends to their college dances and there hadn't been any of his own. Her life depressed him in its simplicity in its predictability. He didn't want to become too involved know who too many people were what they looked like. As it was he'd seen her parents brother various family trips Old World Pennsylvania in the peasant cutouts their house in Cincinnati and he hadn't even given her his home phone number. And she seemed content satisfied with his already minimal effort. And only the second he hoped but no evidence to suggest last date he spent most of the night thinking about Dewey wished he'd been sitting across from her instead. Was it that Kate presented no challenge. Not a good challenge anyway.

The challenge she presented now manifested as how do I get her out of my life without hurting her. The more he knew her the more he saw her saw her small collection of books some Tolstoy *A Farewell To Arms* the more he found out she liked making amaretto sours and had a bottle of Sambuca in her cabinet the more it depressed him but it wouldn't be fair to him to just go along with it. He liked someone else and this was just an obstacle. As inconsiderate as that sounded it was true.

When he was young in high school Hunter Flanagan read *The Rules of Attraction* and liked it quite a bit. It made him feel like he knew what college would be like. He first bought a copy in paperback. Then started to see hard cover first editions in used bookstores and began to purchase those. He ended up with five or six copies of this book. He gave a copy to Eileen for her birthday the year they exchanged presents. Since then he'd taken some of the copies off his shelves to make room for newer more significant texts he'd been reading. He hadn't read *The Rules of Attraction* in a few years. It sort of embarrassed him now that he'd experienced more consequential literature *Moby Dick The Blithedale Romance Light in August* but he always remembered this one line *Nobody ever likes the right person*. It still resonated especially now. How true it was. His current situation was so depressing. He could have predicted something like this happening. Here he was trapped nonplussed.

# 53

He could barely keep track of whom he'd told and whom he'd yet to tell. Among the people he'd only emailed there was Ms. Symkowicz his ninth and tenth grade English teacher. They'd exchanged a few emails this year. He found her address on Google. She taught in the suburbs now. She was the one who introduced Hunter to Joyce Carol Oates and Alice Walker to Salinger to *Julius Caesar* probably started it all for him. Of course they hadn't left on the greatest of terms. His last year at Lab she railed him for fucking up bemused by his actions didn't understand why he wasn't reading anything why he didn't turn in anything. Looking back his behavior couldn't have been any more obvious. He wanted attention needed some kind of support focus discipline he wasn't getting but nobody seemed to really respond to act. Succor came too late to make a difference but could he really have imagined his life without that momentary derailment. He was bored with life at Lab was tired of the same people year after year after year. He might have gone to Bennington or at least away from home had he stayed there graduated who knows might have had a master's degree by now or maybe not maybe a book published but what difference did it make. This was his life. He had a chance to reclaim some of—what—the life that might have been his now. He could go. Wait. He was going. He could not conceive of backing out of not going through with it especially since it was the only offer. He wanted to go and love it and imagine what it would be to alight upon a campus as though it were six years ago and he eighteen and full of thoughts and grunge and hubris and darkness and cigarettes the fall of 1995 and Vermont and not having met Simona or Hilary or any of the rest of them but maybe probably there would have been plenty of girls at Bennington or wherever with names that ended in A or Y and it wasn't as though he couldn't have found a college to go to away from Chicago after Roycemore it was just that he was in such a haze it just never really seemed worth considering.

## 54

Nicole had good things to say. Hunter so enjoyed their Wednesday talks. He felt when they spoke attracted to her but in a distant way. He didn't think about her that way really anymore hadn't since last summer when they met in computer consultant orientation but he still liked her as a friend a friend he appreciated. He valued her cared about her words. She made him smile. He liked looking at her. She interested him because he knew he couldn't have any of her. She had her own world that rarely if ever intersected his. This consulting the only thing they really had in common at least the most she was willing to let them have in common. He had more than once and more than indirectly suggested they go have a drink together this after he no longer was actively interested and she always said no or didn't say no just changed the subject avoided responding definitively. Hunter didn't really fault her for that—whatever—but now he just appreciated their weekly discussions about his dating life.

So how are things going with the stalker she asked.

Hunter feigned embarrassment covered his face before sighing and responded She's still calling me all the time.

She thinks she has a boyfriend Nicole said in singsong.

She does not Hunter insisted. She couldn't think that anyway. So let me tell you what happened with Dewey.

He recounted the events the course evaluations the talk in the entranceway the I don't want to lead you on but Hunter emphasized that he had recovered since then. You know I feel like I invented most of it. I can't understand what I was even thinking.

It's always like that when you want someone to like you or you want to like someone. You totally see things that aren't there she said. I've done that.

It's like I invented her Hunter said. I think I wanted to like her and so I felt more attracted but I really didn't feel that much I don't think.

You know Nicole said a bit reluctantly I had the feeling she wasn't interested.

Why didn't you say anything.

I didn't want to hurt your feelings.

You wouldn't have. *I* didn't feel she really liked me.

It's like what do you say to people. They don't want to hear it they want to see things in this way.

It's so crazy it's like being drunk continuously for a month or whatever.

Well at least you still have the stalker.

That's not funny.

It's sort of the same thing. You know she probably thinks you're giving her mixed signals.

I don't mean to.

You seriously need to just sit down and tell her.

Yeah I was thinking I'd say I'm leaving at the end of the summer so I don't think it would be a good idea to start anything now.

You're leaving. Where are you going.

Oh I got into C—. I'm moving to Boulder.

Oh wow that's great. When.

The end of the summer. August.

That's really terrific. Yeah that would definitely work.

You should move out there.

Yeah right. She laughed.

No seriously or come visit. You like skiing don't you. He wasn't being serious. He was just saying it.

She said in a smaller aside voice Yeah probably not.

Hearing that sort of made him think reminded him of how little they knew each other how they would probably never speak to each other again after they left this campus. He only thought about it consciously for a moment but it seemed to keep resonating after that.

# 55

It was weird. Now when he thought about the stalker he got hard. There was something unmistakably erotic about the last time they were together. Maybe he was attracted to her after all. He spoke to her two nights ago was still pretending to be busy with the end of the semester when in fact he was essentially done.

Last night he rented *Manhattan* after working out made it through only nineteen minutes on the treadmill walked for the last minute sweated a lot felt good afterward. Kate called while the video was on. He ignored the call didn't check the voice mail didn't have any plans for Friday night yet. Did he really want to see her twice in a row. They were doing that typesetting exhibit Saturday. He couldn't talk to her without imagining her in her underwear recreating the scene from the last time they were together. Aside from the cat he really liked her apartment. Her bed was large enough didn't squeak a step up from the twin beds he screwed around with Hilary on at her parents' or in her dorm room in Evanston. They didn't see each other much at the latter. Her psycho roommate—what was her name Eleanor Bethy— Hunter couldn't remember—it felt so long ago—began to complain about his visits even though they had separate bedrooms. They only were there when the roommate was out. The room he began to intenscly dislike though he always tried to imagine what his own living situation would be like in grad school being as far away from Hilary as possible one of the primary criteria at the time. He almost wanted to tell her where he was going not just to brag but to let her know just how different they really were from each other. He wasn't afraid to go to cut the strings to assert himself in another time zone. Well even though he was scared there was a difference between being scared and being intimidated.

Sometimes he couldn't wait to go and started telling people with less reservation started to not feel like it was something to be ashamed of. Christ it was a big fucking deal. What he'd wanted wasn't it. Well it was going to be. He'd gone too far to turn away.

But what to say to Kate. How to tell her. Did he say go to her apartment tonight maybe have a few drinks with her and say it see if she wouldn't want to make out afterward or whether she'd be okay with it and suck his face. Peanut said—well regarding Dewey but what really was the difference—that something like that—the imminent departure—could be good for a woman would let her act more freely knowing subconsciously that there wouldn't be any repercussions because of the fact that no matter how good or bad or erotic things could only last for a very specific amount of time and who could really say what would happen after that. It didn't seem to help matters to tell Dewey. In fact maybe it made things perhaps more difficult. Perhaps that was what she meant when she delivered the now ubiquitously resonating proclamation You come on a little strong. Maybe that was a rebuke for being honest. Maybe with that aphorism Dewey didn't say You seemed so intent on telling me you were going away like I was your fucking girlfriend or something but you really didn't need to do that because I don't or didn't really care that much about you presently or potentially so just keep it to yourself but that couldn't completely apply to the stalker who was after all not equivocating her intentions or feelings and plus he wasn't avoiding saying he was leaving to protect himself to avoid losing her because aside from the new twinges of semi attraction—maybe it could have been any body not specifically hers but any to have fomented his libidinous mechanism—he didn't feel or want to feel any responsibility for feelings. It wouldn't have been fair to either of them. So he might as well see her and get it over with and just deal with the fact that he hadn't when he should have and that he probably had been more or less deceiving her or at least not being entirely candid for what basically a month now and that was just how the events revealed themselves and besides he could always just pretend that he only found out this week.

    But who said Hunter had to be fair. Who had exercised consideration rectitude as far as he was concerned. Who based her actions on how they might impact Hunter's life and feelings. Really probably none of them so why was he so concerned with everyone else's happinesses security well-being. Why was he responsible for everything. Who gave him this sense of rectitude. Anyway couldn't he just protect his own interests expedients and say Fuck it it's her fault for caring her fault for getting involved. Couldn't he just be like that be one of those people just once.

# 56

He drove on the expressway by mistake. He planned on taking Lake Shore Drive to Evanston but was still bleary. It was eight thirty in the morning. He felt already exhausted driving back. The drive to Evanston he was no longer used to and as a result it felt like hours instead of forty minutes. He didn't drive for long periods of time anymore. House to UIC back again house or UIC to father's. That was usually the extent of it. Now with Kate in his life he was driving more to Evanston. He had thought about taking the train parking in his lot at UIC taking the blue line downtown meeting her at the exhibit but she said Why don't you just come here first and he wasn't really sure why that made him feel thwarted but he acquiesced.

This morning he didn't even feel like seeing her. Last night seemed to have cleared up any misconceptions he had had about how he felt any ambiguity over whether or not he liked her. He basically knew he didn't. Last night he took her on in a wave driving slowly through thick gridlock Friday night on the expressway god how painful his car still shaking reverberating sound from the lame muffler good songs on the radio I Won't Back Down and Because the Night and Glory Days all seemed to follow one after another. He thought then he should tell her about grad school. He should do it tonight. No more of this evading.

He imagined the conversation.

He would say I have to tell you something.

She'd say What is it.

I'm pregnant.

Very Funny.

I'm leaving at the end of the summer. I got into C—.

Oh when did you find out.

Just the other day. Then it would be out there and over with.

He lost courage at her apartment. Once there he became concerned with another issue. He examined her. She looked okay her body essentially as he remembered it. Her face he always regarded as though he were seeing for the first time. It had now been officially a little longer than a month that they had known each other and yet he still barely could visualize her when away from her. That and he still didn't know her phone number. He didn't want to remember it liked the fact that he didn't but it couldn't last long. It was an easy number but he always consulted a little scrap of paper the one he first wrote it down on from his night table when and if he ever called her maybe if for no other reason than to remind him of a time when he didn't know it.

Last night they were standing in her kitchen. Hunter pressed into her pressed her against the edge of the sink. He kissed her. He immediately knew that he had just been delusional. Her kiss was as it had always been harsh rough obnoxious. He was beginning to not be so much turned off by it as angered. Why couldn't she kiss better. What the fuck. He circled her waist. Her body felt good next to his. He didn't understand her face when he opened his eyes. It looked so strange up close. Her skin had lines in it looked sort of dry but sort of oily her pores maybe a little enlarged kind of blotchy. She didn't wear much makeup. He reached under her shirt and traced her bra strap. Her back felt a little moist. It was warm outside but not that hot in the apartment. Was she sweating because of him.

You're frisky she said when he pulled away. What the hell did that mean.

I think you're the frisky one he said.

This is sort of a weird place we're standing.

Yeah reminds me of *Fatal Attraction*.

I never saw it.

Oh. There's a scene when they do it in a sink.

Do you want to go into my room.

Hunter thought maybe things would be like he remembered them when it became hot a week or two ago if they were in her bed but sadly this was not the case. Things were strange the choreography odd. He rolled on top of her and then pushed himself off. She moved onto him. This wasn't working. He was completely turned off by the kissing though remained hard. He sort of enjoyed her body but not as much as he thought he had the time before now. He thought god I have to see her tomorrow too. How am I going to get out of this.

He felt his face itch a little and scratched it didn't give a shit about red marks.

Are you okay she asked. You're not getting allergic are you.

No he said. Maybe just a little from out there but it seems fine in here.

Good because Grover has not been in here.

Good.

They kissed more. Hunter pulled away every time she sucked his lip. Sometimes she directed a kiss at what he thought would be his general mouth area but for some reason missed—what the fuck was that—ending up with her lips on his nose or his chin. That was just fucking disgusting. That merited pulling off and beginning a conversation. He didn't want to hurt her feelings but really wanted to ask What the fuck are you doing. That is just wrong but instead said things like I'm really hungry. Do you want to go eat which was true anyway. He'd only had a sandwich at lunch and now it was close to eight.

Where do you want to go she asked. She wasn't wearing her glasses. He noticed this thought it made her look a bit better not to have them.

I don't know. How about the Lucky Platter.

They always ate there. Earlier she suggested they go to the

Little Mexican Café but that was on Sherman and far and probably required a drive.

That wasn't a problem exactly but he said As long as I don't have to sit by the window. I don't want to stare at Market Facts all night. It was across the street.

She said Well we don't have to go if you don't want to. Whatever it was just a joke but at this point the Lucky Platter was closer and that was where they ended up going.

They both ordered cheeseburgers. She had the sweet potato fries. Hunter noticed she put the ketchup on the side this time. That was nice he thought. He had glazed carrots for his side. He ordered the burger medium rare.

Closer to rare he told the waiter who proved to be completely inept. The burger was medium at best. Kate's looked a bit more rare. That idiot probably switched them. He complained to her mildly about it. He didn't really care actually thought it ironic.

I bet he said seventy-five percent of the people who order burgers order them medium or medium well or something stupid like that but get them exactly how they want them.

She said I think it might be illegal to serve a burger rare in Evanston.

You might be right. I think I heard something about that.

They ate. He told dumb jokes said Look it's Frank Sinatra in the next booth. She started to turn her head to look but then stopped.

Hunter you know I don't like to look at other people.

Well it's him I swear.

He poured water in his margarita because it was too sweet ate cornbread ravenously used honey on it kept trying to check out a waitress who seemed not to be wearing underwear beneath a thin cotton dress subtly when Kate busied herself long enough cutting her burger into two parts for Hunter to scrutinize the waitress properly. She looked a little old. Oh well. He was acting like an ass. First thought it was due to being overly hungry but he still kept on even after they'd been eating for a while. Kate laughed when he dipped a piece of cornbread in the carrot glaze. He wasn't trying to be funny when he did that. It was actually good. He told her to try it. She did.

He took fries in his mouth and let one dangle in front of his lower lip and said What. Is there something on my face. She laughed and laughed though was probably embarrassed. He was embarrassing himself. He didn't understand what he was doing. He said incendiary things talked about drinking bottles of Robitussin in high school to get high. Why would he tell her that. He wanted her to stop liking him. It never seemed to work though so it was a waste of time to try. He should have told her about Boulder but didn't couldn't.

It was hard to extract himself when he wanted to go home. More haphazard ill-conceived kissing on her bed followed dinner. She was on top of him but always at an angle. That was weird. He tried to reposition her more directly above him but it didn't work something was in the way poking him. She had her knee bent pressing against his leg like she was trying to block him or something. He tried to push it down but it came right back up.

Why are you doing that he asked.

I don't know that's just how I sleep I guess.

Well we're not sleeping he thought. For some reason this new leg bending sticking him in the side with her knee thing was just too irritating to bear. He hated her idiosyncrasies. He didn't feel like he should have to put up with them. They weren't even going out technically were they. He had to begin to broach the subject of his leaving early since with her it took several dozen attempts before he would actually be released. He didn't understand why she was giving him shit about it mock-struggling sighing looking sad because he was seeing her in the morning. She said he could sleep over.

He said No I can't. I don't have any of my things. I don't have my dental floss.

I have floss.

That's not the point.

She finally let him loose. Fine you can go she said as though disappointed. I'm coming back in a few hours he said and climbed into the elevator. He was glad to go. He didn't want to be tired in the morning but knew he was going to be.

He stopped at the Starbucks when he got to Evanston. He was still early. It was only nine. They agreed to meet at nine thirty. Maybe he could get some coffee and write before seeing her. That would be good. The line inside was long women children men in lycra reading the *New York Times*. A mother and daughter bickered. The daughter wanted a travel tumbler.

It's ten dollars the mother said as though that would clear up the child's confusion and abate her desire.

Hunter bought a tall instead of a grande. The cup was so small but probably just enough. He wondered if he should get her a coffee too but then reasoned it would probably be cold by nine thirty and he really didn't want to appear any earlier though at this point it was nine-fifteen. Anyway he didn't even know for certain if she drank coffee. That was the most cogent argument. Anyway she was unlikely to give a shit whether he brought her coffee or not.

She said her buzzer wasn't working so after he called up she came down to meet him in the lobby. It only took thirty seconds. She was only one floor up. They took the elevator and she looked cloyingly pleased with Hunter's presence. He realized they hadn't seen each other in the morning before now. Well this is how Hunter Flanagan looks in the morning.

He showed her his coffee which was still fairly warm. I gave birth. Isn't this the cutest thing you've ever seen. It's a baby Starbucks.

She received this with a dim smile. I don't think I'm awake yet she said inside the apartment. Do you want some banana bread.

Sure he said and folded his sunglasses.

They took the purple line to Howard and switched there to the red line. The car was sparsely populated. Two girls sat in the seats behind Hunter and Kate. One was very cute. Hunter wished he had better glancing access but sadly did not could only attempt to listen to her over his conversation with Kate. They discussed favorite years. This prompted by certain things Hunter would see from the train's windows parts of Chicago he was actually quite intrigued by especially seeing them from overhead. He might have been on this train once in high school but not since usually only experienced everything from the ground from a car mostly. He was actually enjoying this seeing Broadway and Lawrence and Wilson. When they passed Truman College Hunter told Kate about how much he enjoyed the summer of 1997 taking biology there following Cunanan.

I kept hoping he wouldn't get caught Hunter said. I know that sounds terrible but it was just so exciting the whole thing.

He mentioned other things songs working at Market Facts becoming a supervisor but of course didn't mention being obsessed with Jessica Emerson making out with Jane those other parts of that summer which she didn't need to know about.

1994 was sort of the pinnacle of grunge he said. It was so sad about Kurt Cobain. I liked 1992 a lot the beginning of the Clinton nineties.

She laughed smiled kept letting her head drop onto his shoulder. He didn't want to understand what that meant and asked Are you tired.

No she said sitting back up. I'm actually more awake now.

I think I'm definitely a morning person Hunter said.

Yeah I could tell.

Very funny.

He wished he had more coffee. Her head took several more turns on his shoulder. He wasn't happy about that and thought of the girls behind him. One of them said something about a creative writing class which he wanted to listen to but then got distracted by his own nervous banter. He spoke more quickly when her head was on his shoulder. Why was she doing that.

He spoke about Diana his other sister the older one about

how he thought it was silly for her to apply to colleges out of state. She's just kidding herself. The problem with her is that she doesn't have attainable goals she lives in this dream world. She's not even filling out these applications to schools. She's not going to attend on her own. She wants everybody to help her everyone to hold her hand.

 Well maybe she's insecure.

 I don't know. I think my mother is filling out the goddamn things for her. I wasn't like that at all. I did everything myself. I don't think my parents even knew I was going to UIC until a month or two after I started. She laughed.

 He continued I did it all myself. The applications to undergrad to grad all myself.

 So what are your plans she asked looking at him. This was it. This was his chance to tell her.

 He said Well probably C—.

 That's far.

 Yeah.

 So like in the fall.

 Yeah I'm thinking so.

 That's really soon isn't it.

 That wasn't so terrible. It was a good first step to telling her. It was anticlimactic that she didn't ask more questions get angry demand things. He had expected her to or hoped she'd say something like Well we shouldn't get really involved then but instead she touched his arm maybe a tacit expression of something—what—acceptance—more evidence of the fact that this girl would tolerate anything. Fuck. Why did he keep doing this. Why didn't he just say. Since when was telling the truth so impossible. Did he want it to get worse. Did he want to see how long he could not tell her and then watch her freak out. Did he want to hurt her. There was just no reason for this. It didn't even seem like she was that concerned.

 She touched his arm directly—his skin was exposed—he wore a short-sleeved shirt—a few times. Her fingers were incredibly cold. It was cold in the train car even as more people got on. There were so many stops many more than Hunter was used to from the few times he'd gone downtown on the blue line. He didn't say anything or move at first was actually thinking about his own leaving. He had just mailed the application for housing that morning. What would his apartment be like. He probably should email Hilary and try to get his dishes back the ones he gave her to use when she was at Medill. He wondered if they were still okay. He didn't want to see her. Maybe she could send them with her brother to UIC one day this week. It was finals probably the last opportunity he'd have to get them without having to see her. What could she say. She couldn't say no. They belonged to him.

Ouch he said. Kate touched the bend of his arm. Her fingers felt swollen against his skin like her hand was this bloated cold noncontiguous part detached and groping. That's cold.

My hands are always cold she said. Why do you think that is.

Maybe you have poor circulation. She shook her hands in a cartoonish way like a marionette. They both laughed. Do that again Hunter said.

The exhibit was called the Illuminated Manuscript. They were particularly interested in Andrew Davis's work sketches of large floor to ceiling poems words enjambed all over the place carved letters in bookcases and doors and dressers and little wooden boxes with tops that slid out cemented to a long plank. It was interesting. Along one wall was the text alone broken up into dozens of sonnets. Hunter read *etched in black like whorls of damascene.*

They started trading quotes. He said You're just *swart unauthorized* and I think you're *a great compendium of demons.*

He liked the words felt comfortable alone in this exhibit no one else around *before the portcullis came crashing down.* He felt connected with what he read though a bit distanced *hallucinatory hypnogogic.* He was hungry again. How much of the day were they going to spend together. He didn't mind spending time with her actually enjoyed her company to an extent. They were at some sort of common ground here which was comforting. She interested in visual art he words and writing. It was almost ironic that they would be in such an exhibit reading and looking at such things. He felt like he could stay in that room forever. *Veracity the word itself meant darkness.* He wanted a book of these sonnets. He wished he could write down some of the words but didn't have a pen or really any paper. *The comments sotto voce as he passed.*

Are you hungry she asked turning away from a priapic carving that looked like a doorknocker.

# 57

The formal with Lila. Thinking about it reminded him of the prom his last year at Roycemore. He'd been to the two previous proms. Since there were so few students at Roycemore they invited the whole upper school to the one official dance each May so Hunter knew what to expect by the last one. He was taking Simona of course. He hoped things wouldn't go terribly wrong as they had the year before. The party at the Oxford Hotel which was at first just supposed to be for him and Simona Tom Callahan Suzanne maybe one or two others got fucked up when Jeffrey ended up bringing these Ignatius people who wouldn't leave. Sean Williams Randy Furth Pat DeFranco Brian Coffield others Hunter didn't even know. The reason they all ended up there was that Jeffrey was scoring the cocaine and came late. Tom and Hunter waited in the hotel for him to arrive the girls already headed to the restaurant. They made reservations at three places at the last minute held hostage by Jeffrey and his tardiness. Finally Simona and Suzanne went to Vivo with Jennie Farmer her date and some others. By the time Tom and Hunter had the cocaine and the pot for Tom and had done a few lines in Tom's Saturn they had missed dinner. Simona was pissed off. They went to the dance. She calmed down. They returned to the Oxford afterward. Jeffrey and company were still there lying on the beds watching TV smoking pot.

Simona freaked out told Hunter Get them out of here now

this is our room they don't belong here why are they here how did they get in.

Hunter tried to explain and technically it was Tom's fault.

Tom had said Let's meet them up here.

Hunter said We should do it in the lobby. That way we can leave.

He didn't expect for them to stay even once they came in and Jeffrey said What's the big deal we'll leave in twenty minutes come on what's the big deal we're not going to do anything. But they were still there and Hunter supposed he wasn't putting up that much of a fight against them staying.

He asked Simona Why can't they just stay. He sort of liked that they were there. He had always sort of idolized that crowd liked hanging around them when he was still at Lab but Simona wouldn't have it. There was a scuffle lots of shouting. Simona started crying. Suzanne whisked her away leaving only Tom and Hunter all these small bags of coke. The police came. Hunter freaked. He knew for sure they were going to get busted. Tom stashed everything in the tub drain. They had a mirror on the desk when the cops came in residue all over Hunter's pockets stuffed with empty packages residue probably on his nose his gums numb. They just sat on the couch didn't say anything watched as the cops emptied out can after can of beer into the sink before leaving. They were stunned just looked at each other.

Hunter said I can't believe this I can't believe this over and over. He tried not to think about Simona how he was going to apologize. They rescued most of the cocaine. Some of it got wet. They sat and quickly did what they could of it. Hunter tried to drink some of the wet stuff. Tom went into the bedroom to sleep after a few hours of cursory chat old and black and white four AM movies on TV. Hunter lay on the couch in the living room wide awake nervous depressed wondered where his cummerbund had wandered off to.

The next year he rented a hotel room again. This time it was just supposed to be for the two of them. Simona didn't really bring up the events of the previous year. She'd probably gotten over it. This year Hunter's main concern was Aaron Weinberg whom he was sure wanted to fuck his girlfriend and maybe even had. Hey infidelity wasn't beyond her. He rented a nice room at the Westin put on his tux there before taking a cab to pick her up. He didn't have any drugs this year just plenty of cigarettes. They had dinner at Yoshi's Café. The last time Hunter had been there three years earlier it was a little fancier. They'd changed the menu. Most people were dressed casually which was slightly disconcerting. They had a nice time though no wine. Hunter ordered tuna tartare which she wouldn't try but was intrigued by. Most of the dance Simona was off smoking pot with Aaron Weinberg and whoever else. Hunter danced alone or with others to fast Madonna songs rubbed his crotch against the floor during *Like a Virgin* felt drunk even though he wasn't.

Where's Simona people would ask.

I don't know. I think she went downstairs or something he said.

The prom was at the 95th. Hunter thought his tux looked better than the other guys'. His wasn't rented after all.

Back at the hotel Simona said I want to go to Suzanne's.

Suzanne had rented a suite at the Best Western. Aaron Weinberg was there and so were the Bancroft brothers and Kellie LeTourn. Jennie and Sven had their own room at the Ritz. Sven always had a lot of cash drove a Mercedes for god's sake didn't think twice about dropping six hundred dollars just to be able to fuck his pompous girlfriend in a different bed. Hunter didn't want to go to Suzanne's. He wanted to spend time with Simona alone. They had this room and he had sparkling wine on ice. She ended up falling asleep. They didn't have sex or even fool around. Hunter drank most of the Riunite on his own watching the tourist channel and then went to sleep. He bought her an expensive room service breakfast in the morning. They woke late were kind of rushed for check-out which was somewhat disappointing since Hunter liked mornings in hotels being able to leisurely pour over the *USA Today* sip the really good Starbucks that came with this continental breakfast tray but what could he do. He barely had enough money to pay for all of this.

    So the things he had to do before Friday: he needed to figure out if he had to exchange his white shirt for another one thought about going downtown to do that today but he probably wouldn't have enough time. He was going to get the dishes from Hilary's brother Samuel. That was probably going to be awkward at least logistically. Where was he going to put his car. Where would he put the boxes once he had his car. His trunk was loaded with junk. He really needed to clear some of that stuff out but there was no time for that. Maybe in the back seat. He hoped there wasn't more than one box. He had some short-sleeved shirts in his closet that belonged to her. He had to remember to bring those along. Then dinner with Mademoiselle Mauny now Madame Klaff oh whatever Caroline his old French teacher. She called every couple of months maybe once a year to see what he was doing. She was excited about C—. He told her in an email. She didn't teach at Roycemore anymore. Now she had a French school that she founded on the North Shore. Hunter had to get out there tonight and see her. When was the last time he'd seen her. Anyway he remembered a dinner a month or two after he started dating Hilary. He didn't tell her Hilary where he was going or whom he was seeing. He figured it was too complicated. He didn't want to hear her shit about it. He knew at that point about her female paranoia didn't feel like providing fuel with that. He just said he was working or going to a meeting or something. So then almost three years ago. It couldn't have been that long. Could it. He also probably should order a corsage. Maybe he'd try calling the florist now. He felt like he was lumbering trying to make these arrangements like he didn't know really what to do and was just guessing. He was supposed to call Lila last night and didn't. It was too hot. He lapsed into an all night torpor which included a nap at nine-thirty no reading no writing. After this week he would really have to start reading fairly seriously. He didn't want to just spend the summer watching TV taking naps and jacking off. That wasn't what he wanted to do.

What would this formal be like. Lila would probably look very pretty. Molly also would look very pretty. Maybe too pretty. Perhaps this would be the time Lila would finally make a move or flirt more or something. He didn't think he'd mind having an affair with her. He would of course have to get over this fear of talking to her if things were to become at all significant. He didn't know what the problem was. Maybe they just hadn't become comfortable with each other yet. He felt like he didn't know much about her. Maybe that had something to do with it. Was there anything to find out. Why hadn't she revealed more. They probably just hadn't had the chance. This formal could provide some common experience something definitely to discuss but for how long. She said her dress was maroon. Would that be enough information for the florist. He needed a car wash too. They were taking his car. He was thankful at least for the open bar she said would be there. He really should call her tonight. It probably seemed a bit peculiar that he wasn't. He did email her though so that probably helped. He sort of invited her to see *Rent* with him and might have mentioned the Organic Theater tickets he won during the silent auction at Maya's fashion show. At this point the only out in public dates to actual places not just obscure things and the Lucky Platter or bedroom girl in his life seemed to be Lila. He hoped his face would remain placid just until Friday.

# 58

Finals week was a certainly unique time. The dynamic of the campus quickly changed began to resemble the summer semester considerably fewer people around. What felt odd was not really having a schedule. Hunter worked in one of the computer labs for most of the morning and then ate a sandwich. He typically readied himself for Film and Authorship but that was over with. He could go to the Writing Center hang out or tutor. This week they were having walk-in sessions and probably could have used the help but he was tired couldn't wake up in the mornings. It seemed that having things to do energized him and the absence of those things was debilitating. Right now he sat in a dining hall which was not entirely empty though not as many people as Hunter usually had to compete against outwit outlast for a place to sit.

    He sat across from a girl a table away facing him. She was pretty bright eyes blonde hair a green tank top dark shoulders tan skin. Today was the first day over eighty the first day Hunter had shorts on since last summer. How did she have tan arms already. He liked looking at her felt kind of out of practice looking at a girl and had already weathered several near misses getting caught. Now she wrote underlined a Xerox with a blue pen. Right handed. She had a prepossessing quality. Everything about her the way she flipped through her notes the way she coughed modestly barely emitting a sound the way she flexed her hand rotated her wrist excited Hunter. She took a piece of blue Trident from a folded pack. He liked looking at someone new. He'd been thinking and looking at the same few women for what seemed like forever. He appreciated the variety and such exquisite variety at that. Why was it Hunter had never met this girl before—though she looked familiar—why had he never had a class with her spent an hour helping her fix HTML tags sent a Word attachment in the lab studied pink and brown Xeroxed articles with her. How come that had never happened. All of this made worse by the fact that he'd never have the courage to talk to her. It simply was not within his nature. Even if there were some sort of logical reason to start a conversation with her say something ironic and make her laugh he probably still wouldn't do it. She was too beautiful but that wasn't even the reason because he would inevitably be just as reluctant in approaching a bland looking girl.

He wrote Hilary the night before about the dishes very simply. No Hi how are you no explanation for needing them and she wrote back just as succinctly. He noticed she switched email addresses had a new Hotmail account which must have been equipped with forwarding or something. He wondered if he'd been unduly impassive sterile. He really had no reason to feel like he had to be that formal cold with her but he hated having to talk to her even if it was just an email. He asked if her brother Samuel could meet him on campus somewhere figured that would be the easiest anything to avoid going to her house seeing her or her parents. He couldn't say for certain which sounded more egregious. Probably seeing her. It had almost been a year since they last saw each other—would be a year in June—at the Printer's Row book fair last summer. He really had nothing to say to her. He supposed he didn't hate her exactly but not seeing her or letting her know what was going on in his life not finding out details about her besides the ones he picked up from Google searches seemed more appropriate.

He wished he could talk to the blonde girl wished he could kiss her neck and brown shoulders. Something more unlikely happening in this universe he couldn't imagine. Girls with tattoos—one walked past him a sun with beaming black rays covering her entire lower back—always smoked cigarettes and did drugs. It was almost an infallible correlation. This blonde girl probably did neither. It was a shame Hunter didn't know her. Would he ever kiss someone as physically attractive as Simona again. Of course he thought of her when reckoning very attractive girls who were completely beyond his reach. It depressed him that his relationships since her had been steps down as far as aesthetics were concerned. The blonde girl was writing on her left palm and wrist. Was she preparing for a final. Daring. That took balls especially in college. Maybe she did do drugs recreationally of course. Maybe she took other chances in her life let guys pick her up did her own share of flirting maybe even asked for guys' numbers or called first or had sex on the first or second date or drank a lot. Face it Hunter thought. You will see this person once only now and when you get up she the green tank top the brilliant blonde hair and glinting eyes will cease to be there for you to notice or comment on or get aroused by and that fact had nothing more to do with the fact that life was random ill-conceived disorganized and unfair than anything else did. Despite this Hunter still really wanted her but more than that what he really wanted was some sort of capability some intrinsic faculty to permanently keep every detail about her—the way she chewed the silverness of her watchband the tan arms the darkness of her jeans—inside his head forever to be able to recall without hesitation every piece of her this moment their contexts bordering each other all of it. That way it would always be his and it would mean something perfect. Just knowing that that existed was all he'd ever wanted out of or really because of anything he did but the trouble was the part he had no way of escaping was that he didn't have the power to stop it or anything else from leaving

THE WEEK YOU WEREN'T HERE 257

from changing from ceasing to be his if it ever really was in the first place. Things could only be temporary provisional and anything which seemed to be more than just random was nothing but completely random. Just then she began to gather her things.

# 59

He's drunk or kind of drunk he thought seemed trapped in a situation of sorts. His brow sweaty his left earlobe itchy. Shouldn't drink at school that's just weird he thought but it had been the end of the semester party at the Writing Center. It was insane. Very random. Ricki flirted minimally with Hunter. He flirted with everyone Ricki Emma Jade Peg sort of Marly whom he was sad to note didn't offer her phone number or suggest they go out sometime much to the opposite of what her smiling looking complimenting his writing suggested she was thinking. Fuck. Well then there was Laura Jade Emma some more. Did girls think he was this big lecherous loser. Did he have uncontrollable concupiscence printed on his sweaty forehead. He certainly hoped not. He was still on campus to meet Lila. They said they would have tea. Tea sounded good. Anything to sober him up. The punch was tame. He drank a lot of it. Supposedly it had a bottle of vodka inside. Yeah right. Hunter was not convinced. He couldn't taste a goddamn thing. The same wasn't the case with the shots of Jack and 7-Up chasers after most people left. That worked. He hadn't had any Jack in quite some time. Laura looked pretty fucking left-handed fucking completely uninterested. Oh well. She was probably fat underneath those clothes unattractive in the light. Dewey didn't show up. That was a bitchy thing of her to do. Was it because of Hunter. What a loser she was if it were. Well at least Hunter looked like the mature one. Let her revel in her pettiness let her care hold grudges. He certainly didn't.

That morning he was heading for the Writing Center when he ran into Erica in the hall. He hadn't seen her for a while. She was this girl Hunter liked over a year ago. She was blonde cute. He liked her or started talking to her anyway because of a Sociology class they had. Youth and Our Society. He was still seeing Hilary at the time. It wasn't long before they split up. Erica was twenty seemed flirtatious offered her phone number quickly though things turned out not to be what he thought they were. He lost interest sort of forgot about her only reminded of her when he'd see her.

She said she was tired said she had two finals gotten an hour of sleep fortified by Vivarin tabs and Marlboro Menthols. Do you have to go somewhere she asked.

No Hunter said. He wasn't lying. He really didn't. They sat outside. She smoked a cigarette talked about her new boyfriend who was older.

What is he like thirty-five Hunter asked.

No he's thirty-six she said softly looking away and ashed. He's kind of controlling and that's kind of not like me because I'm a really independent person.

Of course.

Yeah so it's weird you know trying to adjust. We've only been together for five months.

Hunter quickly tried to assess the date of their last long conversation. Longer ago than that. Probably September. He was reading *Sister Carrie* for Modern American Lit just finished it when he saw her and they had coffee together. It was getting cold outside. He was getting a cold. It was a Saturday night and he was reading at school since he had nothing else to do. She wasn't with this guy then. She talked about a different guy that night.

That's not good if he's not comfortable with letting you be independent Hunter said.

I don't know. I sort of want to marry him.

Marry him. Has he asked you.

Yeah he talks about it all the time and the thing is is the longer you wait the more problems you could have you know with kids and stuff.

Yeah but still I think you could probably wait like five or ten or twenty years and still be within a safe window.

Yeah she said cupping her chin with her palm and fingers I guess you're right.

Hunter didn't understand the rush to get married or have children. This guy was obviously a loser but then again maybe he was doing exactly the right thing. Would Hunter have to start wondering about marriage. He wanted to get married someday just to whom was the question. Lila maybe. Yeah right.

Then in the Writing Center Peanut brought up the formal in front of the wrong people. One of the wrong people was Ricki. Hunter had to explain away her jealousy. She acted like she didn't really care busied herself with reading some old newspaper didn't comment or ask any questions but did she really. Probably she did. Peanut later said when they were alone that she was glad he was going.

Hunter said I have no idea what she's looking for. Maybe she just needed a date.

That's possible Peanut said. But maybe she wanted to go with you.

That was just too hard for him to rationalize. He didn't feel attractive. He stuck out so much or maybe blended in so well that most girls just kind of overlooked him—no sweeping gestures just okay so what. He just really didn't ever expect anything to happen. In fact as he thought about it he started to realize that maybe possibly things might be a little easier if she didn't like him if she really only did need a ride or couldn't find anyone else because then he wouldn't have as much thinking to do. He hoped he'd sober up before seeing her. He hoped she couldn't smell the booze on him. He hoped she didn't care about any of this.

His heart sped his forehead sweat he was a mess he was freaking out. I probably look like fucking shit I'm tired I'm sweating he thought. His eyes crossed his breathing laborious everything a challenge. What did he do now. He wondered about these things over and over. He laid his head down for fifteen minutes felt somewhat better upon rising his thoughts lucid somewhat relevant thought he should email Professor Bates about office hours. He didn't feel as bleary as before wondered how loud he'd been breathing when he thought no one else was around when only one guy sat reading in the quiet study area. When he awoke there were five or six. Oh well. What could he say. Now his mouth was dry.

He met her at the top of the CCC escalator. She wore a tight black T-shirt that said Sex and the City in pink letters. He refrained from mentioning it wished not to have the conversation about shirts and what they said. There had to be more important things to discuss.

At a small table in the back of the Pier Room Hunter had a soda. Lila didn't want anything. I just ate and drank she said.

Hunter's mouth ached from the afternoon's debauchery. His eyes scorched. The contacts had to come out tonight. She still looked pretty. She was wearing eye makeup a thin strip of white on the eyelids. God damn it. Did she do this for his benefit. She also mentioned changing clothes on the phone. She had called his cell. He answered it from the library bathroom leaning over the sink splashed water surprisingly soothing almost clarifying. He was fortunately sober now.

She told him more details about the formal. Yeah I guess I like most of the girls. Some of them. Well this one she's pretty mean to me. It's like she's always trying to find something wrong with me. She's never happy with anything I do. She complains about her boyfriend. His roommate is my ex-boyfriend.

Oh well no wonder she hates you.

Lila smiled looked into Hunter's eyes touched her shoe to his. Her foot remained atop his for several minutes. Did she not notice. Did she think Hunter's foot was the bottom of the table leg or the floor. It wasn't just glancing. It settled on Hunter's with no intention of moving. Hunter pulled his foot away quickly when she finally moved. He didn't understand wasn't comfortable suddenly.

I think she's probably jealous of you you know in some way. It seems like completely unearned hostility. I don't get it. You're such a nice person.

Well thank you she said leaning forward touching his shoulder.

So are you going to write about this she asked then.

That's a funny question he said a bit shocked surprised. I might. I didn't really think about—

You totally should but I want to see it.

God no. I couldn't. I mean I've never written when somebody's been one of the characters.

You totally have to do it. I want to read it. I wouldn't be mad.

No it wouldn't be like that. I mean I don't write—

You totally have to.

I was sort of… Who told you I was thinking about—

Nobody she laughed. Nobody. I just had a feeling.

Well maybe I'll probably do it. I mean I'll definitely write something but showing you…

I wouldn't get mad or anything.

He imagined a character going to a formal. Of course he'd have to write two versions—the one she'd see not including any salacious accounts of other women.

I think you'll have a good time she said.

I'm excited he said. He really was. Do I not seem—

No you do. Just think about it this way: how many opportunities will you have—

Well I hope a few.

No but chances to go somewhere be in a room full of people you don't really know. Well you'll obviously know me and Bridget and Len her boyfriend.

The film guy.

Right. Yeah. She grinned again. You read the email. Yeah so you know a chance to be around people without consequences.

That was an odd observation. Hunter didn't quite know what to make of the concept. He guessed he was comfortable enough with himself and his social persona not to have ever thought of things like that.

He said I don't think I—well I guess I feel like I'm pretty much me wherever I go. I don't really generally more or less change how I am.

No what I mean is that you know you don't have to act a certain way knowing that you'll have to well I don't know be responsible for it later.

You mean like you have to since you know you're still in the whole thing with them.

Right. So you see what I'm talking about.

He didn't know what she really meant. Did she think him some sort of ridiculous introvert. Was she having second thoughts about bringing him introducing him to her circle. He guessed it didn't really matter this whole thing only provisionally important to him. He liked Lila but he honestly didn't care barely thought about the thing only really insignificantly curious as to whether or not she would admit anything suggestive with a rum and Coke bolstering. She said she didn't drink much. That was mildly disappointing. Well depending on how he felt he might choose to be temperate moderate in step with her or just work the bar independently. Of course how often had he ever considered the latter. He only had one margarita that night with Kate and look how much trouble being considerate caused. There was something to be learned from that. He needed to assert. He needed to not concern himself with comportment so much. Obviously he wouldn't drink excessively act like an ass take his shirt off but would it be so unconscionable to set the terms just this once just for one night. Of course maybe she'd reconsider once they were there and the death glares and catty once-overs and gum snapping and eye rolling and blasé yawning and ear scratching dissipated. Once the night began to take shape she might change her mind. Maybe what he fancied about her was the way she thought or felt could suddenly change. She still seemed to view the world rather quixotically: There's nothing wrong with an age difference if people are emotionally compatible. Maybe Hunter was the idiot. What did he know. Maybe seeing the world as a twenty-year-old would give him a new perspective a better perspective. Anything beyond his own rigid perimeter could not be automatically deemed negligible. Maybe he liked her for her optimism. Maybe he liked seeing the world through her eyes which were in fact quite pretty which did in many ways resemble his. Hers seemed a bit greener his more blue.

# 60

This free time time of possibilities seemed only to inspire laziness. He went to the gym this morning—that was good—spent time—more time than he might have cared to—on the phone with Renee. She was temping in an office in the dining services department at Northwestern. She wanted Hunter to help her print file folder labels out of Excel. He tried to guide her but found it frustrating navigating without the screen in front of him. He got to campus late—eleven-thirty—felt out of place self-conscious in shorts like he'd come to school with only a T-shirt and boxers on. Despite that it was a beautiful day balmy not that humid bright breezy. The temperature was supposed to drop the news said. He was meeting Samuel in forty-five minutes. Sitting in BSB by himself reading reminded him of his very first day of classes the first semester. He arrived early empty backpack and a copy of *The Informers* sat down at a table. People sat at some of the other tables. He wanted to blend in look less like someone on his first day of college. Probably nobody even noticed him or if they did would they have known it was his first day or even cared. It must have been early most of his classes were at eight that semester and now sitting once again at the clear opposite end last semester last finals week of which he didn't even have any. At first glance it would he thought appear as though nothing had changed. Had anything.

Hunter waited by the back doors to BSB for Samuel to arrive. It was already a few minutes after two. Hunter read the ads sublet apartments Poi Dog Pondering concert in the Soldier Field parking lot signs announcing lectures already passed. Samuel came. He was wearing a blue UIC t-shirt and khakis. They walked to Samuel's car. They had to figure out how to coordinate this. He opened his trunk.

It's only one box and this bag he said.

Oh said Hunter that's not a lot is it.

It's not heavy it's just kind of awkward.

They decided to drive together into Hunter's parking lot. Hunter appreciated this. They talked about the summer.

Samuel was working on campus. You remember I told you about that job working in the Honors College computer lab.

Yeah Hunter said beginning to recall I do. So you're going to do that.

Yeah and take these two classes.

Which ones.

A history and a business.

Oh so history as history not history of business or anything.

No no. Just real history.

They laughed. It was tense sort of. Maybe only Hunter felt that way. They didn't see each other often but Hunter didn't mind seeing Samuel. It was only slightly strange their talking. Their talking which never referenced the only thing they really had in common or ever would have in common. This might be the last time they'd see each other. Hunter thought about this fact. There was so much ponderous intractable finality about all of this the return of Hunter's things. So now Hilary possessed nothing that belonged to him and so they were complete strangers. This was the last conversation between Hunter and her brother so she'd get to keep him and Hunter would no longer have even that part of her. It wasn't as though he wanted to be part of her life anymore. He just didn't like being made painfully aware of the fact that their lives which once had been so indistinguishable so interwoven now basically had nothing in common nothing that would suggest they ever had a past except the fact that they did. Samuel parked behind Hunter's car and took the box out of the trunk while Hunter unlocked the doors.

Samuel said This isn't that heavy and set the box down on the back seat. Hunter took the plastic bag. It was tied up. Clothes he guessed. There was only one flannel he remembered her having this Abercrombie tan-brown sort of shirt. He could make it out through the thin opaqueness of the bag.

Well thanks he said Samuel standing next to him now.

No problem he said. So you're done now.

Yeah but I'm still going to be around working here this summer. Maybe I'll see you.

Yeah.

You should stop by the Writing Center.

Samuel said he might that he'd probably have to work on a paper for history but Hunter knew it was just something to say that he probably wouldn't see him again. Samuel drove off. Hunter sat in the car and untied the white bag. Inside were other shirts shirts Hunter barely even remembered owning let alone Hilary possessing for the last year and two months or longer without his prior knowledge. A black shirt a gray fleece with University of Illinois at Chicago in red stitching above the pocket a J. Crew charcoal and red flannel. He was glad to have these things back but having them depressed him. The shirts were neatly folded in the bag. Had her mother washed them. Had Hilary. Also in the bag folded less neatly a blue suit of Hunter's one which probably didn't still fit him probably didn't even fit at the time. Maybe he'd try it on. Maybe he'd have more success with it now that he was a bit thinner. He considered writing Hilary again to say thanks but she'd already ignored the last thank you email as well as the one where he included his cell phone number for her to give to her brother in case of a mix-up so he figured it was just as well to let it go. He wondered if she wondered what the source for the exigency of this transfer was if it bothered her or maybe she didn't even care. Oh come on of course she cared. Even he'd be curious to hear about such a major development in someone's life even someone he hated or wanted to be free from.

# 61

Having ignored most of Kate's phone calls he broke down and spoke to her briefly on Monday or Tuesday night. Today was Thursday. She called his cell phone each night twice since their conversation. The night before Hunter didn't even listen to the voice mail. If only she were blonde he thought. If only she were a little less—what—less shiny or her face just slightly more attractive he'd have no trouble falling in love with her. Of course she wasn't intellectually his ideal—possibly no such person existed at least not as a human. She wrote a slightly irritated email today admonishing him ineffectively for not writing or calling. He didn't respond. It barely registered. Maybe he could just provoke her into wanting to have a serious conversation and then just end it whatever it was. He was done being evasive. He knew that he didn't want to be with her didn't even want to use her the way she didn't seem to object to being used.

Look he'd say this just didn't work out. I like you you're a very nice person but if I've learned one thing in all of my sort of blind firing—he couldn't of course explain what he meant by that—it's that you can't force certain things to happen. It sounds so stupid to say wrong time but honestly I just haven't been feeling so very romantically inclined and so I hope this doesn't hurt you too terribly.

He could do that. He could take control of the situation what only five weeks and the loss of two or three shirts too late and free himself. Her calls her pleas her entreaties for attention for romantic consideration seemed only to make him less enthused. She was too pushy too overbearing too needy. He needed space. He needed to be alone.

Basically he didn't really need a relationship right now. Wanting someone without the possibility of anything actually happening—that described the majority if not all of the girls he'd worshipped over time. Eileen Lauren Cumin Jessica Emerson that summer four years ago. That's exactly what he wanted and nothing more. Kate wasn't sadly to say that person. She wasn't part of that pantheon. She wasn't even a semi-finalist. Her office wasn't even on the same floor. He had his own combination skin to worry about his own problems with sweat or flies or neediness or intimacy. Kate's problem was a surfeit of intimacy—not a fear of it as was the case with most. It hadn't worked for her and Hunter. Okay. Accept this and go forward. She was after all supposedly popular among the Internet dating pool. Maybe there was some earnest yet dim man out there who could give her what she needed—if she even knew—that was doubtful—then maybe there was some hope for her.

This exigency wasn't inspired by Lila. She had nothing to do with it. Well maybe a little but it was just all the damn phone calls. Did Kate not get subtlety even that it existed in the form of a remote concept. He just didn't get how could she not think that not writing not calling and barely answering the phone could be his way of saying Please double your efforts. He wondered if she'd ever seen a shrink. He might suggest she consider it. He'd have to think of a polite way to broach the subject.

As far as the formal went he was barely prepared. He had his suit though wasn't entirely sure which household closet it hung in. He didn't have cash. His hair was a mess. He didn't imagine it changing much for the better between now and when he needed it to look decent. His car was clean but the trunk wasn't. That would be his morning project—emptying his trunk. What else did he need to do. Not get any blemishes.

# 62

Tie shirt gray suit now loose in the waist held together with a belt. He really had lost a lot of weight from the exercising. Hunter drove on the highway toward UIC. He had plenty of time. Maybe he'd sit in the car when he got there and think about what he was about to do. His hair looked okay. The spray gel actually seemed to work which surprised him.

Inside Lila's room Hunter talked to Len who was her roommate Bridget's date. Len sat in a chair by the window smoking a cigarette watching this episode of *Cops* and interrupted Hunter to ask Bridget for the remote control. Bridget was doing her makeup in the mirror and threw the remote at him without looking. Lila went to put on her dress in the bathroom came back and began to blow-dry her hair. Hunter sat in a chair she pulled out from a desk for him. The room was crowded with desks and boxes of clothes hand bags many pairs of shoes. The white TV-VCR sat on top of a white microwave—It's unplugged Lila said—which sat on top of a mini refrigerator.

It's dorm chic Bridget said.

Bridget wore a blue robe with moons and stars on it. Hunter looked at her and talked to her reflection in the mirror while she applied mascara and eyeliner. He talked to Lila too but not as much. His hands were still cold from the drive. It was actually quite cold outside. He'd wished he'd brought an overcoat.

Len said Girls I don't get them. It takes me five minutes to get ready. There's nothing to it.

Yeah Hunter said if I needed to you know like if it were an emergency or something I could be ready in what a minute maybe two.

Easy for you guys to say Lila said.

Hunter looked at her maroon dress. It was slinky. She was sitting on the bed now fastening a pair of white pumps.

You're not going to be taller than me in those Hunter asked.

No she said I don't think so. How tall are you.

Four eleven Hunter said.

Oh in that case maybe we do have a problem. She punched his shoulder playfully.

She really did look pretty. Hunter thought both of them did. Finally the girls were ready. They walked downstairs and Lila asked another girl to take pictures. They posed. Hunter and Lila in one Len and Bridget in another then the four of them together. Once on the highway Hunter drove quickly Duran Duran Wild Boys on the radio.

Len took out his cell phone. Can you turn down the radio for a second.

Sure Hunter said reaching for the knob.

I need to make some prank calls.

Is that safe in the age of caller ID Hunter asked. Len didn't answer. He called something ordered a limo in a strange Tony Soprano *Godfather* sort of voice. That was weird. Hunter didn't like driving on the highway especially in this direction.

I think this is my least favorite highway he told Lila.

Really she said. They moved quickly. There weren't a lot of cars around.

Yeah I used to have to drive down here not a lot but sometimes. He didn't say the reason why he did that it was because of dating Hilary and that the exit they had to take tonight to get to the banquet hall was the street Hunter used to take to Hilary's parents' house and that was how he knew where he was going without having to consult a map.

He said They change the billboards a lot. That's why I don't like it.

Yeah life is full of changes. The only thing consistent is change.

Heh you're right.

He gripped the steering wheel tightly. He didn't feel uncomfortable yet. In fact he was enjoying himself. Len and Bridget seemed nice and Lila of course was fun to be with. He was actually looking forward to this.

Does anybody know what we're eating Len asked.

Chicken I think Lila said looking at Hunter as though he might know.

Yeah Bridget said I believe it is chicken. I'm not that concerned with that. The only thing I care about is is there an open bar and the answer to that is yes. They all laughed.

That's funny Hunter said to Lila I really never asked you about anything except for if there was a bar. I mean that's what we talked about.

Well there is going to be food. This I know.

Inside the banquet hall Hunter counted four tables on one side of the room separated by the dance floor which was narrow more like a dance column really from two other tables on the side with the bar. They stood still while the girls consulted with each other silently just exchanging nods and glances. People already sat at the tables on the other side of the room. Some girls stood in front of the bar. A blender whizzed. The bartender was older looked like somebody's grandfather in a tux shirt and a black jacket. He stood sullenly over the small bar nodded feigning graciousness really probably could not have cared less about all of this. Hunter felt disconnected. He didn't understand why they were standing and not moving.

Lila whispered We are just trying to figure out where to sit.

Hunter nodded looked at Bridget her eyes darting looked for Len. Where did Len go. He was sizing up the bar. I wonder who gets stuck sitting on this side Hunter asked again noticing the split of the tables.

Huh Lila asked. She didn't hear him. She still looked around confused preoccupied by this table dilemma.

Another girl in a cheap-looking pink dress blonde with her hair in pink clips came over greeted the girls and said You guys can sit with us and so they all went to a table across the dance floor.

Hunter asked Lila Do you want a drink.

No but if you want one… she said.

He didn't answer. He could see Molly from where he sat. Molly had her hair pulled back and wore a flowing elegant powder blue dress. She was smiling. Her date wasn't the tall guy whom Hunter had imagined she would have brought the guy he always saw her with on campus standing outside of lecture centers flirting with her. Molly had her arm around a different guy. This guy was shorter. He had curly hair not entirely different from Hunter's but less in style and texture more in just the general state of incongruousness. Hunter always felt his hair looked incongruous ever since he began to notice how his hair looked ever since sixth grade when he began to spend time in front of the mirror applying gobs of gel spraying in all sorts of products designed to minimize frizz to maximize shine without compromising body and sheen and whatever. Hunter had only recently purchased a small bottle of hair spray non-aerosol of course. It wasn't the same though. Now he was thankful mostly that he still had all his hair. He wasn't issuing blandishments. He had liked his suit. The sleeves of his Calvin Klein shirt were a bit long the collar slightly looser than he would have normally worn but he figured nobody would notice. Who would look at him that closely. He felt like his clothes were all wrong now that he was looking at Molly. What was it about her that fascinated him so. He also thought that it was sort of awkward he sitting at the table with his date Lila who did look rather attractive cute Hunter thought as she silently obsessed over her little clique problems and Molly over there at the table with the sisters Lila did not get along with.

Molly obviously would not come over to say hello. Was he supposed to get up and go over there or not say anything to her. He couldn't ignore her. He liked her. They were polite to each other as co-workers and sort of friendly. Molly didn't try to talk to him really ever. He covered hours for her that she couldn't work. She was actually the only person he'd done that for. Was that her boyfriend. Did she fuck that guy. He seemed to be completely the opposite of what Hunter would have expected. Molly seemed so demanding yet so potentially comfortable with a thick football player with buzzed hair and a dime bag in his back pocket.

Hunter desperately wanted a drink and again suggested he get them something at the bar. Lila wasn't listening. She spoke to Bridget. They both looked around pointed by nodding the smallest of gestures. Len played with his napkin. Hunter watched them speak. He liked the way Lila spoke observed how her eyes widened and narrowed the angles of her face jaw cheeks smoothness of her nose. Waitresses with carts began to circumambulate the room distributing bowls of salad soup tureens glass carafes of white wine thank god. Len poured wine into Bridget's water glass. Hunter reached for the carafe.

I don't want any Lila said.

You don't.

No I don't really like wine.

Are you sure.

Well maybe. Just pour me a glass.

Okay Hunter said and filled her small glass part way then filled his own fully. He sipped the wine. It was chilled slightly bitter a bit thick unmistakably cheap but Hunter was thirsty and sucked it up quickly.

They didn't talk while Hunter chewed his salad. Lila didn't take much of it and ate even less of what ended up on her plate. She spent more time looking around and smiled at Hunter when she caught him observing her.

I'm so glad you came with me she said. I definitely couldn't have imagined coming without you.

Oh Hunter lilted you're so sweet.

She grinned a thank you and turned her head. See the girl in the blue dress she said.

Yeah.

That's the one I was talking about the one who gave me all the shit about rush. She hates me.

What's her major he asked.

Engineering I think.

Oh Hunter said.

What.

I can see why she'd have a problem with you. She's obviously jealous of the fact that you're an English major.

You think so you think that's why.

I'm almost certain of it.

Actually what Hunter thought was that this girl wasn't as attractive as Lila and probably was jealous of her because of that the fact of which made him feel bigger more important in a way. He was cognizant that he had an attractive date and it made him feel more attractive. The other girls' dates looked like idiots cheap suits bad haircuts nothing to say. Hunter looked at other girls at the table when they talked nodded smiled. They didn't really seem to notice or care but that wasn't important. Hunter liked being involved or at least appearing to be. A girl named Harvest spoke loudly drunkenly put her arms around girls around her. Apparently she didn't have a date and sat here with the other dateless girls. One guy a thin young looking guy named Santiago who sat at the end gave her a pink rose which now lay on the table.

She picked up the rose. Isn't he so cute Harvest said.

All the girls groaned. Hunter stopped nodding and smiling shifted his eyes to Lila she seemed small then turned away from the brash loudness. A girl in a red dress and glasses her face pink stumbled out of her seat stood and fell down quickly. Some girls laughed.

One at another table a girl with a dark royal blue dress said

What's wrong with her.

The waitresses began clearing away salad plates clinking and placed them into bins on the cart. Hunter muttered Thanks whenever one of them did something that related to him or his things. The other people didn't seem to notice their plates moving their salad forks taking leave. They weren't aware. Hunter eyed the bar didn't see the bartender but figured he'd reappear when Hunter made his way across the dance floor.

He finally said fuck it told Lila I think I'm going to get a cocktail.

I think the bar's closed during dinner she said.

Oh that makes sense.

The dinner reminded Hunter of Hilary's family dinner fare at the meals she subjected Hunter to countless Saturday nights. Chicken breaded in patties bowls of mostaccoli and small doughy bits Hunter thought were gnocchi. He took some. It didn't taste like potato but then again he reasoned he probably hadn't eaten gnocchi in such a long time that he wouldn't really have a taste memory to compare this to so he decided it would be gnocchi simply because he had nothing else to know it as.

The dinner over cameras flashed pictures of two or three girls their dates the photographers. The entire sorority began to arrange themselves in front of the DJ tables. The men stood in a long line across the room began to situate disposable cameras flashes humming to readiness. Hunter had Lila's camera. He hoped the frame was in focus snapped several exposures. The girls dismantled rejoined dates threw arms around necks hugged each other stumbled back to the bar. The blender began whizzing again. The bartender still looked unhappy. Hunter watched as girls all in basically the same dress all with basically the same hair laughs sounded all the same a cacophony of noises jarring bitter discordant noises mobbed the bar. Kamikazes lemon drops Long Island Iced Teas Rum and Cokes it was as though these girls had never seen an open bar before. It was kind of silly made Hunter feel like the token adult when he wasn't even that much older than these people. He didn't think he was. Their drunkenness became more and more pronounced. There was more crashing into things frenetic laughter eyes half-slits barely conscious numbness. Hunter drank a vodka tonic. He ordered a Skyy. They had three different kinds of vodka—Skyy Smirnoff and Stoli and he was impressed. Having finally persuaded Lila to the bar she asked for a club soda with lime. The bartender looked at her as though trying to ascertain if she really meant to ask for that if she knew that he didn't care that she was only twenty that she could throw caution to the wind but maybe she didn't pick up on that. Maybe it didn't matter to her. Obviously she knew that they weren't carding people. Didn't she. She could always ask Hunter to get her a drink or maybe she didn't want to so as not to seem paranoid. Regardless Hunter gave himself a point for not avoiding the bar simply because she was. Actually he was slightly buzzed from the wine. The goddamn decanter had run out. The waitresses didn't refill it. Hunter's glass had been empty for some time. He emptied Lila's too when she was in the bathroom.

So I got this Swatch band today he told her.

Oh yeah she said. Okay she was listening. That was good.

Yeah he said in Old Orchard.

That's my neighborhood. My parents' neighborhood I guess.

I know. It was really exciting they actually had one. I couldn't find one anywhere. You know Marshall Field's doesn't carry Swatch stuff anymore.

No I didn't know that.

More sorority girls rushed the bar blonde brown hair all loose some down from before others having dismantled their hair or their hair having come apart during too many violent tosses of the neck during the awards ceremony while they ate rainbow sorbet. People started dancing.

Hunter didn't feel drunk enough. He ordered another vodka tonic and finished it while Lila went to the car for another disposable camera. She disappeared for a fairly long time. Hunter decided he now knew how long her absences were how long they would last and could be fairly certain in thinking he would finish the vodka tonic before she came back. Why did it matter anyway. She hadn't exactly placed an injunction on his drinking. He only felt mildly guilty but still didn't know if all this abstaining had to do with a fear of drunk driving—some people made a big deal out of that remaining exaggeratedly sober out of paranoia—so if Hunter could avoid Lila seeing him order extra drinks that was fine but it didn't matter the drinks were watered down severely. Hunter could barely taste anything in his glass aside from tonic fizz and lime tartness. He could tell her Look the drinks are basically like not drinking anything at all but now she wanted to dance. The overhead lights were mostly off green beams coming from the DJ stand the music dance music no words just beat industrial.

Do you dance. She had asked that the night before in the Pier Room.

Well not seriously he said now I dance like a tourist.

She thought that was funny. Now he pulled her close toward him and she remained there. They held hands sometimes. The song changed into a slow song. Aerosmith. The girls swooned. Hunter was determined not to let the music dissuade him. He definitely liked dancing with her. Her body felt small and familiar beside him. His hands were only nominally sweaty only when he noticed. Maybe her hands sweated a bit too. He decided he wanted to dance this way with her that now he was going to see where things would go if he laid out the flirtations purposefully. She seemed to respond positively to everything. He reached for a hand. She returned a hand. He let hers go circled her waist. Her hands closed around the back of his neck. Their movements had this coordination about them. Everything seemed to connect and click and follow.

Hunter asked Do you think there will be any tango any salsa. Maybe just a waltz.

The waltz was the only step I could get down.

You took a dance class.
In high school.
That's so cute she said.
It wasn't anything serious. Just the box step.
Show it to me.
What.
The box step.
Well it goes like this he said and looked down at their feet.
They danced. First people danced beside them moving swaying but then they started to disappear. Hunter didn't mind. It seemed like some sort of mass exodus outside. People reemerged laughing stumbling more swaying over to the bar Ralph the bartender sighing inwardly somebody somewhere probably synchronously recoiling with Hunter at the sight of such blatant foolishness. What was happening. Somebody probably had a joint. He didn't think Lila smoked which was a relief. He liked how she danced. He waited for a real slow song so he could drop the accelerated pretense of a dance step which really didn't compromise their closeness anyway. He liked holding her. He liked the way he felt next to her. He wished his hands didn't sweat so much but what could he do.

She looked around them likely noticing the dearth of people dancing. The banquet hall looked to be dwindling. Were people leaving. Lila looked at Len and Bridget. They stood near a table talking smoking cigarettes.

Lila said Do you think we should leave soon. Let's see if Bridget and Len want to leave soon.

Okay Hunter said cheerily wondering of course soon after if he sounded too eager. It wasn't that he wanted to leave. In fact he was having quite a splendid time. This dancing especially. When he reached for her hand she didn't pull away. She didn't seem to mind his continuing to hold her close to him as the tempo increased. It was as though they had their own rhythm separate from everybody else's. He liked that too but he was her date so he wanted to let her decide when they would leave and that's what he did.

It was quiet in the car on the drive back. Hunter drove quickly confidently not much traffic how to drive I-55 all coming back to him now. Lila thanked him some more.

In the back Len said I'm still drunk. It was that martini that did me in.

They all laughed. Hunter wasn't drunk not even slightly. Maybe slightly but that was probably more from the dancing than the vodka tonics. He watched Lila smile and look out the window. He had the air blowing through the vents. It passed through her hair and picked it up. She pushed strands out of her eyes. She really did have nice hair.

Bridget talked about the sorority girl tension. I just can't believe she thought she was going to start something she said but luckily that girl was just a drunk fool.

They all were drunk Len said.

Well what do you expect it's the first time they've been out of the dorm let alone downtown all semester.

You know Lila said I'm sort of glad this is the last one that we'll at least be free from all of this punctilious pageantry.

It is such pageantry Bridget said.

I mean can you believe the awards the I'm so drunk I look like I'm not. What was that about. Our table won like half of them.

That was because of Harvest.

Yeah she was popular this year.

Hunter liked listening to this. He had two hands on the wheel. He smiled.

I'm still hungry Len said.

You should have eaten more of the chicken Lila said.

That was certainly not chicken he said.

They had real chicken at Tiffany and Claire's table.

Yeah Bridget said I saw that. Why did we get stuck with chicken-like patties.

Hunter laughed. We must not have known the right people

he said.

I'm starting to think so Bridget said.

Let's go to Zorba's Len said. I could go for some breakfast food.

That sounds like a good idea Bridget said.

You guys are invited Len said in Hunter and Lila's direction.

Hunter looked at her. She didn't say anything. He didn't mind going. That could be fun he said.

Hunter parked in the meter lot across from CCC. They walked down Halsted in pairs Bridget and Len ahead of Hunter and Lila. Hunter wanted to hold her hand but didn't know if he should or not. He swung his arm in the general direction of her hand brushed past it hoping she'd reach for it. She didn't. He put his arm around her at one point. They stopped walking at the driveway standing underneath a vaulted brick archway. Hunter thought they were going to go to the restaurant but Bridget and Len continued walking.

I want to get that tape Len said and then called back to Hunter It was nice to meet you. He pantomimed a handshake which Hunter thought was amusing and returned. Bridget waved softly. They disappeared into the building.

More people than Hunter might have expected traveled across the archway. Some leaving probably to get beer some returning. There was a car with headlights idling beyond them in the circular driveway beside the door.

So I had a really great time Hunter said.

I did too Lila said.

They stood close to each other. Lila looked at him. This made him smile idiotically. He couldn't suppress it. He didn't bother trying after a while.

I'm going to make doubles of the pictures she said so you can have some.

I want some definitely.

He imagined seeing the pictures she looking exquisite all the memories flooding back and he next to this sublimity looking dumb. Pictures of him were always hit or miss. He hoped he wouldn't look that stupid in these. Maybe the low lighting would help or would that worsen things.

Anyway I should probably get going she said. I have to be at Borders in the morning.

Shit he said. I so wish you didn't have to work.

Yeah well I do too but you know.

Yeah he said.

She leaned forward opening her arms. They hugged. Fuck he thought just a hug oh well but she didn't move away after or change her stance at all and now he was standing right before her as though they were dancing again just like that.

He spoke then just babbling really Well you know the thing about work is that you have to go well and you know be there otherwise they get pissed and you don't want annual reviews to reflect such blatant disregard.

He wasn't listening. He had no idea what he said. She looked like she wanted to be kissed her eyelids low her breathing steady. He remembered the line from *Dating for Dummies* If you're going to do it just do it don't hover over her and so he leaned forward and touched his lips to hers. There it was. There. He kissed her. They were kissing. It was slow. Her lips were soft buoyant yet tender like some sort of petal delicate softness. Suddenly he didn't know how to kiss. What was he supposed to do. He didn't know. He wanted to record this on an 8mm Handicam. He wanted to know nothing but this kiss forever and always. This was a certain moment in a certain time he might never know again. He knew that right then. He didn't fool himself even in this passionate moment. He had to be aware of that. He also thought of the people coming into and out of the dorms. Luckily they weren't hooting. A car drove down Halsted and honked as it passed. People saw them. Did he care. Why would he exactly. This wasn't wrong quite the contrary in fact. This was quite right.

He pulled away now and looked at her. Her eyes were reopening slightly—barely—as though a great heaviness had overtaken her lids and become suddenly impossible to surmount. He touched her face. He pushed hair from her eyes. What was this. He wanted more. He leaned forward again this time without trepidation. She received him. That was good. This time her mouth opened slightly. He felt her tongue against his. This truly was an exquisite moment. This must have been clarifying things. It was certainly renegotiating the terms of their relationship. However they had interacted up until that point things would be certainly different now. He for one thing could now lean at her lips and she could receive a kiss. That had changed. They didn't kiss the day before or earlier that night though Hunter did consider kissing her on the dance floor was hoping for a song significant enough to foment this inkling but he didn't hear one. He'd just been happy with the dancing. He didn't think much more about it until then when he thought of missed opportunities and standing next to Carlotta in the kitchen at two in the morning arms around each other sixteen years old not doing anything partially because of fidelity to Eileen partially because he didn't have a clue as to how she would react. She ended up lying and saying they did make out which vexed Hunter to no end because he had to apologize—he wasn't quite sure why—to Eileen over something he hadn't even done or months before lying beside Isabelle Rousseau leaning over her his dick hard. He stroked her forehead but ended up doing absolutely fucking nothing. What had been the matter with him.

 Well now that wasn't a problem. He'd done it. He'd made it happen. He'd asserted himself and it worked. So he guessed she had liked him. This didn't seem to be the friendly sort of blow off kiss and did girls really engage in that sort of behavior. Probably not. Kissing usually had a specific meaning not like Hunter's kissing when it could mean I never want to see you again I'm just trying to be polite. Don't call me please. Thanks. No this seemed real especially as Hunter returned again and one more time before finally saying definitively that he was leaving. He liked her kissing.

I should really go.

Yeah she said softly this delicate rapt expression on her face. Could she really have been that blown away by all of this. Hunter could only wish he had the capability of leaving such an impression.

He said I'll call you and meant it too and began to walk away as did she. He turned around as she was turning to look at her. He liked that she turned too. He remembered hearing about the turn around in a book or a movie like *Say Anything* but no that wasn't it. Was it *Pretty in Pink*—maybe a Duckie musing. No not that either. Well wherever it came from the gist of it was that you can tell how a girl feels about you if she turns around after you drop her off somewhere. Say for example she's walking into her building away from your car. If she turns around you know she likes you or something like that. Simona never turned around not even in the beginning and looked back not once. Lila did just then. That was reassuring. He felt slightly uncertain walking away like the feeling of having just left behind that which he would never experience again but whatever—he was being stupid. It happened. That meant something. He didn't want to drive himself crazy with wonder. He just wanted to sort of take pleasure in the moment and fuck for once enjoy something.

# 63

The morning after he left his house and drove to UIC parked took two trains. He'd taken the same two trains before. He remembered that long ago night uncertainty pervaded misapprehended maybe when he went home unfulfilled. Last night something happened. He didn't know what but the odd thing was it didn't happen all at once. No it was a slow diffusing. He wasn't clear on what the responses were supposed to be. Take this for example. He wanted to see her to say something but what. Probably the old second day test would be useful. He always used to think that if something happened with a girl he couldn't be certain whether it was just a fluke or not without seeing what the next interaction would be like. Maybe after a really promising first moment something would go wrong and she would change her mind decide not to proceed instead choose a different course the course of not having Hunter. He had sort of forgotten about that. Maybe he'd stopped caring if things would continue what with all the disappointing turns his divestment the reality induced deflation. Maybe it no longer really mattered. Of course this all still scared him fucking freaked him out gunshy about the precipice because of Hilary because of how hard it had been to rebuild to mean something again to anyone in the aftermath. Maybe Lila didn't even want to see him. That wasn't very likely what with last night. Everything once uncertain now was imbued with purposiveness and a semblance of definition. Motivations made sense though the logic was hard to follow. Why Hunter. Why now. How. He could see at the very least that there was a logic why certain things had happened at different points heretofore only managing to confuse Hunter when he stopped to think about it. This clarity even made other things blur into focus things around him in the Borders merely disparate if he'd seen them the day before: the man in a black turtleneck and black jeans plugged into a Walkman drinking coffee reading in his lap the old woman smoothing out a gum wrapper making crinkling sounds unfolding and refolding papers in her purse that looked like a tapestry the fey effeminate sound booming through the intercom above the Handel announcing the opening of another bank of registers on the Michigan Avenue side the old woman again now in her Saks bag now sitting with—who—her daughter in law who was taking apart a gift bag of cosmetics free with purchase mascara cologne and this—I don't know what this is. You can take it.

No you can have it the old woman said. It's makeup remover.

Hunter itched. He probably was just excited unsure. He hadn't planned out what to say—not really—beyond some small silly things. It would be harder to talk to her if he did see her. She was going to be working the register. The Borders was busy tons of people queuing up to buy cheap pointless books romance novels fat Grisham book just released *Dog Tricks for Dummies The New Encyclopedia of the Dog Olympic Dreams For Dogs*. Didn't anybody care about literature anymore. He passed the new Richard Yates collection actually an old one well anyway he could talk to her about that but she'd really not have time or the patience what with others waiting.

The other woman the daughter in law said I need a good fish cookbook and left the old woman in front of a stack of other cookbooks *Food for Thought The Legal Sea Foods Cookbook*. It looked like she struggled to keep open her eyes. A baby unpacified by its pacifier screamed in a shrill voice from a highchair an exasperated sshhing father Eddie Bauer fleece a lot like Hunter's began making faces while the mother a lumpish dumpy woman in a sweatshirt pushed a spoon and then a horseshoe shaped bottle—There Alistair—at the urchin in a perfunctory attempt to quiet him. He twisted contorted above a pink bib the surly implacable mouth bent seething diminutive rage then settled by a glance something moving to look at a cookie quiet again leaving only the gentle din of café cant the sky a bit darker graying Hunter's coffee warm almost cold.

Something different too in the way he looked at other girls or rather how he wasn't looking at them. He noticed attributes—unaffected posture hair clothes purse—but not the same desperate way he had before. He compared each he saw to Lila though didn't feel right entirely about objectifying her in such a cavalier manner. Maybe he was in lust contrary to the written report he gave Angela in that morning's email. Maybe this thing with Lila—whatever it was—whatever it was to be—meant more to him than he really knew. What now.

# 64

Dinner with Lila tonight. She didn't have any suggestions as to where they should go so Hunter offered Heaven on Seven.

She said Sounds like a good idea. Have you ever been there. I didn't know they had one on Clark.

She was staying at a quote friend's apartment since the hot water was going to be out for a week in the dorms. She called Hunter last night from this mystery place. He had the phone number from the caller ID but decided not to do a reverse lookup. He supposed it didn't really matter if the friend were a boy or a girl. Hunter suspected boy since she didn't use a pronoun in any references. Why would she not say she if it were. It had to be a guy. Anyway maybe that was a good sign. She didn't have Hilary's puritan hang-ups—fears—issues and punctilious comportment as far as guys were concerned. She may have been liberal. Hunter got tickets to *Rent* for Friday night and wanted to take her of course but wondered if he should say anything right away. What if she planned on telling him she acted prematurely the other night—he was thinking of the kiss now—behaved rashly that it was too soon that they just got caught up in the moment and weren't thinking.

There wasn't a lot of thinking that night. Hunter was blinded by the shimmer and sparkle of her dress and her eyes the rapt squint of her eyes as though too flooded with emotion to look at him fully the way her hair blew into her face and how she made no effort to move it. Hunter had reached up standing in front of her and pushed it out of the way pressed his lips to hers. It was perfect a very soft slow careful kiss. She didn't move. It was as though she was entranced frozen still by the gravity of all of this.

He didn't realize it at first but he'd known that kiss and didn't think about how he had known it until that afternoon almost a week after it happened. How could he not have realized it before. My god he must have buried the memory so deep within his subconscious catalogued the sensation so encoded the scene that the feeling had no possible way of revealing itself unprovoked until such a long time afterward. He had known those lips before. He'd felt them only once one tiny moment eight years ago one millisecond in his life which carried the weight the import of six months maybe a lifetime of kissing the pinnacle of his sixteen-year-old mind's romantic inclinations the fragile heart all his desire an apex a plateau a crossing over never to be the same ever again until the glorious reenactment a million miles above the sidewalk pavement floating nothing more perfect Lila glowing no sorority sister could compare—perhaps the most beautiful date Hunter had ever had—their lips touching once and then again again more intentional familiarity in a matter of moments plateaus crossed forever never to be the same again. What was so recently everything now was not at all.

    He'd been there once and only once. Eileen. It happened in maybe March 1993 in an apartment on Fifty-fourth before the stairs leading to the door outside an engine running his mother or Jeffrey double-parked waiting to pick him up hugs goodbyes. He knew he had to do something. This could be the only chance. She had been flirty. She had been sad about her life that night stole liquor from her parents' pantry and was now sort of drunk. He was afraid then of how she'd react but he finally did it. He leaned forward still holding her she swaying gently his heart pounding its way out of his body. He kissed her. They kissed. He didn't go back after. They were both floored. He couldn't move after their lips separated. It was so new back then. Experience did have its merits: at the very least you had a general sense of how even the most uncertain of events would go or if not a sense at least some characteristics generalities of such things with which you could make comparison even stories about other people's experiences a spectrum of similar situations and outcomes with which to refer later. Of course he had none of that back then. He never expected to feel Eileen's lips the first time let alone all these years later but that's what it was. That was what happened. He felt her again.

# 65

Hunter returned from the gym. Not enough time to shower but he had dried off sufficiently he guessed then wondered if he should change out of his shorts. Maybe jeans would be more appropriate. He emptied his pockets took out receipts dollars Chapstick a small tube of moisturizer from one pocket and then his wallet from the other but then decided fuck it—it wasn't worth it. It was eighty degrees outside. He didn't care whether he looked like a dork in his khaki shorts tube socks black Doc shoes. He wanted to see Lila. He found his head heavy with thoughts. It was hard to concentrate on anything. It had been nearly a week since the formal and the kiss. What did it mean. They hadn't discussed it. He needed the second kiss test.

When he dated Dewey the first Dewey they kissed one night at a party. Hunter remembered it quite vividly: Samantha Preston's parents out of town a rowhouse on Wrightwood in Lincoln Park. Hunter didn't go to the party or come late. He went to pick Dewey up. It was snowing. Dewey got mad or something. Maybe he'd said something wrong or flirted with Samantha Preston or was supposed to be there earlier. Dewey was walking down the street. It was snowing harder. Hunter stopped her from moving put his arm on her shoulder. She turned around. He leaned down and kissed her. She had a cigarette in one hand still burning her mouth tasted warm like liquor and Marlboro red. Her lips were perfect. Her tongue fell into a motion a groove with his. He pulled her close to him. Then the next day or days later she called him on the phone said she didn't know if they should get involved wondered if the whole thing had just been a mistake. Hunter was shocked. He wasn't expecting that. He figured everything was set since they'd kissed but apparently not or at least not at that point.

Maybe it all started with Eileen. After their kiss there was never one again. The next time he thought about kissing her she told him she didn't like him. And Dewey needed some more cajoling before she'd wear down enough and start liking Hunter but anyway this was his test: if the first kiss had a follow-up if the second time he tried to kiss whoever she was he was trying to kiss and she didn't reject him then it would stick it would happen something was there. If she pulled away or deflected it or said this was a bad idea or broke up with him then obviously there wasn't anything. So that's what he had to find out tonight.

He was about to leave the house when his cell phone rang. It was Lila calling from that strange number again.

Hunter she asked tentatively without certainty.

Yeah hi he said.

It's Lila. How are you.

When was she going to stop introducing herself. He hated that. It was so impersonal like the sincerely she always used to end her emails with. That was strange at first but then he started to think it cute her signature closing.

I'm okay.

Well I'm not really okay she said sounding frustrated. Is it okay if we reschedule dinner.

Yeah it's fine he said quickly.

I hate having to do this it's just that—well—my job. I hate it. I think I'm going to have to quit and find another one. It's just not what I thought it would be.

Oh Hunter said. Well you know these things sometimes take some getting used to.

Yeah I know it's only been a week but still. It's not challenging. I don't feel like I know what I'm doing. I hate to burden you with all of this.

    It's okay. In fact I'm glad you are you know burdening me. She laughed quietly.

    Look do you want to maybe meet up have coffee or something. I had a weird day too.

    Yeah. Tea sounds like a good idea.

    That's exactly what we'll do. Yeah tea. Definitely.

    Okay I'll call you like in an hour.

    That sounds good.

    At seven-thirty he pulled into the Walgreens parking lot on Belmont. He went inside bought a pack of gum and sat back in the car. Seven-forty-five still no call. At eight he began to grow restless started the ignition pulled back onto Belmont drove around the block. American Pie was on the radio. He started singing. The traffic moved slowly. He stopped parallel to a truck. He turned away stopped singing until the cars began moving again. Why wasn't she calling. What was going on with her. Maybe she didn't even like him. This was so confusing. He would have thought she would have certainly wanted to see him prior to this night if she were at all interested in getting involved with him. Though at the same time he figured that the distance was important. Like this staying at the genderless friend's apartment. He appreciated her independence. She didn't even ask Hunter to stay at his place though she probably made these arrangements prior to last Friday had known for some time about the hot water shutoff in the dorms knew as well that Hunter lived at home. God damn it. Why didn't he have an apartment. He felt like such a fucking loser living at home living at home in a room such a mess with newspapers things strewn about. Winter clothes still lay in piles. Was this how his apartment in Boulder was going to look. He certainly hoped he would figure out how to be responsible for a place before he got there. Lila was the kind of girl that could take care of herself—whatever that meant. She could get herself to work to campus to this apartment and was now handling things in the midst of a crisis. Hunter's instinct was to offer himself to her wanted to protect her in some way imagined Hilary helpless and frightened in the same situation and saying things to her like We'll do this and We'll do it together like he did whenever coming to her rescue but stopped himself. It wasn't appropriate not just because they hardly knew each other but because she was her own person. She didn't need protecting. Basically Hunter just wanted to see her find out if there was going to be a second kiss. He wanted to kiss her again.

She finally called and said she'd meet him at the Starbucks on Clark and Belmont. He passed up one parking space spun around the block found another one a few steps from the entrance. He took *The Pollen Room* out of his trunk which he wasn't particularly enjoying but it was a short book and he could carry it without much effort. He went inside. The barista was on the phone. Hunter thought the Starbucks was closed at first— empty tables the counter lining the wall of windows just chairs without occupants. He spotted a small group of women in the back and figured it okay to approach the barista who said I'll be right with you.

Hunter examined the menu as though he'd never seen it before wondered if he should get something or not while he waited. He decided not to told the barista he was meeting someone sat down at the window counter began reading became quickly annoyed with the dragging diagesis the translation probably missing more than something. This was no *Less Than Zero* though it clearly fancied itself as such. Hunter wanted to look at all the people watch people walk down the street cross at the intersection coming into the Starbucks but kept his head down thought for some reason it would look better if he didn't see Lila first. He wanted to make her see him and come over but not for any other reason than that he hated seeing someone from a distance. He thought it took him longer to spot people due to his weak contacts prescription and that was awkward but also when you did recognize somebody it always seemed to take forever for both people to reach each other and before you did it inevitably felt strange when the person walked toward you because you couldn't comfortably speak until there was a certain proximity achieved—and it always took awhile to get there—so in the meantime you just had to watch and maybe smile dumbly and he'd always preferred just avoiding all of that.

# 66

So do you ever think about reinventing yourself when you start a new job or go to a different place you know like who will your friends be where you'll hang out what you'll be like Lila asked.

They walked down Halsted. She was wearing a white top and blue pants. She looked pretty. Her skin seemed darker juxtaposed with all that white. Hunter wanted to reach for her hand felt like they should hold hands felt like they were a couple so why not hold hands.

I don't know he said. The truth was he hadn't had a lot of experience like that. I guess when I started UIC I didn't really feel like I was beginning anything new. I was so into my job I didn't really pay attention for a couple of years. I was barely there anyway—I took maybe at most six hours at a time. I wasn't serious about school then. So I suppose I didn't change much there.

Yeah that's pretty much what I did my first semester at Madison. I thought about it a lot—who I was supposed to be meeting—but it got to be kind of a hassle. I stopped feeling like me and then when I came back here I lived at home my first year so that was just like more high school.

Hunter chuckled. Yeah. He'd always compared UIC to four or five more years of high school. The expectations were so ridiculously low the effort most of his peers put out minimal to the point of not existing all the ringing cell phones tardiness bad grammar. I don't think I've done a lot of life changing.

You're about to make a big change Hunter. You're moving away. That's a big deal.

Yeah. You know it's funny. It doesn't seem real. I mean it does and it doesn't. Like the other day I heard a commercial for the Madonna concert on the radio and it was for August 28th or something like that and I thought I'm not going to be here then.

That's right. When are you leaving exactly.

I'm not sure. C— doesn't seem to be big on disseminating information. She smiled looked at him as they walked. Her eyes were green maybe looked like his he thought but a little lighter of a tint.

Did she like him or was there going to be a rejection at the end of all of this. This talk of his departure—was that just a segue to something unpleasant. Wouldn't it just be completely fucking ironic if Hunter fell in love with Lila and didn't want to leave. Of course he wouldn't let that happen. Maybe she believed in long distance relationships.

He felt light headed. He didn't like the metaphors he'd been using. He definitely needed to have the second kiss test and see where all of this was going. How ironic was it that he felt like the one who needed things now and that she was the elusive unavailable one who made him wonder and scramble for the smallest affectionate moments hell any sort of contact with her. Did that mean he was falling for her. What did it mean.

# 67

He was starting to really like Lila and that complicated things somewhat. He told Angela about the coffee in an email that night when he got home and about the successful outcome of the second kiss test but that she—Lila—made no moves she didn't suggest anything no casual touching while they walked looked into shops had tea. At Caribou the conversation was decent but a lot of filler. When would Hunter feel comfortable enough with her not to not feel like he wasn't comfortable enough. And why hadn't they had dinner yet.

# 68

Now that Lila couldn't go to *Rent*—I have to work Friday night Hunter you know that of course I'd love to see it with you but my manager has been a dick lately—he didn't know whom he could call and invite. This was bad bad bad. He tried Ammo Coupe. They were supposed to have dinner. He hadn't heard from her. Julianne he kept leaving messages for. He hadn't talked to her in weeks and had no idea what was going on with her. He wanted to go with either of them. Probably Ammo more so since he still felt guilty about not calling her after he heard from C—. He told her Monday when they spoke on the phone. She called his cell. He answered half accidentally thought for a millisecond it was Lila. They had a good conversation though.

    Have you ever been to C— before she asked.

    No he said I haven't. Have you.

    I've been to Denver but not to Boulder. I'd love to see it sometime.

    Well you should drive up there with me.

    When.

    This summer when I have to. You're the only person I know that can drive a stick.

    That was true too. Well there was Jeffrey but as far as Hunter knew he was still in Argentina or wherever with Jenefir—maybe they were already married—so he obviously wouldn't be available. That left Ammo. Ammo dear Ammo.

So you're graduated now she asked.
Yeah.
You majored in English.
Yeah you knew that.
You're right. I did know that.
I also minored in Sociology.
You never told me that. That's so weird. I minored in Sociology.

Hunter tried to remember her major. He was fairly certain it was Communication. Yeah that was it. It was a while ago. She'd been out of school for—shit—three years now. Hunter was so behind it was ridiculous but he was done now at any rate. She made films during college. One was on public television called *Alicia* about a girl from an impoverished community in Indiana. Hunter liked it had it on tape. It was quite good. He wanted Ammo to go to grad school for film but so far she'd just been in Chicago working.

Now she said Maybe I'll go to law school in C—. I've been looking at law schools. Did you know that.

So you're not going to the Navy.

No. I told them no. Do you think that was a bad choice.

No. Absolutely not. I think I've told you before you know this getting in was the big deal. That was the accomplishment. Not going now will be better. You won't have to give up so much of your life like that.

You just want me to go to C— with you.

Well Hunter laughed yeah you're right. I do. I am selfish. What can I say.

She laughed too. We should definitely go out there. Do you know when you have to be there. I tell my boss now when I won't be here.

Sometime in August. I guess I should find out for sure.

Yeah that might be a good idea.

Hey he said playfully I can't know everything.

# 69

Girl pink v-neck shirt hair short brown wavy pulled back in a headband blue Capri pants sandals Nokia cell phone off-white pressed against right ear looked at the stitch of her sleeve talked into the phone.

Yeah she's pretty lazy. It will be really nice for her. I can see her yeah you'd really like her a lot. I know but no. Anyway you guys are so lucky. I'm jealous. You guys should give her a chance. She's really cool. She's Russian but has that whole cheap *Baywatch* look which is her downfall. I'm going to paint your house you bastard. It's my parents' birthday.

She reached into her shoulder bag took out her key chain wallet a small quantity of folded bills Shakespeare abridged. She spoke in Russian then quickly folding the bills. More Russian.

She said U2 concert.

Her earrings looked Southwestern silver maybe from New Mexico necklace star of David silver also. A guy in a hooded sweatshirt came in then and sat down next to her. She got off the phone. He emptied some Tic-Tacs into her palm. She had nice eyebrows.

She told the guy I think I want to go see *Snatch* tonight.

Hunter wanted to leave go to the gym but couldn't extricate himself. He wanted to watch her use a pen. She looked a bit like a young Drew Barrymore but not blonde pendulous breasts which featured a prominent cleavage comment in the v of her pink purple sweater.

She spoke quickly. He doesn't say good night that bastard. Stop stop. Don't make me feel like a crazy girl. I said something silly that night. He put on his headphones. I was like Bastard. He went to sleep and I'm like fine what do I do so I put in *Seven*— great movie to watch before going to sleep—and David walks in. David Goodman. He's the one with the dark skin. I'm sure you've seen him before. He comes in and watches about twenty minutes and he had that look and then he wakes up with that look and I was like Um okay whatever.

This girl kept looking in Hunter's direction met his eyes glancingly a couple of times.

No one ever asks me how my day was she continued. Nobody ever says How was your day. She had pouty lips and talked while looking at the pens in her hands. Because usually it's like Oh my god I had the worst day but like so he goes he doesn't do that. So. She laughed. I need caffeine. She got up and leapt to the counter. Hooded guy followed behind her quickly.

Hunter heard her say How are you in a big overzealous voice probably to the cashier. Obviously she was a café regular or just knew everybody in Hyde Park.

# 70

Some people were still innocent not yet corrupted and Hunter envied them. They had emotional responses to things because what they did and saw was so new and unique to their perspectives. The kids on the train he watched last night they had that innocence. Ironic of course—they probably didn't even realize they had it. Not knowing scared Hunter. He had to know everything. Even things he didn't want to know even things that hurt him to know were necessary. Though he thought innocence an endearing and romantic state it was something he'd be unlikely to actually experience again.

Maybe his reaction to girls how quickly he fell in lust was in a small way a small attempt to recapture innocence. He looked at girls fantasized about them ones he only slightly knew had barely ever spoken to. He'd imagine himself living with or married to them before even dating. It was so juvenile this way of thinking—completely unrealistic. He'd obviously tried enough times obviously knew in his heart that certain girls especially the ones that he didn't even attempt to get to know he would never have a chance with but what chance did he even really want. Girls got close to him and all he could do was think of reasons why it wouldn't work. It had been like that since the beginning. Ten years of dating or whatever constituted dating then or whatever constituted dating now even before that girls he would fall in love with in third fourth fifth grade.

He had these chances to become completely submerged—supposedly what he really wanted. Then he'd tell himself he didn't want to be alone but didn't really want to be involved either. This feeling hadn't changed in all this time. So what did it mean. It was one thing to still wear Doc Martens and flannels it was one thing to reminisce and be envious of teenagers of how he was at sixteen of how brave he had been compared to now but another to keep pushing people away.

He didn't know what to think when he didn't hear from Lila the next day or the day after. He even left a message. He was sort of surprised not to hear from her half-expected something of a deluge attention after the kiss. It took him a while but he articulated the sensation. Déjà vu to five years earlier Labor Day weekend with Simona suddenly absent. Julianne had to explain it to him. They broke up the next day. He didn't even realize it then but knew now: I think she's trying to get rid of me.

His face looked tired and greasy. He looked at his reflection in the back of a stray CD-ROM in the lab. On the shuttle bus over to the west side he watched a couple who sat toward the front of the bus a guy and a girl both in glasses. The girl was very attractive. She had very blonde hair. Hunter felt himself crumpling internally by degrees the longer he looked at her. She had a very delicate face cute in glasses. The boy was tall. He wore shorts and a sweatshirt. It really wasn't warm enough at that point for shorts. His leg looked quite thin hairy tan like an older man's leg. You could see the bones pressing against his skin the way he crossed his legs. The bones looked disjointed not connecting to each other seamlessly invisibly. His hair was short buzzed stood up in the back. Her blonde hair was pulled back held together in a scrunchie not quite a ponytail more like a fist. She wore a gray top and matching gray workout pants. She put her head on his shoulder for a moment talked about a girl and her finals the boyfriend looking listlessly out of the window the bus rolling ahead occasionally causing the girl to lurch forward. Hunter wondered why he never had a girlfriend who looked like this.

There was something so incredibly sexy about this girl like she could do nothing wrong like to be with her would be exquisite three weeks or months of nothing but the best of everything passion tangling together in bed eating breakfast together sharing sections of the *New York Times* on languid Sunday mornings nothing bothering them at all. He'd never had a blonde girlfriend. All of his girlfriends had had brown hair. Jessica Valley had red hair and while that was briefly interesting and a change of pace the relationship didn't last. He barely spent any time with her maybe only ate with her at the Medici once.

This girl on the bus looked like a Jessica maybe a Mandy. Why did she like this guy. How had they met. When did they get together. Had they fucked. She had a very wiry body no chest that Hunter could discern from where he sat but it didn't seem to matter. He could never tire of her body her blondeness the exquisite fucking that they would share. She looked over in Hunter's direction a couple of times. His eyes skirted hers darted away quickly peripherally or maybe he darted because of a reflection in the window he pretended to look out of maybe a combination of the two. He thought he saw her looking at him again. Maybe she was bored of the thin tall bony-legged guy. Maybe she wanted more. They barely spoke to each other. She lifted her arm maybe considered putting her hand on his shoulder but reconsidered laid it across the back of the bank of seats instead. The bus picked up speed. She had a muted brilliance this girl. Hunter's attraction no doubt fueled by how completely ephemeral this moment was—practically no longer existing from the moment he noticed her and when maybe she noticed him. He would get off the bus. He would never see her again. That perpetuated his attraction as did the elusiveness in everything about her he didn't know—her name where she was from how she met that guy. The only things Hunter knew were of course physical specifics—at least ones he could discern from here from sitting in public from having not seen her naked: her hands the faint pink polish her nails were already growing out of the way she twisted her hands laced her fingers together the way she looked at the boy who barely looked at her the way she sought out Hunter indifferently maybe even looking directly through him and then that was it. Hunter rose at his stop and exited the bus.

# 71

Certain things he tried to ignore about Lila—not ignore exactly but just not think about so much. The ignoring actually felt like a mature rational response. The problem was her insouciance her noncommittal reaction to Hunter. It was as though she felt burdened the way Hunter felt about Kate how he'd felt about Hilary toward the end like here we go again every time he'd call or see her as though he were just going through the blocking. Maybe that was what explained the sterility the—what—tension that seemed to frame their conversations and encased all their plans. It wasn't supposed to be like this. They liked each other. Right. This was the period of time the weeks or months where they were impossibly in love loathed separation not being near each other with lots of touching interminable kisses sneaking around not concerning themselves with the business of trivial monotonous details having only each other to think about in a significant way anyway. *Right.* That's what happened *right.* Hunter wondered if he had it all wrong. Maybe he didn't really know how she felt.

Tonight they were supposed to see a movie. Hunter got out of dinner with Linda and Maya even though he was completely hungry and would have liked to spend time with them gave up a really good parking space and dialed her up on his cell phone. The battery was dying but still had enough of a charge for one conversation. He drove down Broadway.

I still haven't taken a shower she said after losing the person on her other line. She only said—no gendered pronoun—somebody is on the other line after they exchanged hellos.

Oh well so do you still want to do something later or... he asked meekly. I could wait. He wanted to sound not like he didn't care but that he understood and could be accommodating. There he went: the same old story. Feeling one thing pretending he didn't but not really evoking any emotion. Christ his life was a broken record.

She said If you have something else to do you know you should do it. Don't just hang around on my account. I feel terrible.

Don't he said it's okay.

You sound upset.

I'm not he lied I was just sitting at a weird angle.

He was stopped behind cars a red light. He didn't feel like speaking anymore.

Maybe tomorrow he asked.

Yeah that might be better. It's just that I need some time to sort things out. I'm just feeling a little cluttered right now. I found a third job today.

Oh that's great Hunter said. That's good news. But was it really.

So you know I have to figure out all that stuff but I really appreciate you being so understanding putting up with me. I'll call you tonight. At the very least we'll get to have a conversation.

Okay he said.

What else could he say.

He didn't want this. He didn't want to feel this way. Fuck. He was not going to be this person. He didn't want to be this person. Things were different. This wasn't just unreturned misplaced affection. He didn't just have a pointless crush without merit. This was supposed to be something. They were supposedly in the process of building something. That's why he was starting to care.

Fuck. It happened again. He lost control somewhere during

the last two weeks and hadn't even realized it. He had no power. He didn't want to be at another illogical indifferent capricious angry yet disarmingly attractive girl's mercy. He'd rather watch TV.

What he'd been doing was telling himself that the space was healthy was important. He'd never really had space in a relationship. The girls he ended up with didn't know the first thing about independent living had never even heard of the concept before and he admired how Lila was a person with agency a person with friends and jobs of her own and more importantly a person who didn't need Hunter as much as just liked him. Maybe she just enjoyed kissing him casually with no visible strings no explicit commitments no bullshit. That's how he always imagined relationships went though he'd never experienced one like that. He'd gathered from watching people like Julianne like Trey that that was how it worked. How it could be. Maybe it was the element missing in Hunter's life the component which would make him content for once not to need to run after a couple of weeks for once. That was what Lila was supposed to be like. That was the person whom she was supposed to be.

Now Hunter didn't know. Maybe he was overreacting. Maybe she still was that person. Maybe she was that and he was freaking out because he didn't know how to handle what it was he thought she wanted. Maybe he needed to ask her what was going on and make a decision but the problem with that was once the adrenaline shock of having been momentarily clear in purpose and intent been brave and definitive like never before after that wore off he'd probably be alone without her to kiss and inevitably more depressed and mixed-up than this this not knowing this wondering and being uncertain and ambivalent and confused.

He'd seen all of this before. None of it was entirely new though granted some factors—some of the criteria—rearranged things reordered the ambiguousness made his course of action less certain than might have existed otherwise but of course he gathered he'd rather have it just as it was because this provided evidence to suggest that all of it—his life his actions the things he did the choices he made the things he wanted and would want and could want—wasn't completely independent of him. Not entirely.